Published by PJTJ Publishing in 2011
PJTJ House, 6 Richmond Avenue
Nottingham NG3 3AT

Prefix: 978-0-9562505
ISBN 978-0-9562505-5-1

Copyright © James C Stuart 2012

First print, Copyright © James C Stuart 2011

Cover Illustration © Steven Forster 2011

All rights reserved. James C Stuart has asserted his moral right under copyright, Designs and patents Act 1988 to be identified as the author of this work.

This book is sold subject to condition that it is shall not, by way of trade or otherwise, be lent, resold, hired out or otherwise circulated without the publisher's prior written consent in any form of binding or cover other than that in which it is published and without a similar condition, including this condition, being imposed on the subsequent purchaser, and without limiting the rights under copyright reserved above. No part of this publication maybe re produced stored in or introduced into a retrieval system or transmitted in any form or by any means (electronic, mechanic, photocopying, recording or otherwise) without the prior written permission of both James C Stuart and PJTJ publishing.

www.dragonstonebook.com

ISBN 978-0-9562505-5-1

GW00535869

Dedicated to the memory of
my father who recently passed away.
And also to my mother who continues
to support me through thick and thin.
My love to them both…

Chapter 1

REVELATION

'Are you certain, Astrophos?'

'I'm afraid so, Cosmolos.'

'How in the Magicklands could this have happened? Surely, we should have spotted the scroll mapping their magick potential?' said Astrophos worriedly.

Cosmolos stood across from Astrophos at the back chamber and concluded some testing on the latest in astrological equipment: The Two-Way Astroscope.

'Well - they aren't the first Magickal family to be missed,' said Cosmolos. 'At least they have been found so they can begin their training,' he said.

'Very true, but none of the scrolls have been purposely tampered with, like this – and if we hadn't received their letter by chance, then surely they would have been lost?' replied Astrophos, sounding very concerned.

'Fortune indeed,' said Cosmolos. 'However, you know the will of the universe: when someone is truly destined to be somewhere, no matter what forces are at play, you will always end up where you are supposed to be,' he explained as they walked back into the main room, under the large archway. 'Nevertheless, I agree, someone has gone to considerable efforts to disguise their scroll chart - the likes of which I've never seen before. Why the dark charm broke when the letter arrived, I have no idea; it is a point for meditation.'

Cosmolos proceeded to set up the room. He added more frankincense to the burner located on the left side of the room on one of the smaller altars. The sweet fragrance permeated the air and the resulting mist surrounded the room, creating a deeper ambiance, perfect for meditation. As he finished, there was a pause and silence, then Cosmolos spoke, again.

3

r friend, I'm afraid this raises other questions; why
do such a thing? Who would do such a thing? How
ess to our room? And what do they know that we
very least, suspect?' he said, angrily, at the fact that
___ penetrated their sacred domain, tampered with their
equipment, and left without leaving a trace.

'Furthermore, how on earth was the house disguised
against the Trackers?' Astrophos interjected. 'OK, scrolls are lost or
damaged, families move on before their time, but the Trackers
always find their man – or family for that matter! It is frustrating
that magick cannot work properly in the Plainlands; we could do
our work, much more efficiently if it did.' Astrophos held his hand
to his head and began to rub it in an attempt to remove some
tension that had suddenly formed there.

'Yes, what a sad day that was,' said Cosmolos, solemnly. 'I
don't know how they live without magick in their lives. Life seems
so much more complicated. As for the house, there is a possible
answer for why the Trackers couldn't find them, though I will have
to go and investigate,' said Cosmolos, revealing nothing more,
furthering the frustration of his close friend Astrophos.

Astrophos and Cosmolos began to pace around the
beautiful, circular, wooden, coned, room. It was intricately
designed with beautifully crafted patterning, combined with a rich
tapestry of golden symbols. Each of them bold, powerful and
meanings designed to protect, enhance and energise the room.
Cosmolos' embroidered dark blue robes were flowing, lightly
behind him as he walked; he did well to avoid the centre altar table
in his deeply focused state. He stopped. His deep blue eyes cast a
gaze as if to look beyond the confines of the room, twisting his
beard whilst doing so.

'Just... just look at this chart. It's incredible!' Excitement
began to rise from the pit of his stomach. Astrophos raised his
hand and muttered, 'Venio.' Immediately the scroll rolled itself up
and swiftly flew over, landing gently in his hand. He opened it and
began to analyse the astrological correspondences closely. His eyes
widened gleefully at what he was seeing and then a shudder went
down his spine.

4

Simultaneously, goose pimples crawled along his skin as if some great ancestor had walked through him from beyond the grave. 'Could he be the one?' Astrophos added. 'You know the one that is mentioned in the prophecy?'

'I'm not sure my dear friend. There have been others with similarly, exciting, astrological information, so it is difficult to tell. If I remember rightly, the prophecy mentions *"the one born of Dragon,"* though sadly we have no way of deciphering this and the other half of the prophecy mysteriously disappeared'

'What does the pendulum say?' asked Astrophos.

'It hasn't said anything in a while.' Guilt suddenly masked itself over his face, tinged with regret.

'I think it is quite annoyed from its last divining mission and it is refusing to talk. I suppose winding him up like that wasn't the brightest of things to do,' he confessed. 'Well, I should apologise, I suppose - mead never really bodes well with me.' They laughed. Fresh colour started to appear in their faces. Cosmolos and Astrophos looked kindly upon each other and smiled. The deep tension that had previously formed on Astrophos's brow began to dissipate as he relaxed.

The mages sat down. Fire drakes zipped around the room, dimming the flamed torches, allowing meditation to take place. Astrophos closed his eyes and began to meditate, whilst Cosmolos seemed to be searching the room for answers. He hoped it would be there, hiding, so he could summon it easily, like a book off a shelf. His blue eyes gazed around the room admiring the solid oak struts that were similar to those of a country cottage, curving upwards, to form a dome.

The altar table was positioned behind him. His gaze took him to the adjacent stained glass window that encircled around the top half of the room. The colours in the window changed intuitively, depending on what they are thinking about at the time. During times of deep reflection, the colours become more intense. An interchange of purple and violet light, emanated from the window, indicating they were in deep, magickal thought. Momentarily, Cosmolos noticed a bit of dirt that had somehow attached itself to his night blue robes, but, with a waft of his hand, the dirt vanished from sight. He pushed back his white hair, which had a few remaining blond streaks in it and continued to gaze in the around the room.

Cosmolos was very particular about everything; the way he appeared, the way the room looked and the way everything was organised. Astrophos wasn't as meticulous: he was untidy and often eccentric, like a mad scientist when he was working; it was therefore strange for him to be the one meditating.

An hour had passed and it seemed that no solution would come. Cosmolos then spoke.

'Astrophos!!' he said suddenly, startling his friend. 'We must consult with Artuk Ra: he might be able to interpret some of these complex alignments in this chart, after all, the Egyptians are masters of this kind of phenomenon.'

'Agreed,' said Astrophos. 'We must also consult the Head of School, the Head of the Elemental Houses and the Governing Council of Elders.

'Yes, but let's see what Artuk has to say first as we wouldn't want to appear over zealous or even worse, idiotic, like a couple of over enthused teenage magicians, with their first fire element experiment. Previous Astro-Mages have made wild claims about various charts and paid for it dearly with their jobs. If there is any truth to the alignments, we need to proceed with caution and let events unfold naturally.' he said, as the stained glass window suddenly turned into a vibrant yellow to denote that logic had entered his thinking.

'Agreed,' said Astrophos, realising that over reacting could have severe consequences. 'In the meantime, we must move forward with the official formalities of introducing the family to our world,' he said excitedly. 'I have to admit, I do like to see the confused look in their faces when they realise they have magickal ability, as well as the shock when they see our world in all its glory,' said Astrophos, teasingly.

'Yes,' said Cosmolos with youthful enthusiasm. 'It brings great joy to my heart to see folk realise that there is something much better to life than living within the mundane realms of the Plainlands,' he said, as his eyes glistened like the birth of two new suns, whilst the stained glass window shone a glowing red and bright gold, showing enthusiasm and power.

'Oh yes. I nearly forgot. I will personally investigate my theory into why the Trackers couldn't find them. If I am correct, it will be a very clever form of hoodwinking – devious, though brilliant.'

'What is it? Tell me,' he said excitedly.

'Ah, my friend, in time - in time…' Astrophos didn't look impressed by this. His face seemed to contort like a teenager being grounded.

'Do you know something Astrophos?' Cosmolos asked, clearly distracted by something. 'Do you know the most impressive thing about the Astroscope?'

'You mean the fact it can display and project the actual star positioning as if we were back at that moment in history?' I did come up with the idea,' he said proudly.

'Ah, yes my apologies my dear friend. But this should really help me finally prove the link between the past and the present, however, there is much work to be done,' said Cosmolos, being taken over with excitable emotion.

'First things first,' said Astrophos suddenly donning the role of methodical thinker. 'We need to contact the communication department to deliver the acceptance letter. Also, the relevant details have to be sent about the city tour and visit. And… oh yes – don't forget the letter to the apothecary; they must prepare the potion so the transition can take place.'

'I'll prepare and send the scroll,' Cosmolos enthused. Quickly, he went to the parchment table and picked out a sheet then said, 'Annoto, Imprimo Invitatium.' The parchment flew over to the writing mangle and it causally began to print the document.

'And the scroll to Artuk,' said Astrophos.

'Artuk, Annoto, Imprimo, decidio,' said Cosmolos. Another parchment was printed. Cosmolos picked up the neatly, sealed scrolls and took them to the Scroll-Porter. He slid one of the scrolls upright into the bracket, and said, 'Incedo Artuk Ra.' The scroll dematerialised into light blue sparks with specks of orange and then vanished downwards towards its destination. He then sent the second scroll.

'The job is done. All we can do now is wait - and Astrophos my dear friend.'

'Yes.'

'I think this year is going to be a very interesting year.'

Chapter 2

CONCERN

The sun had already begun to rise in the Great City, though its rays hadn't quite reached the Political Quarter. The air was crisp and fresh and the sky was beginning to glow its usual vivid blue colour. The smell of flowers from the lavender fields had caught the east wind and was imbuing the area with a sense of peace and tranquillity.

Markus Rome, a political officer to the English Quarter, had just reached the Great Gate where Sedrick the Viking guard was keeping watch. Sedrick came out of his security box, standing very tall and very broad.

'Good Morning Markus,' Sedrick said cheerfully.

'Morning,' said Markus with a distracted tone.

'Are you… OK Markus?' he said sounding concerned.

'Yeah, I suppose. A bad night's sleep and I have a very early appointment with the Governor.'

'Oh dear,' he said sympathetically. 'I do have some of Percy's Pick Up,' he said pointing to the bottle with purple and turquoise liquid. The colours circulated around the bottle, mixed together and then separated again.

'Go on, have it, it's the new brand formula. It really works, just look at me,' he said beaming as if the sun had already reached him. He stood up revealing his massive frame. His silver chainmail was spotless and his helmet, sword, axe and spears sat comfortably next him.

'Wait a moment,' he continued. 'It's a bit early to be having a meeting - it's not even 6am! What does he want with you at this time?'

'Not sure,' said Markus shiftily. 'Though I must be hurrying along,' he said, wanting to get away before any more questions could be asked.

'OK – I understand,' he winked. 'Magick business I presume.' Markus momentarily said nothing.

'Thanks for the drink,' he said, changing the subject.

'That's OK – I have three crates at home. You know the routine Markus,' he continued. Markus walked over to the centre of the Great Gate and muttered something, but what he said was not recognisable to Sedrick's ears. The massive Iron Gate opened and Markus walked in.

'I'll be seeing you later then,' Sedrick shouted.

'Ok, though I might need something more than a *Percy Pick-Up* when I have finished,' he bellowed. He gulped down the drink Sedrick had given him and, true to the Viking's word, he felt a warm tingly sensation rising from his feet and finishing at his head; even the smell of Lavender seemed more intense. He smiled. The gate closed and the city symbol that had separated in the middle, united. The symbol was a massive red dragon. Its claws grasped half a scroll, located on the right hand side, which represented the half prophecy.

Markus proceeded to walk down a dusty pathway putting some distance between Sedrick and himself. The track was now turning into a large stone road that was smooth and easy to walk on. The Political Quarter was located in the middle of the city, each linked by a separate gateway to the other city quarters.

The sun had risen sufficiently now and its rays had passed Markus, covering the city. Markus, alert after taking his *Percy Pick-Up Juice*, took notice of the grandeur of the city.

He walked down the Parthenon Main Street. It was very quiet as most people were asleep. A gust of wind caught his wavy blond hair, which covered his eyes so he simply brushed it back again with his hands. The road was long and in the centre was a huge Parthenon. It sat on a massive marble cliff top that seemed impossible to get to.

Located at the sides of the main street were entrances to other streets, which then branched out to other smaller ones that were perfectly straight and well ordered. The buildings comprised of merchants, bankers, restaurants, cafes, bars and sellers. They looked like miniature versions of the Parthenon, though each had its own unique design and signage.

Markus stopped as he caught his reflexion and adjusted his clothing that was reminiscent of a Jayne Austen novel. He turned and looked at the Parthenon in the distance. It was made of beautifully smooth white marble, though it equally looked menacing because of its size. It was like the unconquerable fortresses of the ancient times and made its Athenian counterpart look like a miniature model in comparison. The Parthenon was where the Magickal Peace alliance was signed to ensure magickal cooperation amongst magickal nations; it is also the parliament of the Great City.

Suddenly, a voice startled Markus, increasing his heart rate and he became rather flustered.

'Allo Markus,' spoke Napoleon, as the statue concrete styled substance suddenly took form.

'Hello Napoleon. Your turn is it then?'

'Oui Monsieur... I couldn't rest, zee uthers are asleep. What are you doing up before zee shops opening,' asked a surprised Napoleon.

'Meeting with the Governor,' Markus said, having the feeling of Déjà Vu, after his conversation with Sedrick.

'Mon Dieu – what - at ziss time!' his surprise clearly showed. 'It must be important. Be on your guard - take no prisoners,' he said reminiscing of his French Imperial days. 'I'll be 'ere for you Monsieur, if you need me.'

'Thank you Napoleon... I'll bear that in mind,' he said courteously. The concrete formed back into a solid like substance. Markus hoped he wouldn't encounter anybody else on his journey, so he hurried along hoping no one else could distract him.

He arrived at the next statue, though no one came through this time. He turned left and he walked down one of the smaller side streets. Markus arrived at another gate and whispered the same words as he did at the main gate to the city. It opened and Marcus walked in. He was now in the political government building sector where all the main governors and staff dealt with the day to day running of the city. The Governor's offices were much bigger and grander than their staffing counterparts and were located some distance apart from each other.

Markus' pulse and temperature rose again, but this time it didn't recede. The heartbeat got stronger and louder and a vein on the side of his head appeared to throb. He approached the gate. His hands and brow became clammy as he approached the Governor's house. The house guard came out.

'Ah! Markus! The Governor has informed me that you would be arriving early. I have to say, he doesn't seem too happy. You better come in,' said the guard. 'I suggest you hurry as he has to go away on business to the Royal Houses, later this morning.' Markus said nothing as his face suddenly went a dull colour and he wished that Sedrick was handing him another *Percy Pick-Up Juice* or something stronger…

He walked up the marble steps past the main wooden gate into the hallway. The wooden door closed suddenly as it was aware of his presence. Coldness pervaded the atmosphere, which falsely tempered his nerves. One of the two sleeping mini fire drakes opened a sleepy eye. It looked at the other drake and then at Markus. You could sense that is wasn't impressed as he knew he had to get up to tend to the torches. The drake hovered causally over each torch, which instantly lit as it passed. It stopped at the last of the torches and bathed in the glistening flames before heading back to sleep. The air warmed slightly, though a chill still remained.

'Come through,' said a commanding, echoing voice in the distance.

'You wanted to see me Lord Balfour,' Markus said, pretending that his invite was some sort of surprise. The Governor said nothing.

Markus walked along a short corridor that had red and purple material hanging, down covering short sections either side of the torches. He walked into the massive rectangular room, which bore no windows. There were several pillars supporting the roof surrounding the edge of the room, while four larger ones sat inside, forming the corners of a large square. A stone altar lay at the south edge and was decorated with a variety of magickal instruments. Lord Balfour stood to lay the table out: there were three black candles towards the back, along with a miniature cauldron, a dagger and incense burner; they were all perfectly placed. Gold symbols where strategically imbedded into the walls and altar. Each symbol bore some magickal significance that helped to support and

12

empower the magician in his workings. The rituals were further supported by larger banners designed with triangular symbols, which indicated the north, south, east and west directions.

'Follow me,' commanded Lord Balfour and Markus said nothing again and did as he was instructed. They walked beyond the south corner of the room and through another door, which then divided into further passageways. They took the middle passage that got colder the further they walked along it, despite the firedrakes floating just in front of them, lighting the torches as they went. On the right hand side, a sign at the top lit up into orange and red sparks, and a voice from seemingly nowhere announced, 'Welcome Lord Balfour - 12th Governor of the English Quarter, to your office.' The door opened and both of them entered. The governor walked behind his desk and sat down. There was a silent pause and then Lord Balfour spoke. 'Please sit down,' and Markus promptly did as he was told. 'I received your message scroll last night Markus – are you sure?'

'Yes my source is a one hundred percent accurate my Lord,' said Markus confidently. His nerves settled at the sound of the Governor's voice, relaxing slightly.

'But how is this so? How was the enchantment broken? The enchantment should have been beyond even Astrophos' and Cosmolos' knowledge – this is quite disturbing. Did you follow my instructions to the letter?' he asked accusingly. 'It took me many years to find these old magickal documents.'

'I'm not sure, my Lord, what happened exactly. I am sure it had nothing to do with Cosmolos and Astrophos. They are just as confused as we are,' he said, assuring the governor. 'It had something to do with a letter they received from the mother. I am uncertain what the connection is.' Markus' heart rate returned to normal knowing that the governor believed him. 'The child and the rest of the family will receive their invite for the usual tour before their entry into our world for magickal learning,' he concluded.

'You know it was for the protection of the child don't you? I'm not sure what kind of protection I can offer him now! It was best for all concerned that he stayed away from our world, though now, a whole can of worms is about to be opened.'

13

The governor's normally assured demeanour seemed tainted by sadness.

'But we are not a hundred percent sure that it is him my Lord. No one knows for sure.'

'True, but if it is, he will be in grave danger and I won't be able to stop the others.' Markus became slightly agitated again.

'You must somehow keep watch. Stay out of sight for now, until we know more,' Balfour instructed.

'Yes my Lord, of course.'

'OK Markus, you must return by Portal so as not to be seen. The city must be bustling by now.' Balfour's mind was working away planning the next stages.

'But I can't travel by Portal out of here. It is the Governor's privilege,' he said, reminding Balfour.

'Ah yes – well you can use mine.' Come with me,' he said, rediscovering his authoritative tone.

Both Markus and the Governor left the room. The door shut and the voice from the door said: 'Take care – until your return my Lord.'

Markus and Balfour hurried quickly into the empty room opposite. Balfour, who had fiery red hair like the fire drakes was slightly stockier and taller than Markus. Balfour raised his hand, pointed his longest finger and said, 'Portus.' A black hole opened up in the middle of the room.

'Home,' replied Markus. At that moment, the back of the portal became a dullish grey and he could just about see the inside of a house.'

'Thank you my Lord,' he said politely.

'I must consult the fires first, and then I will send you a secured scroll with your instructions.'

'Yes my Lord,' he said as he raised his leg to put it into the hole then vanished through the Portal.

With Marcus gone, Balfour hurried back along the corridor and back into the main room. He walked into the centre of the four main pillars where he announced,' I wish to consult with the fires of Esrid.'

Steps suddenly formed in the middle of the square and Balfour walked down into a separate chamber. He put on some navy blue robes and a dark cloak that covered his head. He picked up a shoulder length staff and said a word that was just as inaudible as Markus'. A stone wall lowered into the ground and Balfour stepped into another chamber. As he entered, the torch flames lit automatically and then dimmed; it was as cold as the other rooms. There was a bright red carpet on the floor, with a marble pit that was approximately waist high off the floor towards the back wall. He stood in silence, closed his eyes and seemed to enter some kind of meditative state. Moments later, his eyes rapidly. His jaw was firm and his breathing was deep and purposeful. With his energies all focused, he raised both his arms and said...

'By the fires of Esrid, I summon ye – come COME TO ME!' The fires stirred, rose and cackled. *'BY THE POWER OF THE FLAME AND BY THE ALL KNOWING FORCE – I BESEACH THEE – COME – COME – COME AND GUIDE ME AS TO WHAT MUST BE DONE. SO MOTE IT BE!'*

The flames rose even higher with purpose and ferocity. They changed through a variety of colours and finished at a golden orange. He knelt down on the carpet and a voice began to speak.

Chapter 3

THE BULLY

In a small Derbyshire school called Little Middlings, the bell had gone for the final lesson. Most of the children had gone to the class apart from a handful of pupils.

'Hey Tommy- get 'ere. Trying to run away, again,' shouted Vinnie Sykes the school bully.

'I i i it wasn't me V V Vinnie I swear,' he said quivering.

'Yeah – I believe ya,' he smiled. Tommy looked like he was going to get away with it when Vinnie concluded, 'NOT! Haa haa haa.' Vinnie went for poor Tommy. Before he could grab him, the fear within Tommy sped him away. He ran as fast as he legs could carry him. The teachers' offices were behind Vinnie so there was no way that he could reach their protection. He ran to the only place he could go to, a small alleyway that separated the two halves of the junior school. He turned left to run down it – 'not far now,' he said to himself. *I can reach the teachers from the front of the school*, he thought. He got three quarters of the way down when who should appear? Vinnie's three stooges, Baines, Smith and Howard. They stood in the middle of the path, chatting. Poor Tommy's face was plain to see; it was as if some one had stabbed him, and then put salt in the wound.

'Stop him,' shouted Vinnie to his oversized friends.

'Going somewhere Tommy?' Baines said with the smuggest look on his face.

'Yeah –Yeah,' said Smith and Howard.

'Oh poor little Tommy Thumb,' said Vinnie sarcastically, as they surrounded and circled Tommy like a pack of wild hyenas ready for the kill; he didn't know where to look. His head turning as best it could to see what the bullies had in store for him. His heart pounded so quickly, he was convinced that if he took it out, it could pound the four of them.

16

Vinnie started singing: 'Tommy Thumb, Tommy Thumb where are you? Here he is...,' but before he finished, Vinnie's fist flew out catching him fully in the stomach. Tommy doubled up quickly; the pain in him was clear to see. Baines also lashed out though this time with his foot straight into Tommy's side. Tommy started to cry and didn't know what to do. He couldn't run or hide. The only choice available to him was deciding which side hurt the most to hold. Then Howard immediately thrust his elbow straight into his back.

'Ahhhhhhhhhhh,' Tommy screamed and cried some more; the lack of mercy now clearly evident by his captors. Smith was about to delegate further punishment when Vinnie held his fist up ready to punch him in the face; the evil twinkle in his eyes looking more menacing with each blow. He was about to punch down at Tommy, who had his eyes shut, in the hope of extinguishing the evil before him. Suddenly, Vinnie went flying, tripping over Tommy as he passed, whilst scuffing his hands as he fell to the ground. Slightly dazed, he turned round.

'Charlie?' he said as his eyes beginning to focus. 'Get him.' Baines descended on Charlie like a grizzly bear about to maul its victim. His fist came swift and fast like an upper cut, though Charlie was equal to him. Only the small gust of wind from the passing fist caught him in the face. Charlie raised his leg quickly in the direction of Baines' nether regions and he instantaneously doubled up in pain, just as little Tommy had moments earlier. Immediately after, Smith launched himself to rugby tackle Charlie. Charlie, again too clever and quick for his thuggish friends, simply moved to the side, pushing Smith into the wall as he did so. It was Howard's turn, this time positioning his arms as if he were in a boxing match. His right fist came from the side swiftly followed by his left. Charlie evaded both hits. It was now Charlie's turn. He came forward to hit with his right fist, but he lifted his leg at the same time catching Howard in the shin. Howard grasped his chin as he did so then Charlie hit him with his left fist punching him to the floor. Charlie spun round and guided his leg downward on Vinnie who was about to get up and launch another attack!

'CHARLIE STUART!' shouted an authoritative voice at the top of the alley way. Charlie's head spun round to see the

17

headmaster standing there. Little Tommy picked himself up and ran towards the headmaster shouting, 'Sir, sir, it was Vinnie and his friends - they got me and were beating me up.'

'You snitch, Tommy,' shouted Vinnie, his eyes now burning ferociously.

'Cha…Cha…Charlie came to help me,' he stuttered, catching his breath. 'He was amazing Sir and he took all four of 'em on – he stopped 'em.' Tommy's eye was beginning to darken and the colour spread, touching the freckles on the upper part of his cheek.

'Is this true, Stuart?' the headmaster queried.

'Yes Sir. I was on my way to woodwork when I heard somebody shouting, so I went to help,' he said proudly.

'You got all four of them you say,' said the headmaster sounding impressed.

'Yes Sir he got 'em all Sir,' said Tommy, temporarily forgetting the pain he was in, whilst smiling at Charlie at the same time.

'Thank you Charlie. No one has ever stuck up for me before.'

'No problem,' said Charlie. 'It's a pity that they've never been caught before. You stick near me Tommy and it won't be long now until our year leaves.'

Tommy was starting to feel refreshed despite his battered state.

'Vinnie…Baines…Smith…and Howard!' The headmaster spoke as if announcing a death sentence. 'To my office – NOW,' he said as his kindly old face crimpled showing his anger and disapproval.

'Charlie, you follow also as I would like a word.' Charlie knew that despite his noblest efforts he would get a talking to for fighting.

Vinnie and his band of thugs followed the headmaster, glaring at Tommy first and then at Charlie with an evil look. Vinnie was about to mutter something to Tommy when Charlie leaned forward quickly and purposely, reminding Vinnie of what he did to them. Vinnie looked defeated and he didn't look as confident as he did at the beginning of the encounter. They walked towards the headmaster's office and little Tommy went to see one of the other teachers to tend to his wounds.

Vinnie and his gang were inside the headmaster's office whilst Charlie stood outside. The door was shut and the headmaster was shouting, venting his disapproval at what they had done. Charlie could hear him shouting, stating how he disliked bullies and that he was going to write to their parents. He also gave them play time detention so they couldn't bully anymore as well as lines and litter picking duty until the end of the year, which was now only one week away.

'Charlie Stuart, you may enter!' Charlie opened the door and walked in as Vinnie and his friends left.

'Close the door,' said the headmaster.

'Now Charlie – that was a very brave thing that you did, though it is school policy that I should inform your parents of what has happened here today. Officially, we, the school, shouldn't condone the use of violence, though I have to admit I was quite impressed at the way that you handled yourself.' The headmaster's words were music to his ears.

'Kick Boxing Sir – mum sent me to classes ever since I was four.'

'Four?!' he said, nearly choking on the cup of tea that he had made himself.

'Yes sir. Mum said not to go around saying that I did it as it will cause others to come and want to fight you, so I stayed quiet about it.' The headmaster looked at him with some surprise at the maturity of his statement.

'Well, well, Charlie. I'm sure with an attitude like that you will go far in your new school. Which school are you going to again?'

'Compton Comprehensive Sir.'

'Ah yes, a good school Charlie, you will do fine I'm sure.' The headmaster took out a pen and began to write. He said nothing as he scribbled for a few minutes. Charlie was looking at the soft white hair on the headmaster's head and was amazed that it was all there: all the old people that he knew either looked like monks with a shiny scalp with hair either side, or they just had a few strands that were combed diagonally in the hope that it would cover all the head.

'Take this to Mrs Harrington: this will explain to her briefly what has happened and that you were also with me. That is all Charlie.'

'Thank you Sir.' The headmaster just smiled and Charlie left the room.

'CHARLIE STUART!' said a voice in the main corridor. 'Where *have* you been?' *Not again,* Charlie thought. He looked up and saw Mrs Harrington. He didn't really like her because she tended to prod you as she told you off. He turned around, looked at the headmaster's door, and then looked at Mrs Harrington.

'Er - the headmaster's office miss,' he said sarcastically.

'Don't you cheek me young man,' she said sharply. 'Been in trouble have we?' raising her prodding finger like some viper about to strike its prey. 'Some of you lot won't get anywhere in life... you mark my words,' said angrily.

How dare she? he thought.

'Actually, this letter explains it all Miss,' said Charlie. 'I have a letter from Mr Otterwell explaining what has happened'

'Really,' she said in an equally sarcastic tone. Well - you have assignment work to catch up with.'

'Work?' he said sounding confused. 'But we finish next week,' he said suddenly feeling deflated.

'That is no excuse – and, it has to be in on Monday.' Charlie groaned and muttered something under his breath. Mrs Harrington threw out her arm, but Charlie instinctively moved out of the way.

'Here is your final course work.' Charlie picked up the paper and read as Mrs Harrington walked off. Not good, he thought, and began to visualise doing some martial art move on his tutor. *Well, one more week and I will be away from that old bag,* he thought. Before he could think further on the subject, he heard the bell ringing outside. He looked at his watch and noticed a crack on its screen he had from the fight - he could still make out the time however, and it was home time. He ran outside towards the main gate where he was greeted by his older brother, Emmanuel, and younger sister Lucy.

'Come on Charlie - mum's cooking dinner for us – it's egg, bacon, sausage, mushrooms, beans and toast.'

'Mmmm! Great! My favourite!' His stomach began to rumble. Fighting was hungry work, after all.

'Have I got a story for you brother!' said Charlie smiling.

'What's that then brother?' asked Emmanuel. Charlie closed the gate behind him and proceeded to tell his brother what had happened.

'Nice one,' Emmanuel said on hearing the story. 'High five that one,' he continued as their hands connected in mid-air. Lucy didn't seem too bothered, though she was pleased that she had an older brother that could look after her.

'Good man that Mr Otterwell,' said Emmanuel.

'Good man indeed. Not sure what mum will make of it though… ah well, it's happened now,' he said casually.

Fortunately they didn't live too far away and they arrived home moments later.

Chapter 4

RECORDED DELIVERY

They arrived at the front door and Charlie smelled the food that was escaping from under the door and an opened window. The smell enticed and teased them to come in.

Emmanuel carried the keys to the house. He searched his pockets, but he still couldn't find them.

'Hurry up, I am starving,' said Charlie.

'I bet fighting four people made you hungry,' said Emmanuel as they both laughed.

He found the keys in his bag and opened the door. There was a tiny porch way with a small front room to the left. They walked in through another door just a few feet in front of the main door and they were in the living room. Immediately to the left there were stairs leading to the bedrooms, though the staircase was in full view of the living room.

'Hello my lovelies – have you had a good day then?' their mother asked?'

'Charlie was fighting today,' said Lucy quickly.

'Did you have to tell her now?' Charlie said. 'You are a snitch, sometimes, you know,' he said now sounding cross.

'WHAT! YOU'VE BEEN FIGHTING? YOU ARE SOOO GROUNDED,' said Mrs Stuart angrily. 'Are you OK? What happened? Couldn't you have waited a week?' she said, now sounding concerned and frustrated.

'Mum, it was that bully Vinnie: he and his cronies were picking on little Tommy from down the road. They had him on the ground and they were kicking him and everything.'

'Oh really,' said his mum in an unconvincing tone. 'I knew that kick boxing would get you into trouble - if your father was here…' She stopped and seemed saddened by what she had said.

'Well he's not here is he mum?' said Emmanuel, now getting angry.

'Well it's the truth…' shouted Charlie, 'and actually - Mr Otterwell was…' But before he could finish, the phone rang; she picked it up.

'Hello, can I help you,' she said. 'Yes, this is Victoria Stuart.' There was a pause. 'Ah headmaster, I guess you are calling about Charlie's little incident, today.' There was another pause whilst she listened to the headmaster. 'Yes… yes… yes,' she continued: 'Oh I see - is the poor kid OK, now?' Charlie's ears had perked up as he knew the headmaster was explaining exactly what had happened.

'Oh thank you headmaster…I shall tell him…Thanks again, byeee.'

'Well, Charlie. The headmaster is most pleased with you. Tommy's parents had phoned the headmaster and said to pass on a message of thanks to you for saving him. Apparently, he was bullied for most of the year and the poor boy never told his parents until now. Tommy's mum, Hilda, is going to be writing to Vinnie's parents telling them exactly what their son has been up to.'

'Well then mum - do you believe me now? It wasn't my fault.'

'It seems that you did play the hero, though be careful in future.'

'Does this mean…'

'Yes, you aren't grounded,' she smiled.

'YES!' said Charlie scoring yet another victory.

'Charlie, Charlie,' he turned around forgetting his youngest sister Olivia.

'Awe my little baby sister,' said Charlie excitedly.

'She's not a baby,' said Lucy, who decided to join in the conversation again. Well she was right. Olivia was three and a half, Lucy five, Charlie eleven and Emmanuel the oldest at twelve. Olivia just looked like Charlie with lovely blonde hair and dashing green eyes. Emmanuel and Lucy took after their mother with dark, mysterious eyes and dark brown hair.

It was 3.50pm and they sat down to have dinner in the living room. There was a small table on the other side of the sofa

23

where they sat for meals. All of them were quiet whilst they tucked into their food. The smell was even more intense now the food was in front of them. Emmanuel thought he was in paradise and Charlie picked up some bacon and put it in his mouth. The fatty flavour tantalised his taste buds as he swallowed it down, followed by a bit of sausage, egg and toast. Lucy dropped some of her toast on the brown flowery carpet and went to pick it up off the floor.

'Leave it sweetheart and we'll pick it up at the end. We don't want any germs now do we?'

'Mmmmm, mum, you're the greatest at cooking,' said Charlie feeling the reward of his hard work. His mum smiled and started humming approvingly at what had just been said.

Once they had finished, they started to take the pots into the kitchen. Emmanuel started to go upstairs, as he hated washing up. A verbal summoning by his mum quickly brought him back to the kitchen. As they were tidying up, the doorbell rang, followed by a knocking at the door.

'Charlie - is Lee coming round today?' she said referring to his best friend.

'No mum, that's tomorrow as he's helping me with a project – I'll tell you about it later.'

'No problems,' she replied. Victoria went through the first door, closed it, and opened the front door.

'Recorded delivery for Victoria Stuart,' said Jack, the postal worker.

'Oh – the post is late.' *I wonder who this is from*, she pondered.

'Sign here Victoria,' said the postman. He passed her the form to sign. She did so then collected the round tube parcel. She looked at the postage mark and it said Nottingham, with a stamp mark of a dragon next to it. 'Thank you Jack,' said Victoria slightly confused. *What could it be?* she thought. She closed the door behind her and headed for the kitchen. She went to the cupboard drawers and picked out a knife to break a small seal that kept the tube together. She opened it and pulled out the contents. Inside was a letter and some other documents; she began to read. Victoria's jaw dropped as she couldn't quite take it in. The other children were completely oblivious to what was happening as they were busy

24

tidying up. Even Emmanuel got carried away with the cleaning, getting out the vacuum cleaner and managing to vacuum the entire carpet.

'Come on gang,' said Charlie, taking on the role of leader and coordinator. 'Working as a team we'll soon get this done,' he said enthusiastically.

Victoria read and re-read the letter just to ensure that she hadn't hallucinated. She even checked the packaging just to check it wasn't a fake. *No, it's recorded delivery,* she thought, *it can't be a joke.*

'Anything else,' said Emmanuel.
Victoria said nothing as she was still in deep thought.

'Earth calling mum ha-ha,' laughed Charlie.

'Ooh sorry my lovelies. Just sit down and I'll make us a cup of tea,' she said with a beaming smile.

'Can I put the TV on,' said Lucy hoping to catch her favourite television programme.

'Of course you can sweetie,' she beamed again.

'Is mum OK?' said Charlie to Emmanuel.

'Not sure Charlie. Whatever it is she seems to be very happy. Leave her to it, that's what I say, ha-ha.'

'Yeah, we might get fish and chips tomorrow,' said Charlie.

'Thinking of your stomach again Charlie.'

'Yeah I am. I love food,' he retorted. 'Mum always treats us more when she's in a good mood,' he concluded.

'Charlie - could you get Lucy and Olivia's juice out of the fridge please – thank you,' she said, now bouncing around the house and humming a cheerful tune.

'She's definitely lost it,' said Emmanuel.

'Is everything OK mum?' asked Charlie.

'Oh it certainly is – he-he,' she said like a teenager just being asked out on a date for the first time. 'I have some great news,' she said eagerly. 'I'll tell you all very soon,' she said grinning like a Cheshire cat.

The suspense was now killing them all. They had not seen her in such a good mood for a very, very long time.

'Go on, tell us – please,' they all implored.

'I'm afraid you will have to wait: I'm just about to put the kettle on.'

Lucy made a 'tut' noise showing her disapproval and proceeded to watch the TV. Charlie desperately needed the toilet and hurried upstairs. Emmanuel, found himself in the same predicament as his brother and proceeded quickly to the downstairs toilet, whilst Olivia was very happy playing with her cuddly bears, arranging them in a circle, and then feeding them pretend egg and bacon.

Fifteen minutes had passed and the tension and anticipation had grown so much, it seemed like the walls of the house were about to burst. They all gathered into the living room.

'Come on, tell us then,' said Charlie, his frustration had turned to annoyance.

'OK, now we are all cleaned up and toileted - I can tell you the news I've just received,' she said.

'You mean in that tube that has just arrived,' said Emmanuel observantly.

'Yes that is the one,' she confirmed.

'Well here goes.' She took a deep breath, composed her self and began to read the letter aloud.

Dear Victoria Stuart,

Thank you for your enquiry with regards to the possibility of your son's attendance to Dragonstone School, through our access programme for impoverished families. After careful consideration, and consultation with the relevant department, we are delighted to accept your son's admission pending a provisional meeting at the school.

Furthermore, we will also allow attendance of your eldest son Emmanuel, who will have to be placed on a fast track program to catch up with specialist subjects that are attributed to our school. Your youngest daughter, Lucy can attend the Junior Dragonstone School program, and our Crèche facilities are available for Olivia at Dragonstone Tots.

In addition, we will also assist in providing housing and other financial provision to ease your transition to the area as stated

26

by our Provision and Equality Department for families who cannot afford the mandatory fees for attendance.

Finally, it is customary for families who live outside the area to attend our two day programme. The first day consists of a tour of the city before proceedings can be finalised at the school the following morning. See attached sheet for details.

We promise an experience that cannot be matched by any other school in the country.

Looking forward to meeting you all.

School Headmistress and Principal,

Hecate Winslow

There was complete silence in the room, followed by synchronised jaw dropping, with the exception of Olivia who was too young to understand. They all looked at each other aghast and the silence seemed to last an eternity, until…

'Is this a joke?' Emmanuel asked, still not convinced by what he just heard.

'It certainly isn't my dear. Here is the letter – look – read for yourselves,' she said calmly.

Emmanuel and Charlie both dashed to get the letter, but mum raised it before they could grab it.

'Hold your horses. You'll rip the thing if you're not careful. Just calm down and you can read the letter together.' She gave the letter to Emmanuel to hold as he was the oldest. They sat down side by side on the sofa. Emmanuel positioned the letter so Charlie could read. It took them a few minutes then Charlie spoke. 'Crikey,' he said, trying to take in the magnitude of what he just read.

'I know what you mean brother,' said Emmanuel.

'Are we going to go then mum?' he asked.

'How can we not?' She exclaimed. This is our ticket to a better life. Though I have to admit, I am very surprised to hear from the school. I just wrote the letter a long time ago explaining our situation. What I put in it must have really convinced them. Well what do think about it then?'

'This is amazing! I can't believe it,' said Emmanuel.

'Me too,' said Charlie. 'It's supposed to be the best school in England,' he continued.

'Wait a moment…' said Charlie. 'What about my friends? – Will I ever see them again?' Emmanuel looked saddened at what Charlie said.

'Oh yeah, I never thought of that,' replied Emmanuel. The two brothers seemed upset at the prospect of losing their friends, as they had grown up together.

'Well, we are only in the next county, so I'm sure you will see them at some point.' No one said anything.

Charlie was staring down at the floor replaying old memories of the fun times he had with his friends. Emmanuel seemed to be doing the same thing.

'I want to go,' said Lucy already convinced.

'Listen, I tell you what. Let us go to this tour - see the school and we can make our minds up then. I can't say fairer than that. If you both don't like it, then we have lost nothing as you both still have your schooling arranged for next year. What do you think?' asked Victoria.

'That sounds good to me mum. What do you think Charlie?'

'It's not a good idea – it is a great idea,' said Charlie.
All seemed happier with this choice.

'When is the visit arranged for mum?' said Emmanuel.

'Oh, a very good point, let me look at the itinerary?' Victoria proceeded to pull the second item for the tube and studied the paper.

'Ooh crikey – it is Monday, First of August,' sounding excited. 'I suppose term starts again in September, which only leaves a month to prepare – cripes,' she exclaimed.

'Fantastic,' said Charlie, I can't wait to have a look at the school.'

'Me too,' said Emmanuel and Lucy.

'Oh, I mustn't forget, I must tell Mr Otterwell on Monday about the acceptance to Dragonstone,' said Victoria.

It was getting close to six o'clock. Lucy was still hogging the TV watching her cartoons on Free View. Charlie had gone upstairs to start his project. He walked in the bedroom he shared with his brother, which was small and cosy. The wallpaper had pictures of aeroplanes on it. It hadn't been changed for years as they couldn't afford to redecorate.

'How am I supposed to make this when the school is closed?' he said loudly, suddenly dawning on him that he had to create his project. 'Evil hag,' he said, punching the hanging boxing ball as he went red with rage.

It was a hot evening so he went over to open the single glazed windows to let some air in the room. Charlie sat down to work on his project; Charlie always struggled with numbers and angles. He explained to his brother his predicament and Emmanuel realised that he did the exact same project the previous year with his friend Jonny in his father's workshop. After exploring his old trunk, he found it, giving it to a grateful Charlie.

'Brilliant, thanks mate,' Charlie said with a look of victory on his face.

'Yeah, just redraw the diagrams and you'll be fine.'

'Thanks so much. Once we get our plans done, we can then relax for the rest of the weekend,' he said.

It didn't take long to copy out his brother's plans and he spent the rest of the evening watching a DVD before heading to bed. Charlie, being the younger brother, got the lower bunk bed and Emmanuel lay on the top one.

'What a day hey brother?' said Emmanuel.

'Yeah, crazy indeed,' replied Charlie, as he turned the light off.

'What do think about going to Dragonstone?' asked Emmanuel.

'I think it is a brilliant idea! I can't believe they let us in! The more I think about it the better it sounds to me. If we do go I'll miss my friends that's for sure,' said Charlie.

'Yeah, I agree, though getting out of this place seems like a good idea,' said Emmanuel. 'Oh, I'm heading out with Jonny, Richie, Graeme and Craig to play five-a-side football so I'm not coming to kickboxing.'

29

'Ah, OK, fair enough,' said Charlie.

An hour had passed, and they both lay there thinking about what had happened. Charlie's mind was working through the day's events. He hoped there would be a kick boxing school close to where he was living: it was his favourite thing in the world.

Moments later, Charlie heard some deeper breathing from above and he knew that his brother had fallen asleep. After numerous yawns and stretches, Charlie's eyes became very heavy and were closing. Suddenly, Charlie thought he caught sight of a small shadowy figure and he panicked. He submerged his head quickly under the duvet. A moment had passed and then lowered the cover, slowly, so only his eyes were peering over the top. He remained in this position for several minutes with his eyes doing all the work. He was petrified and daren't get out of bed. The shadow entity was moving around slowly, examining the room.

Charlie's eyes widened further with fear as it approached the bed, but the entity stopped a couple of feet away. The featureless creature just stared at him; he was so scared he couldn't summon the courage to call for help. Seconds later, it vanished.

Some time had passed. He was drifting to sleep and his eyes closed. With one last effort, he opened them. He couldn't see anything and convinced himself it was a trick of the mind. Having conceded defeat to tiredness, he finally closed his eyes and went to sleep.

Chapter 5

FINAL WEEK

'Charlieeee, time to get up,' shouted his mother. The alarm went off moments later.

Charlie stretched, yawned and grunted as he opened weary eyes. *Ah, one more week,* he thought to himself. Charlie sat up, remembering what he thought he saw the night before. He got up checked under the bed and the cupboard. 'Nothing,' he said to himself as he proceeded to the bathroom.

'One minute,' his brother said in a gargled tone as he was finishing brushing his teeth. Charlie could hear him spitting the contents of his mouth into the sink. Moments later, he left and Charlie went into the bathroom. The bathroom wasn't too big and it certainly needed decorating: the dull yellow paint was beginning to peel off the walls, the windows needed replacing as there was a spider like crack in it and green mildew was growing from the bottom of the window and walls, spreading upwards. Charlie never liked the bathroom: he thought it was creepy, so it didn't take too long to get ready.

He went downstairs for breakfast. He saw his mum smiling again as she was setting the table. In fact, the only thing she did do all weekend was smile and hum playful tunes.

Charlie walked towards his mum who was no more than five feet tall. Charlie was certainly close to catching her up. Emmanuel had an inch on Charlie, though Charlie was taller than Emmanuel at his age and slightly broader build.

'Mmmm, porridge,' he said as he sat down.

'Best breakfast you can have,' she said smiling again.

'By the way, Olivia will be going to her Grandma's today, my lovelies - I have a lot to do.'

After breakfast, they all tidied up together, collected their bags and left the house.

As they left, Charlie started thinking about the history of the house. His mother had told him that she, her Grandmother and Great grandmother were born there.

The day was pretty eventful for Charlie as the news of Charlie's acceptance spread like wildfire.

The headmaster was especially ecstatic about the whole thing. Charlie's friends were too, but there was a teary sadness that lingered, knowing that this would be last week they would be all together. One of Charlie's other good friends, Michael, was moving to London as his father had a new job so only James and Lee would remain in the village.

At school, Mrs Harrington didn't seem too amused: firstly at Charlie's acceptance to Dragonstone and secondly, the fact that he and Lee had managed to hand in their project on time.

Much to his amazement, it was in Mrs Harrington's lesson that Charlie saw the shadowy creature, again. He knew what he saw the night before wasn't a figment of his imagination. It was of immense intrigue and amusement to Charlie the manner in which the shadow suddenly appeared; it caused Mrs Harrington to trip over whilst she was cruelly shouting, passing lunchtime detentions to those who had not completed their projects. The shadowy creature also caused her chair to collapse in front of the whole school in assembly. Remarkably, most pupils refrained from laughing, as they knew she would get her own back some time.

Come evening time, the family were at the hospital visiting Charlie's Grandpa - Arthur Stuart. Arthur could be a bit grumpy from time to time, though his stay in hospital simply exacerbated his moodiness. He collapsed, suddenly a fortnight ago with a suspected a heart attack, but it wasn't. The doctors had spent some time in trying to find out what had happened using all kinds of probes, needles, and scans to get to the root cause of the problem. The doctors were very mystified by what has happened to him. He was looking a lot paler than normal and he seemed to have lost some weight.

'Hello dad,' said Victoria.

'Decided t'visit then 'av ya?' he asked.

'We were only here last Wednesday,' Victoria said, reminding him.

'Two flippin weeks I've been in 'ere and they 'av no idea what the blinkin 'ell is wrong wi' me,' he said in his Yorkshire accent, sounding distinctly different from the rest of the family.

'Haven't they brought back the results yet?'

'The bloomin idiots, lost 'em or sumthin' – I dunno.'

'I'm sure that they will get to the bottom of the problem soon dad,' said Victoria in a reassuring tone.

'I flippin 'ope so,' he said now sounding fed up.

'Hey grandpa – guess what?'

'Wha' Charlie?,'

'I, well, er, we've been accepted to go to Dragonstone School and we're going to check it out next Monday,' he blurted out trying to change the conversation.

'Ooh, blumin 'eck, going all posh on me then?'

'I think so, grandpa,' he smiled, quite liking the idea of being thought of as posh. 'We aren't sure whether we're definitely going to go to the school. We're going on a visit before making our minds up.'

'I suppose you don't want t' look after me. I see, pack up und leave me,' Grandpa said.

'Oh dad – don't be silly now. It is a marvellous opportunity to move and start up again. Especially since his... well their father up and left. If I ever see him again,' she said threateningly.

They spent some time discussing the school and other life details, when...

'OK folks – visiting time is now finishing,' shouted a nurse.

'Thank god for that,' muttered Emmanuel.

'Oh, is that the time again?'- said Victoria, 'It seems to go so quickly. Well dad, see you again next week.'

'I might be dead by then,' he said pessimistically.

'Oh dad, don't be silly,' she said, shaking her head disapprovingly.

'Bye grandpa,' said all of his grandchildren, who always remained quiet when they went to visit him apart from Charlie, who was very fond of him.

'See's ya later, then,' he said. He closed his eyes to rest and immediately started to snore.

***

The rest of the week brought much laughter of remembering the old times as well as more tears of sadness for the imminent parting of a near eleven year old relationship of four, close friends.

However, it was within these last few days that Charlie observed another strange phenomenon: smartly dressed men in pinstripe suits with long umbrellas walking up and down the street. They stood out like a sore thumb as you never saw such richly dressed men in an area where Charlie lived. What enthralled Charlie further was that he could have sworn he saw the shadowy creature flying amongst them and then away. He watched them closely over the week to see what they were up to. Disappointingly, for Charlie, nothing much happened.

Charlie and Lee had attempted to find out about the Dragonstone School using the Internet, but sadly, the website stated that it was under construction.

The biggest cheer of the week occurred when the headmaster announced Mrs Harrington's resignation from the school, only to be traumatised by a second announcement that she was going to be teaching in the secondary school, which most of them were heading too.

The biggest event of the week was a surprise disco that amazed everyone. Mrs Harrington, who briefly attended, scowled disapprovingly at the level of noise and promptly left, much to the cheer of everyone.

Charlie, Lee, Michael and James danced away in the smoke filled room, whilst James thought it humorous to try and look up some girls skirts like they used to do. Unfortunately, for him, he got his head trodden on by Sarah Bennett in the process.

That was to be the end. A few more tears shed and they said their good byes and good lucks. It was time for something very different to come along for Charlie.

Chapter 6

THE BUS

'Charlieeeee! Emmanuel... wake up!' Small groans and grunts could be heard coming from the bedroom to their mother's daily call; both Charlie and Emmanuel were still very tired.

It was the morning of their trip to Nottingham and the weekend had passed quickly and without incident. Victoria had been busy planning for the day. She made sure that they were packed and ready the night before. The whole family got excited, as they had never stayed in a hotel before.

'Are you two up yet?' she shouted again.

'Yes mum,' they both said at the same time.

'It's your turn to go into the bathroom first,' said Emmanuel, gloating at the fact he could have a few extra minutes in bed.

'Oh yeah,' grumbled Charlie as he slithered out from between his bed sheets and then walked like a Zombie into the bathroom. He quickly got ready when he realised he was in the creepiest room of the house.

Between them, it took ten minutes to get ready because of Victoria's continual nagging reminding them how important it was that they get there on time.

Once downstairs, they hit the breakfast table and swiftly ate their porridge.

There was an anticipation building up in the room created by them all; it would be the fuel that would propel them onwards towards the bus station.

'Walk quickly you lot,' said Victoria in a frustrated tone. 'We're going to miss the bus,' she concluded, whilst pushing Olivia's push chair.

'We're coming, we're coming,' Charlie said. They both slightly behind as they were holding Olivia's hands. They picked up the pace. Olivia seemed as if she was about to take off.

35

'Ouch,' shouted Olivia, 'you are hurting my arm.'

'Sorry Olivia,' said Charlie as he loosened his grip.

Moments later, they turned a corner and the bus was in sight. As they approached, the doors closed. Victoria who was still slightly ahead started banging on the side of the number 39 bus.

'Hold on,' she shouted.

'Hang on,' they all bellowed. The driver looked into his side mirror. His eyes seemed to narrow contemplating whether to pull off or whether to allow them on. 'Ha-ha,' said the driver to himself. He was going to pull out, when the doors unexpectedly flung open.

'Eh,' said the driver sounding very confused.

'Ooh! Thank you driver,' said Mrs Stuart as she put her foot on the step of the bus. At that moment, Charlie looked up and saw the mysterious shadow creature leave the bus. He wisely said nothing as he knew no one would believe him.

They paid for their ticket and he closed the doors bringing the smell of freshly baked bread from the nearby bakery to Charlie's nostrils, which he enjoyed. It was a-far-cry from the usual stench brought about by the litter. After placing their baggage in the hold, they walked towards the back of the relatively empty bus and sat down. Two old ladies sat discussing the youth of today and how life was so different from what it was in their time. 'No respect,' one of them shouted. Charlie knew they were right, thinking about the likes of Vinnie.

The morning was a little cooler than normal so Charlie put his red tracksuit top on over his black Goonies Tee shirt. Charlie loved the Goonies: it was an old film but he loved the adventure they went on. His blue jeans sat nicely on top of his trainers, which were scuffed from all the running around he did at school. Emmanuel wore similar clothes to Charlie, though his jeans were darker and his trainers were newer than his brother's. Emmanuel also had a black Tee shirt on, though his had some numbers and writing on it. Victoria was dressed nicely, as always, as she liked to make a good impression. She was wearing a blue knee-length summer dress and smart summer sandals. Nice clothing was something that rubbed off on both Emmanuel and Lucy. Lucy was wearing a lovely pink dress, with matching tights, and shoes with little stars on. Olivia almost looked identical to her sister, though she wore little pink boots instead of shoes and her top was a brighter shade of pink.

They all sat quietly. Their expressions were full of mixed emotions: they were tired, excited, and in deep thought all at the same time. Emmanuel's eyes were opening and closing. Victoria was reading a book and Olivia and Lucy were fast asleep. Victoria loved her children dearly and always tried to do the best for them. Being given the opportunity to come to Nottingham was more than she could ever hope for.

Charlie was staring outside; his mind began to wonder. He was thinking about the end of year party, smiling at the great send-off they received. He began to chuckle at James' head being trodden on after attempting to look up Sarah Bennett's skirt. Afterwards, his thoughts began to wonder about the dark shadowy figure that seemed to be following him around. *What is it? Where does it come from? Why is it following me? Well so far it hasn't hurt me, so it can't be that bad*, he thought. Ultimately, he wasn't even scared by the strange apparition. He oddly felt something very familiar about it, but he couldn't quite put his finger on it. He then started to wonder about the school and what sort of things they were going to study and what sports he was going to participate in. His thinking suddenly switched to his grandfather in hospital. He was worried about him and hoped that he would be OK. Charlie's thoughts were interrupted by the smell of the bus after the smell of the fresh bread had dissipated. It reeked of bad body odour so he turned his head the other way, where the smell wasn't as pungent.

Smell asides, there was an anticipation sizzling in the air around them. They had never been to Nottingham before. It was much larger than the Village of Eanor they lived in and considerably more affluent.

Suddenly, the driver made an announcement: 'OK, Friar Tuck Way - final stop.'

37

Chapter 7

FEAR, FOREST & THE UNEXPECTED

They all got up and shuffled towards the front of the bus.

'Emmanuel - please get Olivia's push chair out from the hold for me,' asked Victoria politely.

'Sure thing mum,' he replied. After the second attempt, he managed to lift the pushchair out.

They stepped off the bus and car fumes of the inner city greeted them. Charlie was not impressed by this as he already had to put up with the body odour on the bus.

'Hello there,' a voice said loudly from the entrance to an old pub called the Salvation Inn. 'You must be the Stuarts – pleased to meet you all. My name is Randle Fitwick and I'll be your tour guide for the day. I'll also be taking you to the school tomorrow.

Randle was a tallish man of slight build, elegantly dressed and spoke with quite a posh accent. He seemed a caring, helpful and knowledgeable man who was very fond of architecture and history. He had a way of telling stories, which was quite engaging, and he could draw you in with the slightest adjustment to his voice; they all found him quite captivating.

Charlie eyes opened, realising this man wore the same pin striped suit like the men back in his village, but he said nothing.

He took them on a tour of the city centre, but Charlie never realised that Nottingham had such a substantial history. He loved Nottingham Castle, and he was keen to learn more.

The day finished with a shopping trip to a large shopping centre that was, amazingly, paid for by the school; Victoria was in her element as she had never received such generosity.

After journeying across the city, they arrived back to where they got off the bus. There, parked in front of them, was large bus-coach.

'Terrific!' said Charlie. 'That's a nice coach,' he said catching his breath. It was a bright red bus-coach with a massive golden dragon on the side, and Dragonstone written in large thick swirling letters. The windows were tinted so you couldn't see inside, which made it look important and the belly of the coach was rounder than a normal coach.

From the road side, another man appeared.

'Hello Eric,' said Randle.

Eric moved to the side of the coach and opened a side panel.

'Just pop ya stuff in 'ere then we can be off,' said Eric grumpily. All of them put their shopping into the coach. Eric was quite different from Randle, shorter, bolder and quite large around the waistline. He wore a smart red blazer, but he didn't look smart wearing it.

He closed the luggage hold. Eric kept his head down and trundled towards the coach entrance.

'He looks happy,' said Emmanuel.

'Ha-ha,' laughed Charlie. 'I hope he doesn't go to sleep at the wheel.'

'Ha-ha – me too,' said Emmanuel.

'Oh – don't worry about him - that's Eric the coach driver. He's been doing this for years. A good driver, though he can be a bit of a misery.'

'Well come on then, we haven't got all day,' Eric's voice boomed from inside the coach. They walked onto the coach one by one. Charlie was first and he looked around. It was a very smart coach and the likes he had never been seen before. It wasn't just full of seats. It was almost like a very comfortable mobile home, with a lounge area, TV, a bookshelf with magazines and all kinds of old looking books. There was even a small bar like area, which held all kinds of drinks, snacks and silver looking cutlery. The design was old and very posh. Charlie had seen something similar on TV drama his mum liked, were men wore colourful clothing and strange looking wigs. The windows had very smart silk curtains that folded nicely inwards. As they walked on, they could see some other people on the coach.

'Helloo there,' said a man's deep voice. He was clearly Scottish.

They all looked over and there was another family sat towards the back. He stood up and he was very tall, broad, with thick dark hair and matching beard. 'You must be the Stuarts,' said the man. 'A good Scottish name, aye. Och, sorry,' he said, 'how rude, my name is Andrew Campbell and this is my wife Victoria.'

'That's mum's name,' shouted Emmanuel, before Andrew could finish his sentence.

'Aye and a grand name it is,' he concluded. Charlie's mum blushed by his flattering comments.

'Always the charmer,' said Mrs Campbell.

'These are my children, Bruce, Amanda, Martha and Lottie.' All of which were looking at the Stuarts eagerly.

'Lovely,' said Victoria, 'this is my eldest Emmanuel, then Charlie, and these are my youngest Olivia and Lucy.

At that point, Randle climbed aboard on the bus.

'Ah, I see that you are already acquainted. Good, we can now be on our way. Come now Eric, boot her up like they say in the films.' A grunting sound came from the front of the bus as Eric started the engine. He looked into the wing mirror to check for traffic, indicated, waited and then he pulled off.

Both the Stuarts and the Campbells sat down and they discovered that their seats could transform into comfortable recliners.

'Och Aye – this is the life,' said Andrew. 'After spending all those hours on that train, this is just what the doctor ordered. Have you travelled far Victoria?' asked Andrew.

'We come from a small village called Eanor which is only an hour away,' she replied.

'Oh – not too far away,' he said. 'We were supposed to go on this mini tour of the City, though the train got delayed in Edinburgh…just for a change,' he said sarcastically. 'We arrived half an hour ago, so we just decided to wait here. Did you go on the tour?' he curiously asked.

'Yes,' said Victoria. She began to explain to them all what they had done. This was greeted with nods, wide eyes and gasps, especially when she explained about the shopping excursion.

'I canna believe it,' he said feeling rather annoyed that they missed out.

'Not to worry,' said Randle suddenly interjecting. 'There will be plenty of time to catch up. Trust me – there are plenty more surprises in store for you all,' teased Randle.

Surely can't be any better than this? Victoria thought.

At that moment Randle came round with some drinks for everybody as they were all quite thirsty.

'Hello Charlie,' said Amanda 'How old are you then?'

'Hi Amanda,' replied Charlie. 'I am eleven, and my brother, Emmanuel, is twelve years old.'

'Och! I'm the same age as you and Bruce is twelve the same as your brother. I wonder if we are going to be in the same class?' she asked excitely.

'Probably,' he replied. I wonder why it is just our two families on the bus. Don't you think this is a bit strange? I mean the tour, a visit to Sherwood Forest; and the fact that no one really knows anything about the school?' Charlie said, as took another sip of his drink and scratched a small irritation on his nose.

'Aye,' said Amanda, 'very strange. Did you see those people dressed in smart suits carrying those long umbrellas?'

'Yes.' It all seems a bit creepy if you ask me.'

'Aye,' said Amanda – 'very.'

There was a pause in the conversation as they took another sip of their drink and munched on some chocolate cookies. Charlie then had a thought, *I wonder if Amanda has seen any strange shadowy creatures following her around.* How could he approach such a question to a stranger without looking completely deranged, or at the very least, insane! Ok here goes… 'Amanda, this might seem a bit bonkers, but have you seen anything strange, like a shadowy type thing around?'

'Och no,' she said casually. 'Though I have seen ghosts,' she said casually.

'Really?!!' he replied sounding enthusiastic and curious.

'Aye, I was in a pub with my dad and there he was an old man drinking beer. He looked at me, winked then vanished again. I've seen him a few times. I've seen other ghosts, too,' she concluded. Charlie began to relax as he'd met somebody else who had seen something that others hadn't. Charlie began to tell her all about his experience with the dark entity.

'That sounds amazing,' she said with soft Scottish accent. 'I believe you of course. Like me, no one would believe me when I said what I had seen. Everyone laughed and told me I had an over active imagination and that ghosts don't exist.' They both laughed, took another sip of their drink. Charlie looked around and saw Emmanuel laughing at what Bruce was telling him; they seemed to be getting on fine.

'Och my brother,' she said, 'he's been in trouble a few times recently, getting into all kinds of mischief. The other day he got Martha's teddies and hid at the front of her bed. He held them up as if they were floating and then made spooky noises at Martha - she started to cry. Dad got very angry and it took Martha a week to get to sleep properly.'

'Oh dear,' said Charlie, however Amanda said something that just hit Charlie like a tonne of bricks: the 'D' word. Charlie dearly loved his mother though he missed his dad also. In fact, Charlie hadn't really known his dad, but he remembered having a good time with him when he was around. He always seemed to be disappearing on business and, of course, eventually, he disappeared altogether. If his thoughts had not been enough to cope with, Amanda came out with the dreaded question.

'Where's your father?' asked Amanda. Charlie suddenly felt angry by the intrusion of this question.

'Er – mum and dad separated a few years ago,' he replied. Charlie looked down at the floor and his anger suddenly turned to sadness. He didn't reveal to her the fact that he just upped and left one day.

'I'm so sorry Charlie. I shouldn't have said anything.' Her beaming smile suddenly turned into remorse.

'Oh it's not your fault,' said Charlie, understanding it was a question that he might have to get used to. Anyway, his tone suddenly turned more cheerful, '…we've still got mum and I have my brother and sisters. My dad left when mum just got pregnant with Olivia and I'm not sure that he even knows about her. Lucy was too young to remember him.

'Oh dear,' said Amanda. She looked over to her father who was laughing and joking with Charlie's mum and her own mother. *I canna imagine what it would be like to be without my dad*, she thought to herself.

'Good, good,' said Randle, 'great to see everyone getting along so wonderfully. We're not far away now, so start to get your bits together and I'll collect the rubbish.'

Whilst everyone was getting organised, the coach turned a sharp left into a road at the start of the forest. Everyone was falling all over the place apart from Amanda who was still sat down, hanging on for dear life.

'Eric my dear boy, not so fast,' Randle said with a disapproving tone. 'Just think of our guests.' Eric quietly chuckled like a child who knew that he had done something wrong, but enjoyed it never the less.

The anticipation was growing amongst the families on the coach and their eyes were transfixed by the surrounding trees either side of the road. The coach travelled a little further and there were signs of more life as the coach arrived.

All of a sudden, they were greeted by the flames of fire eaters who were standing either side of the coach. You could see the sweat dripping off their foreheads as they had the daytime heat to contend with as well as the fire.

'Wow,' said Bruce, 'that's fantastic. I love fire.'

'Me too,' said Emmanuel.

'That is really cool,' said Charlie transfixed by the flames.

At that moment, the coach stopped and the doors opened. Sword jugglers as well as floor acrobats then followed, all interlinking and interchanging with each other like some circus display.

'Come on you lot, gerroff,' said Eric. They needed no further invitation to get off the coach.

'Come on Amanda take a look at these guys.'

'Hang on Charlie,' she said cheerfully. 'I just need my dad to get my chair.'

'Your chair,' said Charlie curiously?'

'Aye,' she said. 'I canna walk,' she said giggling, as Charlie turned a bright shade of red.

'I, I, I, I'm sorry I didn't know,' said Charlie feeling guilty.

43

'Och Aye,' she giggled. 'Don't worry about it. I'll tell you all about it later,' she said calmly whilst smiling at him. Charlie composed himself a little.

'Dad,' she said.

'Aye, my little angel...I'll get it for you,' he said, instinctively knowing what she wanted.

Minutes later, they were nearly all off the coach. Amanda's wheel chair was outside waiting for her with Charlie at its side. Amanda's father came off with her in his arms and placed her in the wheel chair. Charlie then took it upon himself to push Amanda around, even though she was more than capable of manoeuvring by herself; he was trying to be a gentleman.

'Hello there,' bellowed another voice. 'I am Robin Hood – welcome to Sherwood Forest.' A man dressed in typical Robin Hood attire spoke as if making an announcement or proclamation. 'Who would like to be my outlaws?'

'Meeeee,' all the children shouted.

'Great stuff,' he said. He reached into a large bag and handed out some suitable Robin Hood outfits, which they put over their clothing.

The whole area was getting very busy with different coaches pulling up with other tourists and visitors turning up. The Stuarts and Campbells walked through another large wooden framed entrance.

On the other side were men and women dressed in costume. There were a variety of stalls and designated areas where people seemed to be doing different kinds of craftwork: making pots, tools, cooking, face painting, to name a few. There was even a man forging swords and another making bows and arrows.

The time went quickly. Charlie especially enjoyed the sword making with a man called Barnaby, whilst Amanda received a free bag of herbs from a kindly old lady on the stall.

The evening was drawing to a close and, after a meal, Randle invited them to the evening's festivities: a medieval pageant involving archery and jousting; it was a delight to be sure.

At the end, Randle approached and spoke. 'Now, there is one more event set aside for those belonging to future

Dragonstoners,' he said. Randle's tone managed to arouse further excitement and expectation from everyone.

Charlie began to think. *What more surprises are there in store for them? Surely it cannot get any better than this? Why would the school go to so much trouble to put on such a display?*

'OK – five minutes and we'll be heading into the forest.'

'The forest, spooky,' Emmanuel said. All the children started looking at each other with wondrous delight. Even the adults couldn't wait to see what was to come, apart from Charlie's mum...

'But it's getting quite dark now,' said Victoria.

'Yes,' said Randle, perfect timing for the next activity.' They gathered their things together and started to follow Randle. Both the families reunited with each other and it was all was very quiet as they headed into the darkness.

The temperature was dropping and there was a fresh smell in the air. All you could hear was the procession of crickets and grinding of soil beneath feet as both families and Randle walked along. The sun, at its lowest point, shimmered, a beautiful orange whilst the moon was full and bright. Some of the stars were becoming more visible as the sun was setting.

Lucy was gripping her mother's arm tightly as she was slightly afraid of the dark, and Olivia was almost dropping to sleep. Emmanuel and Charlie were walking side by side, though each was looking around to see where it was they were heading to, but their final destination wasn't obvious. Charlie's mind began to wonder again, thinking about the events that had gone before him as he often did. He was thinking about the castle, pageantry and all the swords and armour and wished he lived in such a time.

Suddenly after walking for what seemed an age, there was a small glow ahead: it was a small fire.

'OK,' nearly there,' said Randle.

'What are we doing here,' said Mrs Campbell sounding rather nervous.

'Nothing to worry about,' said Randle. 'All will be revealed when we get there.' Minutes later, they arrived. Charlie looked around and there, beneath the fire, was a stone circle and all around there were various symbols surrounding a larger circle.

'Please - *tell* me what is happening,' demanded Victoria Stuart. 'This is all very peculiar.'

Randle nodded courteously and spoke. 'You are about to witness something quite unique - something that is not witnessed by many.'

'What?' Andrew demanded.

'It is an ancient rite, a druid ceremony that has been performed for many centuries. Don't be alarmed when you see them. They are a peaceful people who work with and respect nature and humanity.' As soon as he spoke, people came from the woodland from all directions and headed towards the circle. Their appearance was timed perfectly as the sun finally went to rest. All of them jumped when they first saw them. They were wearing long white robes with hoods covering their heads. They came donning flowers and laid them in front of them.

Still fearful, both families seemed to be joined together even closer to form a protective barrier.

'Fear not,' said a voice. One person came forward and pulled the hood back. It was a beautiful lady with smile that seemed to warm all those around her. 'Blessed be, for it is an honour to receive such distinguished guests.'

'Blessed be,' said the rest of the group.

'*Why* have we been brought here? What *are* we doing here?' said Andrew now rising very tall. 'I never realised it was Halloween. Is this a trick or treat or something?' he asked defensively.

'Hello Andrew,' said a familiar voice. Another person came forward and pulled his hood down. It was Randle. No one had noticed him disappear and they were shocked to see him all dressed up.

'It isn't Halloween and it is certainly no trick or treat,' he laughed. 'It is like I said - you are here to witness a unique ceremony…that is all. I can assure you that not many people will see what you are going to see, and I can further assure you, by mid-morning tomorrow, the whole thing will make a lot more sense. You are about to receive a blessing from our kind, that is all. If you wish you can leave, it is your free choice.'

'Let's stay mum!' pleaded Charlie. 'This looks very interesting,' he said, sounding unperturbed by what was happening.

46

'Can we stay dad?' pleaded Amanda.' 'I've seen documentaries on these kinds of things…'

'Please mum,' said Emmanuel.

'Well, I'm not too sure' said Victoria. 'After all, it is way past your bed time.'

'Please, please,' they all begged together.

'What do you think Andrew?' said Charlie's mum.

'Och Aye, - we'll stay if the children want to stay.'

'Mum, mum please,' said Charlie.

'Oh, OK then – but I have to say - this is highly irregular.'

'Take these,' said Randle giving them some warm robes to wear as it was getting cold. They put them on and they sat down. Charlie was sat by Amanda's side.

'What do you think to this,' asked Charlie.

'This is really cool. I don't know why, but something seems familiar about all this,' said Amanda.

'I know what you mean,' he said.

A drum began to beat slowly which brought a natural silence to proceedings.

One of the druids came into the centre sprinkling salt on the ground whilst muttering some strange sounding words and then walked three times in a clockwise direction around the circle. A second druid then came round with a flamed torch and also started muttering some words and walked around the circle three times. Then, a third one came wafting some kind of large incense stick, muttering words and walked around like the others. There was a fourth one who walked around, whispering various words, though this time sprinkling water around. Finally, another druid came into the centre of the whole circle, lifted his hands high and said a few words.

The druids then retreated to the outskirts when the women who greeted them came forward with a large staff and started turning around in the centre with the staff pointing towards the ground. As soon as she started, a chill pervaded the area and a tingling sensation went up their spines; they shivered. Both families seemed transfixed by the whole proceeding and were keen to see more. The lady who drew the staff around and around seemed to

47

make an invisible door way in the air. One by one they entered the circle.

Other druids then took it one by one to etch invisible symbols at various points of the circle once they were in. Then finally, two more people went in raising their arms and then bowing whilst making further incantations.

Charlie suddenly looked up and there, sat beyond the fire, was the shadowy figure. This time it was bearing a smile. It winked with one of its large eyes he had never seen before and then it disappeared again.

'It was over there again,' whispered Charlie to Amanda.

'There was what?' asked Amanda.

'That shadowy creature I told you earlier. Did you see it?' quizzed Charlie in the hope that she had seen it.

'Sorry Charlie I didn't,' she whispered back regretfully.

'What is it?' he said to himself? He was now feeling the frustration of not knowing.

Amanda's eyes went as wide as plates and her mouth opened.

'Look,' she pointed.

'Look at what?' asked Charlie.

Amanda said she saw some golden glowing figure in the centre. It came towards her and then it disappeared again.

'See what,' asked Charlie.'

'I'd never seen anything like that before,' she said, explaining to Charlie what she had seen.

Charlie looked surprised but then began to wonder why she could see nice glowing things and why he could only see dark shadowy things.

The drum stopped, which brought back Charlie's and Amanda's attention again. This time, one of the druids brought forward a large silver goblet. It was held up in the air and magickal sounding words were spoken. The goblet was then held by the beautiful lady who had spoken to them earlier and all the other druids came and placed various ingredients into the goblet. The goblet was swirled around to mix the added ingredients. 'So Mote it Be,' the lead druid said.

The rest of the druids said the same immediately after.

'Come my friends,' the lady spoke. 'Drink with us this special night. It is our gift to you.'

'What is it?' demanded Andrew sounding suspicious.

'It is a consecrated drink, mixed with fine herbs and berries. It is an ancient formula passed down only by word of mouth.'

Charlie fearlessly sprang up and went forward to the lady.

'It's an honour to meet you,' she said to Charlie.

'Thanks – you too,' Charlie nodded respectfully.

He took the goblet and took a sip. He rolled it around his mouth his mouth then swallowed.

'Mmmm,' he said. 'This is good. Come and have a sip of this,' he shouted. Sure enough, they all went up to have a drink from the goblet.

'It is done. Blessed Be, So Mote it Be.'

***

The day's events had exhausted them that much that they seemed not to take an interest in the hotel. Charlie and Emmanuel were sleeping away peacefully in the partially moonlit room they were sharing, when suddenly something seemed to disturb Charlie's peace. He began to panic: his body went rigid, his breathing became quickened and erratic and his head turned side to side, eventually turning as rigid as his body. More disturbing was the fact that Charlie wasn't seeing anything, no dreams, no images, nothing. Trying to open his eyes he barely managed a squint; what madness possessed him in the darkness?

He tried to scream but couldn't. He tried to move again but couldn't. The only movement that came from him was a tear rolling down the left side of his cheek.

Charlie couldn't understand what was happening to him and, disturbingly for Charlie; it was for the first time that he felt the fear of being powerless. Never before had he experienced such anxiety as he was always so confident.

Charlie tried to fight it further, but the harder he tried, the tighter the madness gripped him; he began to sweat profusely.

He had all but given up. He couldn't even cry when at last he managed to make a small whimper of a plea, 'Help,' Charlie croaked. As fast as he whispered it, the shadowy figure flew into the room, somehow comforting him. It flew around him so quickly that a cool breeze formed around him. Emmanuel, who was completely oblivious to Charlie's plight, picked up on the coolness and wrapped himself up further in his duvet. Charlie momentarily forgot his paralysis and looked in wonder at what he was seeing. Whatever the shadow was doing was working; Charlie's stiffness was reducing and he could wiggle his fingers and toes. Minutes later he was completely free.

'Thank you,' said Charlie gratefully as the shadow entity flew through the main door.

Charlie's experience had exhausted him further but he reluctantly went back to sleep, frightened the experience would return.

Four hours had passed and Charlie was disturbed by something else. His reaction was to move his hands and arms hoping he wasn't paralysed. He did so effortlessly, which instantly calmed him down. He realised it was only his mum knocking at the door.

'Charlieee…Emmanuel…time to get up.'

'OK mum,' said Emmanuel surprising Charlie.

'Ooh you scared me,' said Charlie nervously. 'I didn't realise that you were awake.

'Yeah, I've been up a while. I just woke and I couldn't get back to sleep. I slept well though. Did you?'

'Er – yeah,' said Charlie, lying to his brother.

He knew that he wouldn't believe him if he told him what had happened, so he didn't say anything.

After breakfast, both the Stuarts and Campbells went outside to a fed up looking Eric, who was to take them to school.

Chapter 8

DRAGONSTONE SCHOOL

A small slit in the gate opened and a pair of hazel eyes were looking through.

'Come on then - open up,' said a frustrated Eric.

The guard's eyes narrowed, sneering back disapprovingly at Eric's choice of words.

Slowly the enormous wooden gate creaked open dividing down the middle. The surrounding wall was so huge, not even a fire engine's ladder could have reached the top.

Eric put the coach into gear and began to enter the grounds. To the left there was a small hut type structure with a large built man sitting down operating the controls to the gate. Both the Stuarts and Campbells had their faces glued to the windows, trying to glimpse what was, until now, a complete mystery. As they looked, their mouths went into a fly catching position, totally flabbergasted at what they were seeing.

'This is Dragonstone my dear friends,' said Randle. 'Marvellous isn't she? Wait until you see the rest.'

The grounds were absolutely, massive with fields as far as the eyes could see. Groups of trees were huddled together and deer roamed the grounds. There was a massive building sat at the top of a long gradual sloping hill.

'Now, this magnificent structure was the first Renaissances buildings in England built in the early 1500's. It was completely out of context for the period of course.'

'What do you mean,' asked Charlie?

'It means that in this country we still had older medieval structures compared to renaissance inspired Europe, so this would have seemed very strange over here.

'Oh I think I know what you mean,' said Charlie.

'Interesting,' said Mrs Stuart. 'I like this more and more.'

'Aye,' said Mrs Campbell. 'I did have my doubts, but I think it is going to work out just fine,' she said relieved.

The building was beautifully designed: it had two enormous dragons in front of the building that were moulded into a protective stance. They looked menacing and magnificent at the same time and the children couldn't wait to have a closer look at them.

The school appeared to be abandoned; term time hadn't started yet. Charlie looked over to Amanda and noticed her staring into the distance.

'What's the matter?' asked Charlie.'

'Oh, I could have sworn I saw a group of people over there. Oh, it must be my imagination,' said Amanda as Randle looked curiously at her.

A lovely cool breeze greeted them at the top of the hill and Charlie took a deep breath taking the fresh air in, instantly relaxing him. With the massive school to the back of him, Charlie looked around - he could hear no noise. There was a peace in the area that brought about an instant quietness and stillness; even the traffic couldn't be heard in the distance. This, coupled with the warmth of the sun that gently caressed the skin, made for a perfect moment. He looked down the slope and he could see birds quite happily fluttering from tree top to tree top as well as small clusters of deer grazing in the freshly cut grass; the whole scene was remarkably evocative for Charlie. He turned around slowly and he was instantly greeted by the large dragon that stood to the left of the main entrance. Despite its lifeless stone mass, it made Charlie jump, bringing him completely out of his moment of wonder.

He steadied himself and he examined the two dragons closely, followed by the school itself. Charlie remembered what Randle Fitwick was telling him about the school being from the Renaissance period and it certainly looked different from any of the other buildings that he had seen previously. Either side of the centre front of the building were two huge towers. Between the towers was a gap filled with many classrooms. There was centre tower that was even taller than the towers and approximately five times the width and beige in colour. *Someone made this into a school,* he thought – *wow.*

Charlie then went over to join the rest of the family, and they arranged themselves into a makeshift circle to discuss what they thought about the school and they were all equally impressed as well as surprised. Emmanuel spoke. 'I can't wait to see inside: I wonder what the classrooms are like?'

Charlie looked over to the other side where he observed the Campbells were discussing similar things, apart from Bruce who decided to climb the dragon.

'Hey...Bruce...Get down,' shouted Andrew. 'Ya shoudn' be climbing up there...get down, now!' Emmanuel laughed, Charlie grinned and Lottie wished he'd just fall off for all the cruel teasing that he had given her.

Randle then spoke. 'Oh, I hope you like the school grounds, but before we continue, headmistress, Hecate Winslow, would like to see you all now.' They were eager to meet the headmistress whose letter had greeted and surprised them.

'Follow me,' said Randle.

They all proceeded up through a multitude of steps, apart from Amanda, who was pushed along by her father on the flattened pathway leading into the school. Shortly after, they were all in the vast hall with two staircases leading upwards from two directions. Beneath the stairs were more doors that led into different areas of the school. There were also some lift doors. Dark wooden flooring covered the entire area, matching the colour of the doors. Surrounding the outer part of the wall were suits of armour from the medieval period, all decorated with different colours and individual Coat of Arms. There were four stands propped up against the wall with long broad swords slotted in them, but one was missing; it reminded Charlie of the sword he tried to make in Sherwood Forest. Placed high on the thick stonewalls were old fire torches that weren't lit and there was no sign of modern lighting anywhere. There was a definite old smell that seemed to excite Charlie, and Randle spoke again as they were all admiring the area. 'This pays tribute to the Keep that used sit here.'

'A bit like Nottingham Castle,' said Mrs Stuart.

'Yes,' replied Randle.

'This is a grand location for a school. Where are we going to live?' asked Andrew.

'All will be explained shortly,' he said reassuringly.

'This is so cool,' Emmanuel muttered. 'This makes Compton Comprehensive school look tiny.

'Yeah - and just *look* at those cool knights over there!' said Charlie.

'Ah said Randle. I'd noticed in the forest that you had a particular interest in swords. I bet fencing would suit you.'

'Fencing?' said Charlie looking confused.

'Oh yes – of sorts. The school offers quite a large range of facilities and activities for students to participate in,' said Randle, finally divulging some information about the school. 'Come on then, time is ticking – we mustn't keep the headmistress waiting,' said Randle looking at his watch.

They all took to the left hand staircase and made their way to the top, whilst Amanda got into the lift with her father. As they walked up, Charlie imagined himself sliding down the banister, brandishing a sword. He noticed that the whole area was quite dark despite the daylight coming in through the large window. It didn't bother him as it just added to the ambience and mystery of the school.

They all arrived at the top and went through a doorway. They walked through and found themselves in a narrow corridor that looked completely different to the main hall. It was brightly decorated with a bright red carpet, with subtle oil light fittings positioned every six feet or so. The walls were tall and had golden striped wallpaper reaching down to an intricately designed wall divider that was gold in colour, with wooden panelling making up the rest of the wall to the floor. Along the corridor were four doors, each very different from each other.

'Ah here we are,' said Randle as Charlie noticed there was no name on the first door they came to. What made it stand out was the triangular wooden carving that was the top of the doorframe. Randle knocked.

'Come in,' said the Headmistress. Randle pushed the handleless door open and they walked into a very large office, which had a similar décor to the bus. Hecate Winslow sat behind a semi-circular desk. It had golden trimmings that were similar to the wall divider in the main corridor. The desktop was made of a highly polished deep red wood. You could see the curved rings from the tree bark in it.

Charlie looked around and he couldn't understand why there were no doors leading in from outside the room like he saw in the corridor. *Surely the doors would have overlapped into this room,* he thought.

'Welcome, welcome,' said the headmistress. 'Please come over here and be seated.' They all walked over to some comfortable looking sofas that had velvety pillows on them with tassels hanging off each corner.

'Make yourselves at home – after all, this will be your new home,' she said with some certainty. 'You must have so many questions regarding the school and why we go about our business in the way we do.'

Charlie looked at her and you could clearly see why she was a headmistress: she had an air of authority about her and her voice was quite commanding, but pleasant. She was tall and smartly dressed. She wore a long dark green skirt with a matching jacket, which supported an ornate broach that gave her a regal appearance. Victoria Stuart spoke. 'I have to admit, it does seem rather extravagant just to come to a school interview,' she said suddenly.

'My dear, you will find that there are many extravagant *things* here at Dragonstone!' she swiftly responded. 'But first, a toast to your arrival - after which, everything will be made clear.'

'Randle, would you mind,' said Hecate, signalling to him to pour the drinks.

'Not at all,' said Randle pleasantly.

Charlie stiffened up slightly after being reminded of the events that followed the drink he had in the forest. Randle walked over to a cabinet and opened it. He pulled out what looked like an old whisky decanter and the right amount of similarly looking glasses. He placed them on a silver tray, poured the drinks, and then carried it over.

'There you all are. Not to worry it is non-alcoholic,' Randle chuckled, as Andrew looked disappointed.

'If there is anything with a bit more of a kick to it for the grown-ups, I wouldn't mind sampling a bit,' teased Andrew.

'Typical,' said Victoria Campbell.

'Oh, I'm sure you'll find this will have 'Kick' enough,' Hecate reposted.

Randle handed the drinks out. They all had a sniff. Charlie swore the drink smell changed from liquorish to chocolate.

'Mmm – this is nice, it smells nice too,' said Charlie. You could see that everyone else was enjoying it.

'A toast,' said Hecate, 'to our newest members of Dragonstone – to Jarv!'

'To who?' Emmanuel queried.

'I'll explain later,' said Randle. 'Ah – this looks to be Percy's best batch yet,' he smiled.

They all knocked back their drinks, when…

'Ooh…I feel kinda funny. What is this?' said Victoria.

'Me too…' said Victoria Campbell. 'What was that?' she said staring at the desk.

'Oh, *not* again!' said Charlie as his ankles, wrists and heart all began to tighten up again, though this time there was an intense burning sensation, before he dropped to the couch. Amanda passed out. Those that remained standing began to sway. Andrew's vision was all a blur and everyone he saw began to triplicate, before he too collapsed onto the couch. Emmanuel had fallen into an uncomfortable heap on the floor and Bruce doubled up over the couch's arm. Lucy, Olivia, Martha and Lottie were all fast asleep. Charlie's eyes were the last bodily movement that remained defiant. Charlie heard Randle and Hecate whispering about him and a prophecy, before losing consciousness.

Half an hour had passed and the Stuarts and Campbells were still unconscious in the room. Randle and the headmistress were running around. Partly in anticipation at what had happened to their guests and partly because they seemed to be putting things in order.

'How long before they wake?' Randle asked.

'I'm not quite sure. Each case is quite different, though I'm quite sure that they will be fine,' said Hecate.

'This has taken some time for the drink to have its effect,' he said nervously.

'It does seem unusually long,' said Hecate, agreeing.

'Yes – far too long,' said Randle. 'I hope that they are OK with this.'

'Ah, once they see our world, today will become but a memory,' said Hecate confidently.

'True,' said Randle. 'Though, there was the unusual case of Mr Jones who went slightly mad at what he saw. His mind simply couldn't accept this world. A good job we had the 'Memory Blank' potion here. Poor Eric had to drive all the way to the south coast to drop him off.'

'I remember him, poor fellow. Well, at least he's happy now, I suppose,' said Hecate, reflectively.

'Are you sure the Astro-Mages' are correct about this?'

'Oh yes,' she said confidently. 'Why would someone go to such lengths to invisibilize their charts is a complete mystery, not to mention quite worrying. What kind of person or persons would deny their family this rite is beyond me,' said Hecate. If it wasn't for Victoria's letter arriving at the school thus breaking the dark charm, they could have been lost forever,' she concluded.

'What is more worrying is that there could be many more families or individuals in the same boat,' said Randle.

'Yes yes,' said Hecate. I hear security has now been doubled at the Astro-Mages chambers and Philbus is now in charge.'

'Philbus?' exclaimed an alarmed Randle.

'Yes, Philbus,' she repeated. 'Astrophos was furious that someone had managed to get into their space.'

'Well, I'll be surprised if they try this again with him in charge. God help them if he catches them. There hasn't been need of an inquisitor for years. I suppose he'll be glad of the work.'

'I assure you he's revelling in the role,' said Hecate.

'Once they discover how things work, should we tell them about the scrolls disappearing? Or should I say hidden,' asked Randle.

'Probably not a good idea; there are many factors that we do not understand ourselves, including, why the dark charm broke.

Cosmolos has a couple of theories that he's currently investigating. For now, let's just see what happens. There could be other consequences as the result of this,' said Hecate sagely.

'How do you think they'd react to all this?' asked Randle.

'I have no idea. In most cases, it is generally well received. Well, we've prepared them and many Plainlanders' as much as possible before entering our world. We have even influenced their television and movie making. It somehow cushions their acceptance of all things magickal,' replied Hecate.

'Oh yes, I have to say some of their films have been excellent recently. There is one that seems quite apt, but as they will learn there is a lot more to understand about magick than they realise.'

'Yes,' said Hecate, 'there is so much for us to learn, also. The last of the greatest wizards died an age ago, taking the magick of the old with him. I would love so much to uncover more about the ancient mysteries.'

Fifty minutes had passed and there was still no sign of consciousness. Randle was fidgeting nervously and even the calm Hecate Winslow was showing signs of agitation. Randle was pacing up and down the room. He then sat down, got up, sat down, before pacing around again. Hecate was sat by her desk tapping her fingers and drinking some cold water. Suddenly, someone spoke. 'Och – my head,' said Andrew as if he'd woken up after a Friday night out with his friends.

Randle and Hecate breathed a sigh of relief and headed for the door. Moans and groans then sounded from the rest of them and then, gradually, everyone started to regain their faculties. Charlie was the last to wake up. He wasn't looking particularly happy.

'What happened?' asked a startled Victoria Stuart.

'I have no idea,' said the other Victoria.

'This is getting beyond a joke,' said Andrew angrily. There are too many strange things happening here and they still haven't told us a thing! Have they?' bellowed Andrew. 'Let's go here, *drink this*, drink that,' he continued to rant. 'What have we got? A sore head and no explanation.'

'He's right,' said Mrs Stuart. 'Where have Randle and Hecate gotten too?'

'Aye,' said Mrs Campbell. 'They've done a runner.'

'This is like some sick practical joke. What a waste, what a waste,' said Andrew getting angrier with every breath.

'Look at the time,' said Emmanuel. 'We've been here over an hour.'

'AN HOUR!' fumed Andrew. 'Wait until I get my hands on them. I'll turn them both to haggis.'

'Is it me, or does everything seem a little brighter to you,' said Victoria Stuart observantly.

'Aye – you're right. Things do seem a little more vivid. It is like everything is sticking out a little more and the colours are more beautiful,' she said feeling less apprehensive.

'Drugs I tell you. That's what they've given us. I bet they would have operated on us next,' said Andrew in frenzy.

'No drugs and they'll certainly be no operating either,' said a voice from the doorway.

'Who are you? Why have you done this to us?' shouted Andrew, curling up his fist and beginning to walk towards him. A man stood at the door wearing dark blue robes with a prominent, blond and white beard.

'Please forgive me and all that you have experienced this past hour or so. My name is Cosmolos and I'm an Astro-Mage.' His words made Andrew stop in his tracks. 'I am part of small number of people who decide who can come to the school, as well as…' Cosmolos said, when…

'An Astro what?' said Emmanuel interrupting.

'Astro-Mage,' said Amanda out of the blue. 'A mage is someone who works with magick… my grandma told me.'

'That is correct young lady, very good.'

'Magick - what utter tosh, rubbish, no such thing,' said Andrew recapturing his aggressive tone.

Amongst the furore, Charlie suddenly realised that he might actually get some explanation about his experiences.

'A trick, you think,' said Cosmolos. Cosmolos raised a shoulder length staff he was holding. The top had a silver ring with a small silver ball at its centre that was now beginning to swirl round. A golden glow began to emanate from the sphere and grew slightly larger as he held it up.

'It's all a trick,' said Andrew, as he decided to move forward to confront Cosmolos.

'Apanus,' said Cosmolos pointing his staff at Andrew, and he began to rise off the ground.

'What the…' said Andrew lowering his voice. Everyone just looked amazed at what was happening and then Cosmolos lowered him down.

'Look, look,' shouted Lucy excitedly as some vines appeared on the boarder at the top of the room.

'Look over here,' shouted Martha pointing at the flowers on the desk: there were tiny white, pink and green spheres circulating around the unusual looking flowers. The spheres flew in, disappearing within. As the green sphere left, an amazing fragrance filled the room, bringing a sense of tranquillity.

'Er…Aye…Er,' said Andrew stuttering.

Both the Victorias were standing together absorbing the scent through their nostrils and enjoying the fragrance, though Charlie was still a little apprehensive about the whole thing. Emmanuel was frozen to the spot and Bruce just sat down, his mouth was wide open, looking rather pale. Amanda and the rest of the girls were all excited. They moved around the room, chasing the phenomena trying to examine it.

'Drugs, I tell you. We had these in the sixties,' said Andrew with a final bit of defiance.

'Drugs,' laughed Cosmolos. He swung the top of his body round with his staff and the other arm pointing at the door that instantly flung open. In flew the miniature firedrakes that went immediately to the torches and open fire. Once lit, the flames grew tall and the heat became intense. Andrew was about to open his mouth again, when one of fire drakes flew over and stung his bottom. Andrew began to run around the room with the firedrake in tow.

'Drugs he says,' said Cosmolos chuckling.

'OK, OK,' shouted Andrew. *Please* stop this…er… well whatever they are.' Cosmolos closed his eyes and took a deep breath.   Moments later the firedrake flew off to meet its companions. The flames receded and the room cooled down.

'Why? - Why us?' asked Andrew.

'Why?' said Cosmolos – 'Because you all have magick,' he said.

Chapter 9

A WORLD OF MAGICK

Silence pervaded the room. Cosmolos placed his staff back on the ground and the metallic end slowly began to stop. Before it did, Cosmolos muttered something under his breath and a pleasant cool breeze now entered the room.

'Air was always my favourite,' said Cosmolos. A *tut* of disapproval could be heard spitting from the fireplace. The air brought calmness, liberating the mind of any anguished thoughts.

Both the Stuarts and the Campbells stood united and, for once, they were speechless. The magick that had unfolded around them brought with it a sense of fear and wonderment at the same time. The atmosphere seemed tangible and bright. The vines on the ceiling seemed to pulsate as if to nourish the room and the spherical lights that surrounded the flowers moved on to some other flowers that had suddenly appeared.

'This must be very confusing for you,' said Cosmolos. 'I then ask you all to sit down and I will try to explain to you all.' Both families sat down, trying to look at Cosmolos to hear what he had to say. However, they were all a little pre-occupied with the wonder that had so suddenly entered their lives. Before Cosmolos could say anything, the main door to the room opened and Randle and Hecate entered the room. Hecate was still wearing her dark green suit but Randle had changed back into his druid clothing.

'Feeling more comfortable?' said Cosmolos to Randle.

'Much. Plainland clothing can be so restricting.'

'Excuse me,' said Victoria, but can you *please* tell us what is happening. We've been waiting so patiently, though now I think we deserve to know what this is all about.'

'I apologise for the distraction. I will begin immediately,' said Cosmolos. 'Thousands of years ago, existed quite a different world to the one you already know. Some of which has existed as mythology through the legends such as King Arthur, Merlin, and

Hercules for example. Back in those days, magick was very real and was practiced as a daily routine by those who could. Powerful magicians such as Merlin, Gideon and a few others were important advisors to the success of the kingdoms.'

'What happened?' asked Amanda.

'Well, those who had abilities were scoffed at by those who did not. A few centuries after Merlin, Lord Gideon Mortus became the most powerful wizard. He was wise and advised the ruling king of the time. However, an equally powerful wizard named Prince Zordemon who was son and heir to the king, had other ideas with what to do with the future of the world. The story got confused over the years as to what happened but what we do know is that, Gideon made arrangements for those who had magick and for those who did not to live separately. Gideon didn't like the idea as he knew that ordinary men neither had the knowledge nor insight to rule properly. Unlike Prince Zordemon, Gideon respected the free choice of men, so went about creating an agreement. However, Gideon made sure that traces of magick existed in the Plainlands.'

'What do you mean?' asked Victoria.

'Well, for all intents and purposes, you can't obliterate magick completely, it is impossible. The whole world is joined together by magick forces. However, Gideon made sure that these traces extended to sensory and some visual experiences.

'Like the cold tingling sensations in the forest?' Victoria Campbell asked.

'Exactly,' said Randle. 'And more…'

Cosmolos continued. 'Enough magick existed to ensure that people had retained some memory of it, so there has always been an interest in magick and some can even practice it to an extent. Look at your world today, look at the surge of interest in so called new age works; even your films have explored magick. The whole magickal concept aches terribly in the conscience of folk. Even those who do not believe are always drawn to such things; this is the power of magick. Remember, magick can never be destroyed, it is always there. Ultimately, it is up to you to decide whether to use magick and if you do, how to use it.'

'You mean for good or bad,' said Mrs Campbell.

'Yes,' replied Cosmolos. 'Sorry, as I was saying, shortly after a battle, Zordemon was defeated. A contract was signed so magick practically became virtually redundant in the Plainlands, so all kinds of witches, warlocks, wizards and magicians moved on.'

'So how does this place exist then?' asked Victoria Stuart.

'A good question! Well, all those with magick had to go somewhere, so Gideon made sure that there were places where magick folk could live. He and some other powerful wizards did this wonderfully. Sadly, there were some Plainers who sought to eradicate the very memory of magick and thousands of people were tortured and burned, as was most of the literature of the time. Most of the people killed were innocent, but some were real magick folk who chose to live on the Plainlands to keep an eye on what was happening and, without their powers, they were defenceless. History was re-written. The old ways became stories, myths and legends instead of facts. Centuries of numbing down has resulted in what you believe today to be real. For centuries, magick was seen as evil and something to be feared. Yes there are dark aspects to it, as there are in all things, but there is a beauty and intelligence that reaches far beyond the Plainland concepts. Plainers tend to associate magick with fear, which is completely wrong. In the modern era, the media and filmmaking has helped to re-introduce the concept of magick, even though most of it is still, sadly based on fear. People like to be on edge, excited by dark ways distorting the true representation of what magick is about. It is quite devious really, as it stops people from exploring their own power and true potential; if you fear magick, why explore it? Gideon knew that magick cannot be eradicated totally no matter how hard you try,' said Cosmolos. 'There is a prophecy, or should I say a half prophecy that states that a greater balance will return to the world one day. Until this day, we have no idea of how it will happen. Most folk either have given up or do not even care. This realm has become so much a part of our lives that most magick folk do not care much about what happens to the Plainers; life here is very comfortable.'

'What do you mean a half prophecy?' queried Charlie.

'Well, for some reason, half of the prophecy disappeared off the face of the earth. What happened to it nobody knows.

Over the centuries, a massive search has been underway to recover the lost half of the prophecy as magick folk believe it will answer all their questions.'

'Why us? What do we have to do with all this? How come we have magick? How do you know we have magick?' asked Andrew, now feeling much calmer.

'Good questions. Each person is born at a specific point in time. I assume that you have all heard of astrology?'

'Yes,' they all acknowledged.

'Yeah, its load of old...,' Andrew thought twice about saying what he was going to say, after all he didn't fancy being suspending in mid-air or being attacked by another firedrake.

'Ahem,' said Cosmolos, raising a brow.

Andrew just put on an innocent face and Cosmolos narrowed his eyes at him, like the gate guard did to Eric.

'Well, the astrology that has become popular in the Plainlands only covers part of what actually occurs. Yes there are predictive values which incidentally, most can be changed, but there are other deeper elements to their readings. Each person has a hand crafted chart or an Astro-Chart. Within these charts there are key signatures or traces for magickal potential. Magick exists within families and nearly all are born and live here,' he explained.

'What happened to us?' asked Victoria Campbell.

'Well, for some reason, some families escaped us but, eventually, we do catch up with them. That is why Randle and some of the others you saw volunteer to become what we call Trackers. I believe the name is self-explanatory.'

'So that's what happened to us then, we got found?'

'Yes... eventually,' said Cosmolos.

'With magick not being able to function as effectively in the Plainlands, it is quite difficult to keep account and to track everyone. It is quite frustrating to be honest. This is why we remain in contact with the Plainlands. There are some here, who wish to cease all communications with the Plainlands and say to those with magickal abilities born there it is tough luck. What they don't know won't hurt them et cetera. Of course, this is nonsense as we all originated from the Plainlands. As you have recently found out, the school is a gateway to the magickal realms and it was

65

one of the first to be created. As you will undoubtedly find out, there are various ways to travel and communicate between communities, towns, cities et cetera via magickal lines.'

'Fascinating,' said Victoria Stuart. 'You say we have magick. Does this mean we can do the things that you do?' Everyone seemed to listen more intensely.

'Yes…' said Cosmolos, '…with a bit of practice.'

'How?' Emmanuel asked.

'Well it is like anything, you have to learn it,' said Cosmolos.

'That is why we're here, at the school I mean,' said Charlie. '…But what about mum, Mr and Mrs Campbell? Surely they don't come to school, they're too old.'

'Thanks a lot,' said his mother.

'Oh…er sorry, I mean grown-ups don't go to school like we do,' he said recovering.

'You are absolutely correct,' said Hecate joining in.

'Well, there is special place for grown-ups called Dragonstone School for Adults and for the very young ones, there is Dragonstone Tots. For those of Lucy's age there is Dragonstone Juniors. Simple, but it works.

'I see,' said Andrew. 'Do we go there full time?' he continued.

'Yes,' said Hecate. 'You have to as you will be out of sync, magickally, with everyone else. You are never too old to learn.'

'Fantastic news!' Victoria beamed.

'So where are we going to live?' enquired Mrs Stuart.

'Well, as you know those attending the school will live here. We have a wonderful Campus full of all kinds of activities, societies, and ways to learn magick. It is quite similar to the universities in the Plainlands.'

'Great,' shouted Charlie, as the rest of them cheered and looked equally as excited.

'However, the rest of you will head to the Village of Wondle. Here you will live with families with similar backgrounds to yourself. Virtually all of your neighbours are friendly and they will help you settle in, and adjust to your new life. Believe me when

I say this world is very, very different from the one you are used to and there are many things to learn,' said Hecate.

'What about Granddad?' Charlie asked.

'We are monitoring the situation,' said Randle. 'We have found over the years that those who are too old find the transition very, very difficult so we tend not to disturb them. Also, those who are quite ill, like your grandfather, find that going through the transition could cause further health problems as there are physiological and mental adjustments to our world. We'll have to see. This is not to say that all old people are discriminated against. Each case is treated individually. Of course, you are free to visit him anytime you like…well as long as you don't miss any lessons that is. But a warning, it is forbidden to discuss this world with your Plainland friends.'

'When does term start?' asked Emmanuel'

'Oh the same times as the Plainlanders start their term. It makes families visiting friends over there easier. However, during holiday time, those who are resident at the school will head back to their families. In this case the lovely Village of Wondle.

'Will Amanda and I be in the same class?' asked Charlie.

'Yes,' said Hecate. 'You are both different elements, but yes, all classes are mixed now.'

'What do you mean different elements?' asked Charlie.

'Each person born under a sign has a predominant element attached – Earth, Fire, Air and Water. Those born under these signs are assigned to an elemental house. You all have potentially a great ability to use this element, but one of the ultimate aims is to be a master of all of them. Needless to say, there aren't many people that can. You can use your element for all kinds of things, including dematerialisation transport.'

'Demat what?' asked Charlie.

'You'll discover soon enough. You will learn that there are many forms of magick and its uses. This school also promotes the development of all creative endeavours like art and music to name a few. There are also fitness activities that I'm pretty sure will be to your liking. After all, magick exists in all things…what expands our minds and bodies expands our understanding of all things and enhances our magick. We are made up of many levels of being and all of these parts need to be satisfied in some way. As for me, I have had many revelations and epiphanies whilst courting the canvases,' said Cosmolos.

'What do you mean by revelation and epiphany?' queried Amanda.

'It means that many things have been revealed to me whilst my mind was engaged in other activities. You will understand as time moves on.'

'Now, before we go on, I must point out that you must make a firm decision whether to enter our world or not. You have received a taster of what could be, though the main ethos of the school is that you always have a free choice whether to enter the delights of our world or not. If you choose not to, then we will return you to your old homes. We'll leave you a few moments with your families to discuss this and then we'll obtain your final answer on our return,' said Cosmolos. Hecate, Randle and Cosmolos turned around to leave the room. The door this time opened automatically for them and they left.

Both families went back into their family units to discuss what had happened. It wasn't until they got back together that they began to realise the gravity of the situation. They all spent some time deliberating, but the pull towards the magick world was too strong for them all. Charlie took the longest to decide, worried about anymore paralysing experiences happening, though what finally swayed him was the fact he could finally get some answers.

Cheers and celebrations could be heard from both families and they huddled and shook each other's hands.

'Well well, you all look happy,' said Hecate, who stood with Cosmolos and Randle. Do I take it that you have all decided to join the magickal community?' she said cheerfully.

'Both the Stuarts and the Campbells will be delighted to enter this fascinating world,' said Mrs Stuart.

'Well then, let's not wait a moment longer,' said Cosmolos. The energy of excitement was now bustling so powerfully, it was like magick in itself.

Cosmolos raised his staff like he did before. Andrew gulped as the last time he did that he ended up in midair.

'Apocalypton,' said Cosmolos, commandingly. Both families where looking excitedly at where Cosmolos was pointing. Suddenly, the doors that Charlie observed that should have been there in the first place appeared. 'Ah', said Charlie now realising what had happened - *but surely these must lead to the main corridor,* he thought. The doors and, most of the wall, were covered in vines and leaves. Each door was decorated with a unique pattern.

'Charlie,' said Cosmolos. 'Choose a door!'

'Me? Why me?' he said looking very surprised.

'Why not,' replied Randle.

'I suppose,' said Charlie.

He walked forward and examined the doors. He walked past the first two doors and nothing. He couldn't explain, but he didn't seem too bothered about them. He walked past the third and fourth doors and still nothing. Minutes later, he walked past all of them again and still nothing. Then, Charlie saw the shadow entity, but this time, its head was poking out between the fourth and fifth doors. He walked towards where the entity was and, there it stood, in the wall, looking at him.

'Look,' the entity whispered. Charlie jumped slightly, as he was not expecting the entity to speak. Charlie gazed hypnotically at the space where the entity was, and then it disappeared. He put his hand on the wall and another door began to appear.

All were in shock at what Charlie had just done, but Cosmolos just stroked his beard.

'I choose this door,' said Charlie confidently. As soon as he spoke, the door also spoke.

'Welcome,' it said simply. 'Enter.'

Chapter 10

THE ILLUSION LIFTED

Both the Stuarts and Campbells moved tentatively towards the door. Cosmolos, Hecate and Randle followed behind. As they passed through it, they found themselves back in the narrow corridor they entered the room by.

'Oh,' said Charlie.

'What's the matter?' asked Emmanuel.

'After all that, I thought we'd enter into some strange new land or something,' replied Charlie sounding disappointed.

'I see what you mean,' said Emmanuel.

The expressions on the rest of the family suggested that they were all thinking the same thing.

The corridor seemed relatively quiet compared to Hecate's office, but it was just as vivid and it somehow seemed very cosy compared to the first time they entered it.

'This way,' said Randle and lead them back into the main entrance hallway. It was empty. There was no one about. Charlie was half expecting it to be bustling with people, but it was like a ghost town.

As Charlie moved down the staircase, he looked round to see the knights' armour and the swords. Like most of what they were seeing, the suits seemed brighter and animated in some way and the swords shone, vibrantly.

'Wow, look at that!' he shouted. 'This is really cool.'

'That's nothing,' said Randle. 'Just wait until we get outside.' Everyone's head lifted and a gentle tingling sensation passed through them.

As they approached the door, there was a change in atmosphere: there was a feeling of happiness and freedom. Hecate then walked to the front and stood at the door.

'Welcome Headmistress. Hope you are having a great day. I see we have new guests in our world. It brings joy to my heart,' said the door very kindly.

'Oh yes, Cyril…new guests indeed.'

'It is going to be a good year, I feel,' said Cyril the door. Both the Stuarts and the Campbells mouths were wide open.

'The doors talk?' said a startled Mrs Stuart.

'Some… but there is more to them than what you think. You will learn more in your studies,' said Randle.

Expectations were building and building. Their experiences were a continual peak that never seemed to stop. Even Charlie's apprehensions eased slightly as he was in awe of what he was seeing and now hearing. On reflection, he was starting to feel quite bad about the amount of times he booted the door at home. *I wonder if it was alive and never knew it,* he thought.

'It is like the whole place is alive – amazing!' said Amanda.

'I canna believe it,' said Andrew.

'Lovely, fabulous,' said Victoria.

'Look,' said Lottie pointing at the vines that were pulsating and vibrating with energy.

'Why do these vines appear on the walls?' asked Emmanuel.

'They help the school,' said Randle. 'They come, when they feel the need to be here.'

'Uh?' said Emmanuel.

'You'll understand in time,' said Randle. 'If I tried to explain it to you all now, it wouldn't make any sense.'

'Ah – OK…' said Emmanuel, looking confused.

'However, they are here to greet you and they are also happy to see you,' said Cosmolos.

'Oh,' said Charlie, not knowing what to say to that. After all, they were just vines – or where they? Still perplexed, he realised that he didn't actually know that much and decided to wait to see what else was going to happen.

'Don't try to figure it out,' said Cosmolos softly. 'Just enjoy it for now.'

'Hello, Cyril,' said Randle.

'Hello Randle,' greeted Cyril. 'I will open up now.'

'Most kind of you,' said Randle.

'A pleasure,' said Cyril.

Charlie was now itching for the doors to open.

'Everyone here is very polite,' said Victoria. 'What a refreshing change,' she said approvingly.

'Aye indeed, everyone is so nice,' said the other Victoria.

Silence pervaded the hall. The door started to open. Both families moved slowly and were nervous at what they were about to see. There was a hesitancy in their movement as they proceeded to walk outside, treading on the ground carefully as if it was not going to be there. They walked down the many steps that were in front of the school, apart from Amanda who went down the side pathway with her father.

'Well,' said Cosmolos. 'Aren't you going to turn around?' Both sets of families heads were fixed to the grass in front of them which lead towards the large gate and with excited fear, they were routed to the ground, frightened at what they were about to see. Hearts were pounding and breaths quickened. Charlie could feel the vein in his neck throbbing and panicked slightly in case he was about to have another paralysing experience. When he realised this was not going to happen, he gave a sigh of relief.

Slowly but surely they began to turn around. Mouths dropped and with eyes wide open they froze, apart from Bruce, who attempted to jump in his mother's arms but he realised he was far too big for that so he stopped well short of doing so.

'Welcome to Dragonstone,' said Hecate with real pride. Well this was the icing on the cake.

'I, I, I, don't understand…How…Er…What?' Mrs Stuart said fumbling her words.

'This has got to be the most amazing thing I've ever seen,' said Charlie.

'I second that,' said Amanda.

'How could this happen?' said Emmanuel.

'I'm totally flabbergasted,' said Andrew.

'Well, let's show you around,' he said.

What they were seeing was something very different to what they first saw when they first arrived. The main building was enormous and several more buildings appeared. *How could something like this remain hidden from so many people?* Charlie thought. Even the landscape had changed and the sky seemed more vivid.

Cosmolos walked to the front, raised his staff, and said, 'Venio Taperatum Megalus.' From the other side of the main school a large rectangular object flew towards them and they looked nervous as the object came closer. Moments later the object landed within a few feet of them, and they all looked.

They still hadn't completely fathomed what was happening to them. It was pure shock on an unimaginable scale.

'Is that a…flying carpet?' asked a buzzing Charlie.

'Oh yes,' said Cosmolos happily. 'It is my personal favourite. There is plenty of room as we all have to get on.'

'We're gettin' on that? You mean we're gonna fly on that?' asked Andrew. 'Aren't we too heavy?' he said, sounding very unconvinced.

'Yes…it is a flying carpet,' Cosmolos chortled. 'Hand crafted by the Arabians themselves. Oh, this carpet can handle more than what you think, so no need to panic.'

'Oh' said Andrew, 'as long as you are sure.' Andrew knew it was wise to say nothing else in front of Cosmolos.

'Well come then, get on,' said Randle sounding more like Eric than his usual self. They walked tentatively on to the carpet, the same as when they took their first steps out of the school.

'What if we fall off?' asked Mrs Stuart.

'Don't worry, you won't… trust me…' he said softly, attempting to allay their fears.

'Why are we going on this?' said Amanda curiously.

'Well, can you think of better way to see the school than to view it by air?' asked Randle.

'I see,' said Charlie. 'At least Eric isn't driving this carpet,' and they all laughed.

One by one they all stepped on. It was a beautiful carpet that was woven red with black square and angular patterns on it. What enhanced its beauty was the large golden dragon that sat neatly in the middle of it.

Andrew was the last person to step onto the carpet. As he

73

stepped on, the carpet took off. They all held onto each other for dear life as Hecate made a small chuckle.

'Don't worry!' Hecate said. 'Look!' Hecate was about to step off the carpet when Victoria Campbell shouted, 'Don't do it.' But as Hecate leaned forward over the edge, Andrew went to grab her. Before he did, Hecate was instantly pushed back by some invisible force. 'See,' said Hecate, 'it is perfectly safe.'

'Ah yes, the shielding addition to this carpet thanks to my old friend Astrophos. He's a great inventor and thinker. Slightly erratic but that's what makes him a genius and a good friend,' said Cosmolos, fondly.

Cosmolos stood commandingly at the front, steering it as if by thought. The carpet flew up and up and over the building they first went in. Once past it, they looked around. It was an amazing site to be sure: there were similarly large buildings that formed a gigantic circle. Cosmolos then guided the carpet to the centre of it.

'If you look towards the corners you can see the elemental watch towers. Each tower represents an element. I assume you can see which is which.'

'Ooh yes,' said Victoria as they were admiring the elemental display at the top.

'Just a quick lesson,' said Hecate. 'The North tower is represented by earth…' You could see the pulsating vines covering the top of the tower, changing shape and moving. It was as if it knew they were there and it waved them a big leafy hello. 'South is represented by fire…' As soon as she mentioned it the flames roared to greet them and even changed colour, turning red, orange, yellow, green, blue, indigo violet and purple. Andrew was only glad the fire didn't attempt to do the same thing as before and sting him on his bottom.

'Wow!' all the children said.

'I've never seen fire do that before,' said Charlie.

'Impressive,' said Andrew.

Hecate continued. 'West is represented by water…' The water was very visible as it caressed the top of the tower like mercury on a table top. It then changed shape swirling around the middle forming a whirlpool. Then it suddenly spurted upwards forming a powerful jet. It changed form again, but this time it looked like a

74

whirlpool in reverse. It finished by sending a light sprinkle of water at them as they flew past. They felt the small patters of water droplets on their faces; it was refreshing to be sure. 'And East is represented by air...' The east tower had a visible covering of air. It was almost liquid in nature, though translucent enough not to be. Like the other towers before them, the air started to perform its own dance: it lifted upwards and started to spin around gently. It then got faster and faster until it formed a tornado, swirling menacingly. The two other smaller tornados came out from near the top and they looked like a pair of arms, waving triumphantly.

'This is incredible,' said Mrs Campbell.

'Yes, the elements are powerful forces. They can be as gentle as a mother bathing her child or as violent as a storm on the seas. You will learn much more about them when you start your classes,' said Cosmolos.

Cosmolos then reversed the carpet so they could see what was below. They could see a massive circular courtyard that was divided into four by a pathway dividing the sections. On the outer edges of the courtyard stood two study blocks to the left of the circle and two to the right. These sat inwards from the Watchtowers. The buildings were joined up by corridors, linking the study blocks. Directly opposite the main building was another large building, but it was smaller than the main one.

'Lessons will be held in all these buildings. Each elemental block is dedicated to learning an element, so the closest block to the elemental tower belongs, in effect, to that element. Now, we must move on,' said Hecate. 'But it will all make sense when the new term starts.'

'Agreed,' said Cosmolos. He turned the carpet around and headed down the field.

'To your right is where we hold our assemblies. We prefer them to be outdoors so students can get a breath of fresh air and remain alert. If it rains or snows we do have our magickal covering to protect us.'

Cosmolos guided the carpet to some buildings that were located at a distance, directly opposite the assembly area.

'These are the living quarters of our pupils. Magnificent

aren't they?' said Hecate pointing to a series of small buildings that made up a miniature student village.

Cosmolos then flew up more towards the centre of the vast field.

'As you can see, there are all kinds of other buildings and marked parts of the fields. These are to do with the magickal and creative societies. There are too many to mention, though we are very keen for students to further their skill range and create new friendships. Some societies have changed, though you will get your full listing when you start term,' said Hecate.

Cosmolos then flew further down the middle of the field until they approached a massive hole in the ground. There was no mistaking what it was: it was a huge underground arena.

'What is that for?' asked Charlie.

'Ah,' said Randle, 'this is what most students enjoy the most: it is the Arena of Orberon. It is a special arena where students can pit their wits and magickal talents against all kinds of scenarios that we put against them. It is fun, safe, and it helps students to revise and encourages them to learn new things. It is the most popular form of entertainment here at the school and quite possibly, the most popular in the land. You can build alliances with anyone from your year. The rules will be explained later on. In fact, I'm sure your new friends will explain it all.

'What are the houses?' asked Charlie.

'There is the House of Ghob that represents the earth element and the House of Gjin that represents the element of Fire. Also there is the House of Paralada, which represents the element of air and, finally, the House of Necska, representing the element of water. The names come from the genuine founding Kings of the elements, dating back thousands of years,' answered Hecate.

'Sounds fascinating. The schools where we come from all have houses, but nothing like this,' said Emmanuel.

'Yes, where do you think they got the idea for houses from?' Hecate said with a little chuckle.

'This all sounds very interesting. We have so much to learn by the sounds of things,' said Mrs Stuart.

'I wouldn't worry too much,' said Randle reassuringly. 'We find that most pick up the basics of magick pretty quickly. There are very few who investigate magick's full potential and what can actually be achieved by it. Just don't panic, take each stage as it comes. Just flow with it and the magick will help you on your journey.'

'Have you seen the time? We need to move on,' said, Hecate.

'Yes, we must move on. There is more to the school premises, though you will discover all of these whilst you are here,' said Cosmolos.

'Where to?' said Mrs Stuart.

'To the Village of Wondle!' said Hecate. 'You will now see your new and wonderful abode,' she said proudly.

Cosmolos immediately spun the carpet around and soared upwards. They could feel the force of the wind on their faces and their hair flew back in response to this manoeuvre; it felt refreshing and powerful. The carpet paused and floated majestically in the air.

Cosmolos raised his staff and spoke again. 'Portus Megalus,' he said commandingly and the air started to distort several feet in front of them. A large vortex appeared. As soon as it opened, you could see rows of houses either side of an open road. The image looked greyish and wasn't completely formed; it was clear enough to see where they were heading, however.

Like a swooping bird of prey, the carpet headed towards the vortex. 'Amazing!' said Charlie. The youngest girls screamed and Emmanuel and Bruce shouted cheerfully at the air as it did so. Seconds later, and without much fuss, they were in Wondle. Cosmolos guided the carpet down the street. They were all looking excitedly at the village they were all going to be living in.

'I wonder which is going to be our house,' said Victoria Stuart.

'Aye, I wonder whether we are going to be neighbours,' said the other Victoria.

'Yes you are,' said Randle. 'We try to do our best to make sure that we put families together that get on.

'It's beautiful,' said Victoria Stuart. 'It is so oldie worldy…' she said, as her eyes were in awe of what she was seeing.

Chapter 11

A NEW HOME

Cosmolos steered the carpet down the street as Randle began to explain.

'Tudor inspired,' he said. 'Oh yes, a wonderful place it is…so sophisticated and elegant. It is one of my favourite places and I regularly like to have a quiet drink in the *Old Witch Tavern*; it serves beer and ales like no other.'

'Now you're talkin' my kinda language,' said Andrew.

'I didn't think druids did this sort of thing,' said Amanda.

'Oh yes,' Randle laughed. 'There is nothing wrong in enjoying some of the physical pleasures as well as the spiritual. As Cosmolos will tell you, it is all about keeping your life in "balance and proportion," isn't that right, Cosmolos?'

'Indeed this is true,' said Cosmolos. 'Ah here we are - your new home.'

Cosmolos and the families descended onto the back garden of the first house. The whole thing looked like everything else in this new world, vivid and beautiful; qualities that are so often drowned out by the melancholic glumness of the Plainlands.

The air was fresh and clean. The flowers gave off a hypnotic scent and the wind blew the long grass in the adjoining field at the back of the house. Just beyond that there was a mixture of hills and woodland.

'Stuarts, you are in this house and Campbells, you are next door,' said Randle.

Cosmolos dropped off the Stuarts first and then glided the magick carpet towards the Campbell's new home. Hecate had some errands to run in the village. They weren't too far from each other and they could quite happily chat away. The land was plentiful and a range of flowers and trees existed, some known and others unknown.

'I've dreamt of a garden like this…' said Victoria, admiring the upward and downward flow of the water between two pond segments. At the top of the garden, a large tree stood firm with large overhanging branches that spread as if to keep shelter.

'What tree is that?' asked Mrs Stuart.

'It's known as a Crainus Tree. It is a relative of the Willow, though much older and wiser. It only exists in our world. Many varieties of plant and wildlife exist here, each making a valuable contribution to our learning, the environment and ourselves. The school has many varieties and some of them are quite amusing.'

Amusing! How can plants be amusing? Charlie thought.

'Lovely. I love a good garden. I'm not sure I could manage to look after this myself, though.'

'Ah my dear, one cannot be expected to look after this by yourself. There is help, if you so require it,' said Randle.

'Help? From whom?' Victoria asked.

'The elementals,' replied Randle. 'What you saw at the school were the elements in their raw form. Each element has its own kin, its own representation. They are experts of nature and it is the root of earth magick. There is more respect between our two kingdoms than there is with the Plainlands. Many stories have been written about elementals, but you will learn the truth, soon enough. Put it this way, they can help or cause you much grievance depending on your attitude. There have been many younger pupils who have not quite handled or summoned an elemental properly and, in some cases, they've literally gotten their fingers burnt. Fortunately, there are teachers on hand to help resolve any issues. However, they're many who do help us out with day to day activities, one of which you have seen, today.'

'That fire thingy,' said Emmanuel.

'Yes, that is correct. That fire thingy as you call it is a fire drake. They love smaller fires and love lighting and sitting in the flames. To them, it is the equivalent of sunbathing on a beach somewhere. OK,' said Randle,' lessons later. You must be curious about your new loggings so let's head inside.'

'The house is beautiful and so big,' said Victoria with some delight.

79

Randle moved forward and whispered something to the door and it opened slightly.

'What did you say?' asked Charlie.

'Ah, it's a type of magickal password. You'll all have your individual ones when you start school. In the mean time you will have to make do with a key.' At that moment, a set of golden keys gently oozed out from the front of the door and a handle appeared.

'My password is now redundant,' said Randle. 'When you get your magickal password, you will then be able to enter as I have done.'

'When do we get that?' Victoria asked.

'When you go to your respective schools of magick,' Randle replied.

'Well, how come a password wasn't needed at the school when we first came out?'

'Well, passwords will be used at times that require access to something personal or secure. The whole process is complicated, but it is really effective. There is no conning an access point that uses your password, the door will know whether you are lying or not. Cyril is aware of all the members of the school, so there is no need for the password in that instance,' said Randle.

Victoria got the set of keys and entered the house with Randle. The house was very impressive, large and spacious. It was beautifully Tudoresque in design. It was laced with hand crafted wooden furniture. There were many rooms, including four living rooms, three dining rooms, eight bedrooms, six of which had en-suite, and another main bathroom. There was a play area, an attic room, and even a drawing room, full of old books.

'Are you sure that we are going to live here?' Victoria queried.

Randle laughed. 'Of course! This house is tailor-made for you.'

'I see you have TV here, said Emmanuel. 'Is it the same as the TV we watch back, well, on the other side?'

'Just Wizard TV, I'm afraid. There is plenty to choose from. Though trust me when I say you will be too busy to watch much.'

'I'm thirsty,' said Charlie.

'I believe your food stores are well stocked. Let's head to the kitchen.' They all followed Randle into the kitchen, but before anyone could say anything, the fridge started to protrude further from the wall and it opened. It was fully stacked with a range of drinks.

'There are a lot of drinks in here. Where is the rest of the food kept?' asked Charlie.'

'Oh, I keep forgetting, things work a little differently here. Just close the door and whatever else you need will appear,' said Randle.

'Wow, what a great idea,' said Charlie.

'Amazing!' said Emmanuel.

'Might I suggest this drink if you are thirsty?' Randle leaned forward into the fridge and pulled out *Percy's Thirst Quencher for all Occasions - Magick Bean Root flavou*r.

'Would you like a glass?' asked Randle.

'Ooh, yes please,' said Charlie.

Everyone else was just looking to see what other marvels would transpire. They weren't disappointed. A cupboard door swiftly opened at his request.

'I guess the glasses are in there but I can't reach,' said Charlie. Suddenly, the part of the floor he was on lifted him up towards the cupboard. Everyone's mouths opened up like they did in Hecate's office.

'This is awesome,' said Emmanuel beaming.

Charlie picked his glass and the floor lowered again. He walked to the table top and started to pour the drink. It went from a bright red to a dark red. Then Charlie caught sight of the instructions on the bottle "the darker the colour it turns, the thirstier you are and the more potent the thirst quencher becomes."

'This is so cool,' said Charlie. 'We have nothing like this where we are from.'

'Oh, you must be thirsty,' said Randle. Charlie showed everyone what the bottle said.

Everyone else clambered towards the fridge to get a drink just to see what colour their drinks would change to.

'Of course, there are drinks for all occasions and they are all natural ingredients, with a bit of added magick to it,' winked Randle.

'Is there any ice?' said Charlie.

'Ooh, over there in the bowl,' said Randle.

'The bowl?' said Charlie looking rather confused. Charlie went over to the bowl and saw some blue sweet wrappers.

'Aren't these sweets?' asked Charlie, as he began to unravel the blue wrapper. Then low and behold, there it was, an ice cube, inside.

'Now that is impressive,' said Victoria. 'It's amazing that the whole thing doesn't melt,' she continued.

'A true genius that Percy, he's thought of *everything*,' said Randle. 'Anyway, I must show you this,' he said leading them to the drawing room. The casings were packed full of all kinds of old-fashioned bound books. 'These books will help you understand the world of magick, though these ones must be read first. It covers some of the topics we've covered already and more. It is kind of a dummies guide to magick.'

'Thank you Randle, though another question. I've noticed the word Magick is spelt with a K on the end and not a C as we normally see back in the Plainlands. Why is this?' asked Victoria.

'A good point,' said Randle approvingly. 'You see, we have spelt it with a K on the end because it defines real magick and sets us apart from what's been before. With the K, it gives the word more meaning, power and potency.'

'Fascinating,' said Victoria speaking on behalf of everyone. 'I can quite honestly say that we are completely overwhelmed by this; incredible…amazing…speechless! Never in a million years would we have ever imagined a place like this. It is it something, only made in fantasy. In fact, the more I think about it, the more I need to be pinched to ensure that this is real,' she said in a hurried tone.

'Mrs Stuart, you will find that all fantasy has its foundations somewhere. Well actually, most of what the Plainers call fantasy is actually reality!'

Charlie and the others just listened and then began to think again at what was happening. Victoria had brought it home to them

82

how an unbelievable experience this had been and so, so different and alien, from what they had been used to: buildings that have life in them; talking doors; magick carpets; cupboards that seem to read your mind when you want something. *What else exists in this world? What other experiences and bizarre things exist here?* Victoria thought. In fact, the more she thought about it, the more confused she became.

The room went silent and Victoria wondered whether she had done the right thing by exposing the family to this; it seemed to take her breath away.

Randle caught on to the vibe of the situation and spoke. 'I sense this might all be a little overwhelming and understandably so. It will take some time to get used to. I can assure you that you are in the best of places where your potential can be fulfilled and your dreams realised. There is a beauty here that cannot be found anywhere else and it is how things should be. Admittedly, not everything is perfect but, compared to the Plainlands, it is paradise. Much of what comes from the Plainlands is born out of fear, manipulation, and the absence of real colour and creativity. People are shaped and live by what others say they ought to be doing and end up living, comparatively, mundane lives; people exist rather than live and achieve a fraction of their potential. Of course, not all of it is bad or a complete waste of time, but there is so much more that humanity could gain if they could simply open their eyes...' His passionate words seemed to calm them a little and the room fell silent. There was a knock at the door, which brought them out of their reflective thinking.

'Hey, how's it going?' said a familiar voice. It was Andrew.

'Hi Andrew,' said Victoria sounding pleased to be hearing his voice. Do come in.' Charlie opened the door. The Campbells and Cosmolos were standing there.

'Come in guys,' said Charlie. He was pleased to see them, especially Amanda, who he had warmed to. They entered the house and looked very excited.

'Amazing,' said Andrew. 'Absolutely amazing... I canna believe it, I reckon I'm going to enjoy this place,' he said enthusiastically. 'Things seem so much easier here as well as cleaner. We had a look outside into the small town area and it is immaculate. Back home there is litter, dirt and children up to no good. This place will be ideal. I have to admit, this will take some getting used to.'

Victoria just looked at him. It was like the roles had been reversed as it was Andrew who first showed the greatest apprehension to all this.

Afterwards, they spent some time exploring the house and the ornate craftsmanship that had gone into creating it. The house was tall and consisted of four floors, with an oak staircase.

'I want the top room,' shouted Charlie and ran towards the stairs. He stopped suddenly when he realised that Amanda had no way of getting up. 'How is Ama…' Before he could finish, Randle pointed to another door that fitted neatly under the first stair case. Charlie opened it and much to his amazement, there was a lift.

'Hey Amanda check *this* out,' he said excitedly.

'Yeah, she said, we have one exactly the same at our house. In fact, this house seems identical to ours.'

'Marvellous! Did you check out the fridge,' he said whilst they entered the lift.

'Aye, it was great. Bruce was rather thirsty and he opened the fridge. Looks like these Percy drinks are very popular here. I love the way they change colour.' Charlie pressed the button for the fourth floor, whilst Amanda was talking to him.

'I had a *Percy Cola – Extra Fizzy*,' said Amanda. 'It was amazing, though bright blue did put me off to begin with. Then, my brain fizzed with excitement once I drank it.' They both laughed and the lift stopped. Charlie opened the door and, amazingly, the lift was not in the same place, but down the corridor just outside a bedroom door.

'Wow!' said Charlie. 'It's like this house knows everything.' *How does it know everything*? He thought.

As Charlie approached the door, a handle appeared. Charlie turned the handle and the door opened up.

'This is the best room I've ever seen,' said Charlie. It matched the rest of the house in terms of design. Charlie began to explore. It had a king size bed at the top of the room, a door leading to a personal bathroom and a giant walk in wardrobe. At the bottom of the room, there was a giant TV screen fixed to the wall. There was a large study desk on one side and another fixed table. It was made out of marble, though strangely, it fit in well with the rest of its surroundings.

'I wonder what this is for,' queried, Charlie.

'Not sure,' said Amanda. 'I've got one exactly the same in my room.'

Charlie maintained a puzzled look, but managed to turn around and observe other parts of the room. There was a large window overlooking the back of the house and dotted around the walls, were small oil lamps, which looked similar to ones outside Hecate's office as well as two unlit wall torch holders. *So isn't it dangerous to have torches?* he thought.

'This bed is amazing,' said Charlie to Amanda. He took a run and jumped onto the bed, before jumping around.

'It is huge, brilliant, it's…oh…this room is just for me…no more sharing. I have to admit, I did have some fun with my brother so it wasn't all bad,' he said reflectively, thinking about the bunk bed he shared with Emmanuel.

'Just imagine having a bed that could fill a room,' he said to Amanda. Suddenly, the bed started to creek and it started to expand width and length ways.

'Crikey,' said Amanda as she wheeled herself quickly out of the way.

'What is happening?' Charlie bellowed. The bed continued to grow and grow. Amanda wasn't waiting to see. She backed out the room into the passageway and then turned to face Charlie. The bed was about to hit the side furniture, when Charlie shouted: 'Stop, please STOP!! The bed stopped expanding. It had nearly covered the room and the bed sheets had miraculously grown with it.

'Ha-ha-ha – wow!' said Charlie again, and he began to laugh and run around the bed. 'Amanda, Amanda,' he shouted excitedly, 'this is brilliant, just blooming brilliant…I so want to be here, right now,' he was brimming with excitement. In that moment, Charlie had forgotten about all his anxieties and worries he had about the magick world.

'Charliee, Amanda,' shouted Victoria. 'We need to get going,' she continued.

'Going?' said Charlie. 'But we have just arrived,' he said to Amanda.

'Amanda. What are you…?' Victoria's mouth just opened as she stood just behind Amanda. 'Charlie Stuart. What have you done to this bed,' she said sternly.

'But…I…it…er…the bed, it just grew,' he said.

'What do you….' said Victoria.

'Ahem,' a voice came from behind her. It was Cosmolos. Moments later, there was a small audience in the hallway.'

'I see you have discovered some of the wonders of the magick houses,' he said calmly, as the rest just stood aghast whilst Randle laughed.'

'What happened?' asked Charlie.

'Well, you must have asked for it,' said Cosmolos.

'Ahhhhh, I did, but I was only joking about it to Amanda,' he said looking puzzled.

'You've heard of the phrase be careful what you wish for?' asked Cosmolos. 'This is never a truer statement in Magickal Law. However, this house is designed to cater for your needs and for the most part, responds accordingly with your wishes. However, no harm can come to you in your own house.'

'Cosmolos, why are we going now?' asked Charlie grumpily.

'Remember this is just a visit, but don't worry, this world is your real home now so there is plenty of time to explore. For now, you must head back to the Plainlands to settle your affairs. Randle will fill you in on the details of what you are to do next.'

'Oh deary me,' said Victoria. 'I'd completely forgotten. It seems that we've been here for ages.'

'And not a moment too soon,' said another familiar voice: it was Hecate. 'I have some paper work to do before the new term starts.'

Five minutes had passed and they were all outside, in the back garden, and on the Magick carpet. Cosmolos raised his staff and uttered some familiar words, 'Portus Megalus.' A great vortex was summoned and back to the school they went.

Chapter 12

FIRST DAY

The month had gone quickly and the Stuarts spent some time concluding their business in the Plainlands with their family and friends. Before they left there was a big party in the house. Mum was very vigilant and did well in keeping the grown up drinks away from the children, despite Lee's efforts to acquire some. "Boys will boys," said Victoria, half amused by their efforts, but ironically, she managed to get a bit of a headache herself from drinking too much and, in the morning, she kept telling everyone to keep the noise down at every given moment. Emmanuel did his best to tease his mum by crashing cupboards, pots, doors and other items, much to her displeasure; he'd obviously been hanging around Bruce, too much.

The journey back to school was about an hour and they were all very apprehensive. Randle, who seemed to have the knack of picking up on these things, spoke. 'Now, I know you are all going to be very nervous, but don't worry, there will be plenty of help. I hope that you have been reading your basic magick books, as this will really help you. Remember, keep calm and within a few weeks you will be in the swing of things.'

***

Eric honked the horn at the school entrance. The slit in the gate opened and some steely eyes narrowed, looking at Eric, and Eric responded in kind. There was a strong impression that the two didn't like each other, though Charlie thought it was all amusing.

The gates opened and the bus entered. As it entered, the school was beginning to reveal itself in its full glory, though this time it was bustling with children, teachers and families.

The bus moved around and upwards towards the school. 'Move out the blooming way you imbeciles!' shouted Eric. Some of the children were sticking their tongues out and making gestures towards the driver to wind him up further.

'Ha-ha-ha-ha-ha,' laughed Charlie and Emmanuel. Even Randle seemed to have a smirk on his face.

The bus pulled into the parking area. Randle stood up to speak. 'OK, this is the plan: Charlie and Emmanuel, you are to head towards the top of the main entrance, and you'll both be directed from there. The rest of you are to coming with me to the Village of Wondle to settle in. In two days, you will be taken to your respective schools to begin your magickal training. Oh, something else to mention; only teachers and special guest visitors can use the Portus charm to leave and enter the school. It is quite a new ruling, but it was introduced because pupils thought it was a great way to play truant.'

'Where's Cosmolos?' asked Charlie curiously.

'He's in the Great City. The Astro-Tower is there. He shares it with Astrophos who is helping him on some venture. I do hear that he will be taking on some subjects to teach at the school this year at the invitation of Hecate.'

'I like him,' said Charlie. 'I have a few things I'd like to ask him, but hey that's for another day.'

'A silly question, but what is the Great City,' asked Victoria.

'It is one of the magick world's finest achievements. There will be a visit there and you will see first-hand,' said Randle. They all got excited.

'What about our schools things?' Emmanuel asked.

'The school will provide you with everything that you need,' said Randle. 'Sorry to hurry proceedings. You both must head up to the school for your induction. And don't worry; you are in very capable hands.'

Charlie and the rest of the family spent a couple of minutes saying their goodbyes. Victoria was rather tearful as she wouldn't be seeing her sons until the holidays. The sudden severing of the umbilical cord created a feeling of insecurity within Charlie; it was a feeling that he wasn't used to. Things didn't seem as straight forward anymore, like sorting out Vinnie in the playground, but he'd have to get used to it.

As Charlie and Emmanuel turned again to wave his mother and sisters away, a portal opened. In a flash, they had gone and the brothers were on their own. Even Randle wasn't there to guide them. They felt alone so they would have to fend for themselves.

Charlie moved closer to his brother for security and then walked quickly past the dragons before standing at the main entrance, next to the door.

Charlie placed the book he was reading; *Choosing your Own Name* by Dr C Namewise, in his bag, then a voice caught him unawares.

'Hello Charlie,' said Cyril the door, 'how are you?'

'Oh, er hello,' said Charlie feeling slightly uncomfortable at having to have a conversation with a door. 'I'm fine thank you. Er, how are you?'

'Oh, all the better for the new term starting. I love talking to the teachers and pupils. I'm busy all the time you know.'

How can he be busy? He's a door. Charlie thought.

'Well, it's good to see you again and I hope you enjoy your year at school,' said Cyril.

'Thanks Cyril, see you soon,' said Charlie.

Charlie couldn't figure it out, but he felt quite happy at having a conversation with a door.

'Charlieee,' shouted a familiar voice. Charlie turned around and Amanda was a few feet away from him with her familiar smiling face. She was waving at him. Bruce stood next to her and was waving also.

'Hey guys, so glad to see you both,' said Charlie 'When did you arrive?'

'Oh, ages ago. Eric dropped us off and said he was heading over to pick you guys up. It has been a little boring to begin with, standing here until everyone started arriving. Don't they look smart?' she said. You could clearly spot the first years over the other children: they didn't have any uniforms. The other children wore black trousers for the boys and black skirts for the girls. They all wore stunning blazers with bright white shirts and different coloured ties. Some also wore capes with collars pointing upwards and had a metal chain connecting the two sides at the top. It reminded Charlie of a Count Dracula film he saw one night he stayed up late with his brother.

'We do look a little out of place…' said Emmanuel. 'But I can't wait to get our uniforms. They do look rather good,' he beamed.

'First years, this way,' announced an unfamiliar voice. They looked over and there was a funny looking man who was slightly stooped with a hunch back. 'My name is Goodwin Albright. I am the assistant to the year head. Follow me to the tailor's office so you can receive your uniforms,' he said in a dull announcer's voice.

They all proceeded to one of the doors under the staircase they first went up and then proceeded down a similar looking corridor. Amanda pointed upwards towards a ceiling that was decorated similar to the Sistine Chapel in Rome. There was a figure of the ancient god Poseidon holding his fork of power with all manner of mythical sea fairing creatures swirling around. It was as if Poseidon himself was observing the newcomers with curious interest. Afterwards, he dived into the sea, creating a splash that sprinkled over everyone.

'WOW!' said Charlie. 'That was amazing,' he said, breathing in the sea air, as all the first years stood with mouths wide open.

'Come along now,' said Goodwin nasally.
They proceeded further along a corridor until they reached a door. The door opened automatically and greeted them as they went inside one by one.

'Form a line please,' Goodwin said in a dulcet tone.
A man came running out enthusiastically.

'Welcome, welcome, welcome, welcome. My name is Antonio Trapitoni from Trapitoni Tailors from the Great'a City, the besta tailors in the land. One by one come and standa on the marble stepa, say your star sign for your elemental house, and we'll take your measurements for your uniforms.'

Each pupil did as he said. As soon as he stood on the strange marble step, 'Aquarius,' announced Charlie.

Then, the magickally-enchanted-tape-measures, whizzed around him taking their measurements. One impatient tape measure even tapped Charlie on the arm as if to say raise 'your hands I need to measure your waist and chest.' A stunned Charlie raised an eyebrow as well as his arms. When the tape measured had finished, the step glowed red and he was then ushered to a wardrobe. By some miracle, a perfectly formed uniform awaited him. Steam escaped from the sides of the strange cupboard and there was noise similar to a steam press every time a garment was made; it was a well-organised production line.

After they collected their garments, they went to a changing area to put their uniforms on. Charlie, like most of the other children, had problems with their ties, but Antonio and some very small helpers lent a hand. Whilst Antonio had no problems in reaching, Antonio's dwarf helpers stood on boxes to help them. The dwarves said nothing and calmly went about their business. They also handed out cards that said '*Antonio's Helpful Tips for Tying Ties and Looking Good,*' and Charlie put one into his pocket to study later.

After a time, all the pupils were ready and all looking immensely smart.

'Look at you!' said Amanda to Charlie. 'You look amazing.'

'Thanks. You, you're looking great yourself,' he said repaying the compliment.

'What house are you in?' asked Charlie.

'I'm in Necksa. It's a water house. I'm a Pisces…'

'Oh, cool. Not quite sure what it all means, but I'm sure it will make sense. I'm in Paralda,' said Charlie.

'Oh yes, Paraldians are air signs,' said Amanda.

'Yes, I am an Aquarian according to my Astrology book,' said Charlie.

'OK guys,' said the monotone voice of Goodwin. 'Let's go next door so you can get writing materials and equipment for your studies.'

In an orderly fashion they all proceeded through an adjoining door and walked down an old and slightly crooked corridor. The firedrakes that had fascinated Charlie so much were lighting the torches as Goodwin led.

They entered a large circular room that was dark as there were no windows. The sun was unable to penetrate. The room was like a library of empty shelves with bags in them; there were hundreds of them. The shelves were labelled with glowing nametags that were in alphabetical order.

'Please go and get your bags. Those whose surnames begin with the letters A to M, go from left to middle, and those whose who begin with N to Z, go from right to the middle. Don't all rush: we don't want any accidents or any arguments.' Goodwin left the room, leaving the students to their own devices.

Charlie and Amanda separated and Emmanuel ran up to meet Charlie. As Amanda wheeled herself over to her shelf, her wheel accidently caught the foot of another young girl.

'OUCH,' shrieked the girl. 'Hey watch it wheelie,' Felicity said nastily.

'I'm really, really sorry,' Amanda said apologising.

'You will be…Hey girls, we got ourselves a Crooky over here,' four more girls gathered round. 'I think she needs to be taught a lesson. Look at my *foot*. Well, at least mine can getter better,' she said venomously.

Amanda was mortified and completely dumbstruck by Felicity's reaction.

'Let's send her on a little journey,' she said with an evil grimace now forming across her face. Felicity grabbed Amanda's chair and, with the help of one of her other friends, Annabel, pushed the chair forward, knocking over three pupils as it crashed into the shelving. The chair tipped over, throwing Amanda to the ground.

'Oi, you,' shouted Bruce.

'HEY,' shouted Charlie, whilst Emmanuel looked very angry. All three of them ran across the room. Bruce picked up his crying sister with Emmanuel, whilst Charlie headed straight for Felicity, shouting, 'SHE'S MY FRIEND!'

Felicity went to kick him with her pointed shoes, but Charlie instinctively knew what was coming to him and blocked it with his leg. He then sent her flying with a forceful push of his hand from close range. Annabel tried to grab his hair, though as her hand touched his head he spun round, blocking her hand with an upward thrust and span around again, this time sweeping with his foot across her legs, taking them out and she crashed to the floor. The other two girls, Greta Gobbins and Phoebe Mulbright, were about to move to get him when Emmanuel and Bruce stepped in and grabbed them.

'I suggest you stop there if I were you.' The whole room looked on in horror and it went deadly silent. 'Anyone thinking of picking on Amanda or any of my other friends will get the same treatment. I hate bullies and bullies hate me,' Charlie said, sounding very self-assured.

'Thanks Charlie,' said Bruce. 'This is my sister and I suggest, if you don't want to feel my fist in your face, you stay well clear of my sister. DO YOU HERE ME?' asked Bruce angrily.

'What's going on in there?' asked Goodwin.

'Nothing,' said Charlie quickly, knowing his actions were enough.

Felicity just looked shocked then gave a look that could destroy a building. Felicity's friends gathered around her in some final defiant show of force. Something about them said that they were used to getting their own way but they had now met their match in Charlie.

'Are... are you OK?' asked Charlie softly.

Amanda wiped the final tears from her face and spoke, 'Just about,' she said. 'Thanks Charlie. Where did you learn to fight like that?' Charlie began to explain to her all the training he had done ever since he was four. He then told her of the similar story of Vinnie and little Tommy.

'That's amazing,' said Amanda.

'I tell you what: I'll teach you some basic moves you can do with your hands. It's amazing what you can learn no matter what disability you have. Bullies deserve only one thing,' he said working himself up.

'Thanks,' said Amanda. 'I'll enjoy that,' she said sounding more cheerful.

'Good moves brother,' said Emmanuel sounding approving.

'Thank you brother; I hate people like that,' said Charlie, repeating himself.

'I know what you mean,' said Emmanuel. 'Cowards the lot of them... they always go for the easy targets. Well after that, I guess everyone will know who you are,' he laughed.

'OK guys, follow me. We need to go to the assembly area now as the headmistress and some of the other teachers will now introduce themselves,' said Goodwin.

Everyone looked excited and the atmosphere returned to normal, but Felicity and her gang were huddled together scowling, making provocative, whispering, gestures to each other. Charlie just ignored them knowing better than to respond to petty gossiping.

They walked down a few corridors until they reached the outside. This time, they had a ground view of the school and it was very impressive. It seemed so much bigger and more mysterious compared to the first time they'd seen it riding on the back of Cosmolos' carpet.

They walked down some steps and headed into the circular courtyard. It was amazing. There were statues, a fountain, and there was a range of flowers that weren't there before, with all manner of creatures and light faeries all around.

'Ooh, look at these newbies,' said a voice.
Charlie, Amanda, Emmanuel and Bruce all looked around at each other. Charlie looked down at some flowers with large yellow petals heads; they were talking.

'Flowers can talk?' said Bruce.

'Oooh, flowers can talk, nu, nu, nu,' said the first flower called, Neil, cheekily.

'You're kidding me,' said Charlie laughing.

'Don't laugh at me you whipper snappers,' said the flower.

'Hey Malcolm... wake up! Check these first years out. Looks like they think they know it all,' he said.
The second flower opened its eyes and just looked.

'Achoo!' sneezed a flower on the end.

'What's the matter with him?' asked Amanda.

'Hay fever,' said another flower called Brian.

'Hay fever? But he's a flower,' said Charlie.

'I know, embarrassing isn't it,' said Brian.

'He's an embarrassment to the flowering world,' said Neil.

'Ha-ha-ha-ha-ha-ha,' they all laughed. However, Frank the sneezy flower, didn't seem so amused.

'Come along you guys,' said Goodwin. They looked round and realised that most of them had reached the outdoor assembly area, so they began to run across, whilst Bruce pushed his sister along. Panting, they eventually made it and looked to find their seats. Charlie looked up and there were hundreds of pupils sitting down on seats organised in sloping arrangement following the curvature of the hill.

'Hurry up and sit down,' said Goodwin. 'Your seats are just over here. Amanda, there is a gap there especially for you.'

'Thanks,' said Amanda.

'Emmanuel and Bruce, being in the year above makes you second years. Your seats are in the next section up.'

'Good luck guys…see you later on,' said Emmanuel.

'You too brother, and you too Bruce,' said Charlie.

'Be good,' said Amanda.

'Aren't I always?' said Bruce.

They all went to their respective seats and waited. A lady approached the front stage area and the chattering figures all went silent.

'Good morning to you all,' said Hecate, speaking through a magick microphone, but no speakers could be seen. 'I said, good morning to all,' she repeated.

'Good morning Headmistress Winslow,' they all replied.

'Better,' she said. 'I trust that you all have had a great summer holiday and are eagerly awaiting the new term. First years at Dragonstone - a very warm, welcome to you all. I'm sure you will enjoy all the delights our school has to offer and I wish you all the best on your endeavours. Most of you are aware of the rich history that our wonderful school has. However, there are some aspects of our magickal history that, we do not understand. Enchantments remain in the older, medieval parts of the school as well as some from recent history.

The function and purpose of most of these old spells remain a mystery so we advise caution if you ever come across any of them. One of these includes a peculiar door that has come to be known as, The Door of Mystery. We definitely advise staying completely away from this ancient enchantment. *Best avoid that then*, thought Charlie. 'Any moment now, your elemental house masters will be arriving. In fact I can hear something now.' They all looked up. In the distance they could see something coming at them very quickly: a ball of flames came scorching towards them at high speed amongst screams by some of the first years. It got closer and closer and got as far as the stage where Hecate was and it rose ferociously into the air. It landed, transforming itself into an Egyptian wearing ancient clothing, much to the shock of the new students. Various small fire elementals hurtled towards the ducking students, twisting in the air then disappearing again.

'Let me introduce you to Artuk Ra, the Fire House Master.' Immediately afterwards, the earth appeared to distort and reshape as something else was hurtling towards them. As it got close, the earth shook violently, shaking everyone in sight. Standing before them was a stern looking Native American Indian.

'May I introduce you to White Eagle, Elemental Master of the Earth House. He will be joining us as the new house master replacing Dr Hume, who is currently looking after his new born child. Can everyone please give White Eagle a warm Dragonstone welcome?!' The students roared like dragons then clapped. As they did so, something else flew out of the sky swooping down and landing on White Eagle's arm.

'WOW, that's why they call him White Eagle,' said a voice amongst general mutterings. 'Yeah they're really rare,' said another child. Perched on White Eagles arm, *was* a White Eagle. The bird was incredibly rare in the Magicklands and extinct in the Plainlands.

'It's beautiful,' said Amanda. The eagle bowed its head then flew off. Now all the students from all the years were now sitting on the edge of their seats, waiting in anticipation to see who was coming next.

The sky then began to darken, and a large grey cloud approached in the swirling wind.

Torrential rain began to fall followed by sparks of lightning and thunderclaps.

'That's new,' said one of the third years.

This time, two people appeared. A man dressed in ancient Greek clothing and someone else familiar to Charlie: it was Cosmolos.

'Now may I introduce to you the returning Elemental House Master of Water, Archimedes, and our new Air Elemental House Master, Cosmolos, the great Mage and astrologer who has kindly taken on the role this year. Cosmolos has kindly allowed the older students who are studying Advanced Astrology to go and look through the famous Astroscope as part of your studies for astronomical phenomena; this will be a wonderful addition to your magickal training and learning. Thank you Cosmolos,' said Hecate. Cosmolos bowed his head in response. Charlie smiled.

'Now, a real treat for you… for those undertaking your knight training we have a special addition to our team.' Charlie's eyes widened and he went all tingly. Did he just hear correctly or were his ears deceiving him? *Did she just say knight training?* 'And our special guest is…Sedrick the Viking, also known as Sedrick the Brave and Sedrick the Strong!' The student's gasped for air.

'Wow, great, brilliant,' said the students, amongst other appreciative gestures.

'He's my favourite by far. How big is he?'

'He's really big. I've only seen him in posters,' said another child. 'I've got the latest one with me.'

'And here he is, making a special appearance… Sedrick the Viking!' The pupils were looking left and right. There was a bang and a massive blanket of smoke appeared; even teachers were waving their arms trying to clear it with their hands.

The smoke slowly dissipated and the pupils sat on the edge of their seats. Standing there, mighty and strong, was Sedrick. He easily towered over the other teachers and he looked to be over seven feet tall. He was as broad as he was tall, wearing chain mail that covered his thick muscular frame; Charlie just about fell of the edge of his seat.

'I bid ye welcome warriors of the future. By Odin, the mighty Thor and the lovely Goddess Elin, I will make you the best of the best,' roared the Viking's voice. 'Let us see who has the ability to make the Magickal class of knight. I am looking for one amongst you all to receive a special prize. But that is a long way off,' he said scanning the audience with his piercing blue eyes.

'Well I'm glad he got your attention,' said Hecate who approached the front of the stage. She stood next to Sedrick and was like a dwarf by comparison. Nevertheless, she looked unperturbed by his sheer mass. 'I am sure that you are all looking forward to your new term at school and it is great to see some more magickal families joining us from the Plainlands. I am sure that you will all do your upmost to help them settle in, after all, it isn't every day we received Plainland families. Now, I trust you will all go and settle into your accommodation that is everyone, bar the first years as you are now eligible to decide your Magickal names. Please follow our Head of Estates, Winston Denton, to the main building. He will take you to the magickal booths to give you your name. I hope you have had time to think of something appropriate. If someone else has your name the booth will tell you. Once you have your name, you may then proceed to your campus accommodation. I'm sure you will find it to your satisfaction.'

Charlie had remembered reading about the magickal names in his book: it allows access to the dormitories as well as access to other personal information and secured items. The book also said that with the name comes the real power that will help enhance your magick. It was a perfect system as the name is magickally enchanted to be inaudible to everyone other than the user. He thought of a name prior to attending the school and, as it happened, he got one, quite quickly.

Winston led them back the way they came, heading back towards the talking flowers.

'Is it me or have the flowers moved?' said Charlie.

'Is it me, du du du, mi mi mi,' teased the first flower they'd encountered.

'Oh yes, they like the sun,' said Winston. 'Just like me,' he said in his cool Jamaican swagger.

'You mean, they move around?' asked Charlie.

'Oh yes,' said another voice coming into the fray. 'They are a rare species commonly known as Un-Potted Plants. They move according to where the sun is,' said the gardener.

98

'Good morning Reginald. How are we today?' asked Winston.

'Absolutely marvellous! It has been a wonderful summer. I had a little problem with the Trickster Trees hiding my tools, though I got them back eventually…China of all places. Oh! More first years I see. Hello, I am Reginald Bloom, the gardener,' he said in a very well-spoken voice.

'Hello,' said Charlie and Amanda as well as some of the other pupils.

'Anyway, I must be off… see you at the meeting Winston.'

'Always rushing around Reginald, you should take it easy,' said Winston.

'Easier said than done, anyway, pip, pip,' said Reginald as he moved quickly down the courtyard and into the grounds.

With that, the pupils headed towards the school to see what else was in store for them.

Chapter 13

A MAGICKAL NAME

Charlie, Emmanuel, Amanda and Bruce walked towards the rear entrance of the school main building. They were discussing the marvels that they had seen. Charlie loved the way the elemental house masters could transform from their respective elements into full body figures and back again. As for Sedrick the Viking, he was just in awe of him. He couldn't quite believe that one of his lessons was how to learn to use swords and, potentially, become a knight and consequently, he couldn't wait to start. Emmanuel, Bruce and Amanda were equally impressed, though Amanda was fascinated by the white eagle. The talking and walking plants were something else: no one believed that they could do so.

Charlie looked at his emblem and he could see the house badge. There was a Pegasus and a lightning bolt with other magickal details. The whole image was set inside a thin yellow circle forming the outer ring of the badge with the house motto, *Cogitatio est Magicus* written on. Charlie was about to open his bag when Winston spoke.

'OK first years, you need to follow me and stay close to each other. We are heading down to the depths of the school, through the earth corridors.'

Winston was wearing a loose round neck purple tunic with a white long sleeved undergarment, and a short black hat. The garment was held together with a twisted gold and white cord tied around the waist. He wore a purple cape that flowed down to the ground that was hanging off the shoulder. Winston reached inside and pulled out a wand that looked like a twisted bread stick. Around the middle was a single bright silver thin strip that seemed to have something painted on it, curling around the middle. There was a red jewel embedded at the bottom and various engravings towards the bottom edge. As he lifted it, you could see a yellow jewel protruding out of the top of the wood.

Winston lifted his wand and said the following incantation, 'Fotios Sapheara'. Several balls of light came out of the wand and flew down the corridor, hovering at appropriate distances, lighting up the darkest of areas of this strange and creepy tunnel, leading into the earth. The walls were made of mud, rock and vines that seemed rather slimy and unnerving. There was an earthy odour in the atmosphere that seemed rather dense but not oppressive. Only the patter of footsteps could be heard as the daylight from the tunnel faded as they went down. Charlie was pushing Amanda and then he said, 'Where on earth are they taking us?'

'I have no idea. This is all a bit creepy don't you think?' replied Amanda.

'It sure is, Amanda. I don't remember these corridors being mentioned in the Magickal Name thingy book we got.'

The frightened first years continued for a few more minutes until they reached a levelled area. They approached an archway with a curved stone top and entered a large strange room. Slowly but surely the pupils entered.

'Telios,' said Winston loudly, making some students jump. The spheres of lights came back speedily and re-entered the wand. Momentarily, the room went dark, followed by some screams from some of the pupils. Seconds later, a low red light filled the room.

'What is this place?' Charlie asked Winston.

'This is where you give your name,' replied Winston.

'But why do we have to come to this creepy place?'

As soon as he spoke, a wind passed through, creating a moaning sound as it did so. Everyone froze.

'Ah, this is one of the oldest parts of the school. No one knows how long it has been here. Magickal names have always spoken to the earth kind, who embed and then take the name to where it needs to go. See it as a kind of grounding, a confirmation of your power. There are places like this located at many points. Your parents will visit a similar place Charlie,' said Winston. Charlie stood back, surprised that he knew his name and family.

'He's from the Plainlands,' uttered one child. The thing Charlie was trying to avoid was out: he was not born here in the magick realms. Felicity gave a devilish smile and looked to be scheming something, but Charlie didn't see.

'So what?' said Winston, uncharacteristically.'

'Now everybody, go and find a booth. Don't be frightened; though approach it with the highest respect then listen.'

They scattered down the maze of corridors trying to find a booth and one by one, they all entered the strange enclosures. Charlie entered his. The natural looking booths began to close, creating some sort of chrysalis effect.

'Speak your name,' whispered the booth and Charlie uttered it.

'Accepted,' said the booth. 'Speak of this to no one… until it is time.'

'Close your eyes and trust,' whispered the voice.

As he closed his eyes nervously, something touched his throat very quickly. Charlie opened his eyes immediately and he felt like he had a frog in his throat.

'No person will hear your name. The words can be spoken casually, but no one will hear it when it counts.'

'Thank you,' said Charlie. The booth unravelled itself and Charlie then left.

Minutes later it was all done. Everyone had given their name and they could now go about their business.

What does this all mean? Until 'what' time would his name be known? Charlie thought to himself.

Winston lit the way again and they quickly departed.

'Thank goodness for that. That was too creepy. How weird! How strange!' said Emmanuel. Everyone agreed.

'Where do we go now?' said Bruce, who was still regaining some composure.

'Now everybody to your residence, follow me please,' said Winston.

'Great,' said Charlie. 'I'm bursting to see where we are going to live. If it is anything like the new house it will be great,' he enthused.

After passing the Un-Potted Plants, which, as it happened, had moved a little further to stay within the confines of the sun's rays, they moved beyond the courtyard and proceeded to the halls of residence. Charlie and the rest of the gang turned left down a path and went through a large arched gateway and they entered what looked like a mini city. There were buildings to the left and right and they were all similarly designed to the main building of the school, but the designs seemed sharper somehow. The accommodation blocks were at least ten stories high, with a balcony protruding slightly from each room.

'This is incredible,' said Charlie.

'Aye.' said Amanda. 'And just think, no parents telling us what to do,' she smiled.

'But…but… I don't know how to cook,' said Charlie, slightly panicked by this.

'Well maybe food can be magicked,' she said coolly. 'If the fridges can provide us with drinks, then why not food?'

'True, true,' he said feeling more cheerful. 'Do you know what? I think this is going to be really good. I wish my old friends could see this place,' he said reflectively.

'I know what you mean. I miss some of my friends too,' said Amanda.

'Hey Charlie,' shouted a voice across the way. Charlie looked around and saw his brother waving at him from a balcony at the top of one of the buildings. Charlie waved back. On the balcony next to him was Bruce, who sat on reclined chair with his feet up. He said hello by holding up a Percy drink with a straw sticking out from the top.

'Watch this,' said Bruce. He held the drink down and a straw grew upwards to greet his mouth. Bruce made a cheeky wink to say 'this is the life' and then started sipping his drink.

'I wonder what flavour drink that is? It's turned black!' said Charlie, raising an eyebrow.

'I've no idea but the colour suits him,' said Amanda. They both laughed.

In the surrounding edges of the main path was a grass field that flowed in and around the accommodation blocks and beyond. Trees were dotted here, there and everywhere. Flowers were neatly placed in pots and hanging baskets. The light faeries delighted in fluttering between pots tending to flowers. One faerie waited for a bee to leave before it disappeared within the flower. They seemed to illuminate the area further, creating a tranquillity that made everything seem more serene. The air was fresh on the soft wind that carried the sweet scent with it.

Winston walked with a floating scroll that flashed up which students were going where each time they reached a building. The process took a while, though Charlie was just a few blocks down from his brother. Winston read the following names, 'Thomas Feldrew, Amanda Campbell, Nicholas Rhoads, David Moarns, Steven Coldwell, Samantha Rome, Imogen Braithwaite, Charlie Stuart, Raphael Guessepi, Timothy Morden, Helen J Kennedy, Parveena Badhan, Elaina Marcounis, Michael Shaw, Melay Cheung, Pierre Alfonso, Heinz Mogol, Freya Antony and Melissa Jones.'

'About time,' said Charlie, 'I can't wait to see my room. I hope it is as good as my room in my new house,' he said eagerly.

'Me too, I hope the bed stretches out like it did in your room,' laughed Amanda.

'Now remember, now I've read your names, the door will recognise you as you enter and leave. However, you must use your Magick name to enter your bedrooms. Full instructions of how to use your room are in all your rooms. Enjoy!' Winston walked down to the next block with the rest of the children. Charlie and the members of his group walked into the building and moments later, they were all standing in the hall. It was like the main entrance hall of the school, covered in dark wood flooring and walls, only more square. In the centre of the ceiling was a round medieval chandelier though, its flames were extinguished.

'Greetings house,' boomed a deep voice. All the children jumped at the sound of his deep voice.

'I am Sebastian, guardian and keeper of the house.'

'Hello Sebastian,' said the children congregating around the door.

'If you require an early wake up call, please let me know the night before,' said the faceless door. The main door will lock after 9pm, so if you are late, you will have to use your magick name to get in.'

'Thanks,' said Charlie.

At that moment, something else caught Charlie's eye.

'Er... Sebastian... what is this?'

'Charlie Stuart – welcome. Of course you have taken the wondrous journey from the Plainlands. The item you speak of is a Scroll-Porter: you send messages with it.'

'Oh!' said Charlie.

'Here Charlie,' said another pupil. I've got to send this to my mum. She worries a lot so I promised her that I would send her this. The child took the rolled up parchment to the machine and placed it in vertically and said, 'Incedo mum.' The scroll dematerialised into light blue sparks with specks of orange and then vanished. The boy brushed his brown hair and proceeded to wait.

'Fantastic,' said Charlie, but before he could say anything else, something else materialised, falling into one of the pigeon holes located at the wall behind the machine. A name appeared on the green card naming the helpful student who sent the message to his own mother: Thomas Feldrew. Thomas went over to the pigeon hole and said his magickal name. The scroll flew out at him and landed in his hand. As it did so, a green seal with a golden crested crown on it vanished and the scroll unravelled itself keeping firm as it did so. The following words appeared:

Hello my little darling, glad that you have arrived safely.
I can't believe that you have your Magick name now –
you're all grown up now sweetums. May your magick
flourish.

> *Go gettem Tiger ;o)*
> *Love Mum and your family*

A pair of magick lips flew out kissing him on the cheek, leaving a red mark on his freckles.

'I wish she wouldn't keep sending those, it's embarrassing,' said Thomas wiping the red lipstick off. Everyone laughed and playfully teased him as Thomas went a brighter shade of lipstick.

'That is just brilliant,' said Amanda.

'So you are both from the Plainlands then,' said Thomas enthusiastically. 'Oh sorry, my name is Thomas, my friends call me Tom. Tom shook hands with both Charlie's and Amanda.

'Hi Thomas, er, I mean Tom. My name is Charlie and this is my friend Amanda. Yes, we are both from the Plainlands,' said Charlie proudly.

'Great!' Tom enthused. 'I've never been so you'll have to tell me all about it.'

'Yeah sure,' said Charlie feeling more at ease now he had befriended his first Magickland friend. All the other children seemed to be interested in them and Charlie and Amanda shook hands with everyone.

'Do you know lots of magick?' asked Amanda.

'Just a bit: everyone's magick really begins to work once you have your name you see. Mum made me remember the sending spell and expects a letter every day. She drives me nuts. I see you're with the Air House,' he said to Charlie. 'And you Amanda are in the Water House,' he said observing their badges. I'm in Earth House. A bit harder to travel I hear than Air, you lucky thing.

'Er, Ok,' said Charlie not being sure how to respond.

'Ah, sorry Charlie, you have probably no idea what I am talking about. Well, I'll tell you as much as I know as we go along,' said Thomas helpfully.

'Thanks,' said Charlie. 'We would really appreciate it.'

'I don't know about you, but I'm dying to see my room,' said Tom.

'What room are you in?' asked Charlie.

'I have no idea. Let's check the board,' replied Tom.
Everyone hurried over to the main notice board to check their room numbers.

'Brilliant, Charlie, you're on the top floor next to me,' enthused Tom.'

'So who am I sharing with?,' enquired Charlie.

'Sharing?' Er, no-one shares, we have a room to ourselves. Great isn't it…'

'You're *kidding*!' replied a stunned Charlie.

'Boy, you certainly have a lot to learn about the Magicklands. The board says you are in 10a and I'm in 10b. This building is going to be our house for the next few years, apart from holiday time of course. You know all about that I assume?'

'Yes Tom, Cosmolos told us all about it when we first came,' said Charlie.

'You've met Cosmolos,' said Tom curiously.

'Yeah, we took a ride on his carpet when we had a tour of the school,' said Charlie.

'Wow! You never! You *lucky* thing!. I've always wanted to go on one.'

'Oh right!' said Charlie sounding confused. 'I thought that everyone would have had a go on one?'

'They're quite expensive to buy. Normally all the top households have one – well, all the decent ones.'

'What do you know of Cosmolos?' Charlie asked.

'Just that he's a Mage, the next stage above a Magician and below Wizard in terms of magick. There haven't been many true wizards for centuries, though mages are extremely powerful. He's a brilliant astrologer and he looks after everyone's chart. Some say he knows everything about everyone. He works with Astrophos, another great Mage.'

'Ah yes, he is the guy who invents things,' said Charlie.

'That's right. He's brilliant!'

Charlie, Tom and Amanda proceeded through some double doors, which lead to some other rooms. The first door leads to communal room where everyone could socialise together. There were nice sofas like the ones on the bus and in Hecate's office. There were also pictures and posters of different magickal folk left over by the previous occupants. One was of Sedrick, the man taking them for Knight training. He was holding up some sort of trophy. It said '3 x Winner of the Orberon.' There were a couple of fridges and a kitchen area and a TV hanging above the massive fireplace. On one of the tables there were some board games. As Charlie glanced, he saw a game called Wizopoly.

'Hey Charlie, come and check this out,' shouted Amanda. Charlie was so pre-occupied he failed to notice that Amanda had wandered off.

'Over here,' she said excitedly. Charlie and Tom walked over to Amanda.

'See… what do think to this?' she said.

'WOW! Er, what is this room?' asked Charlie.

'It's the room of reflection,' replied Tom.

'A what?' asked Charlie and Amanda.

'Come in and see. See the stained glass windows change colour to what you need and help you come up with solutions to problems. It is very clever. Not too sure how it works. Think of something,' Tom said to Charlie. '…Something that you would like an answer too.'

Immediately Charlie thought about the shadowy thing, and the experience he had in the hotel. The light in the room turned green, violet then purple. Charlie's mind went unusually still, and then he opened his eyes.

'Good isn't it? Whatever you were thinking seemed quite important. I know purple means important magick stuff. Sit for long enough and, you should be able to come up with a solution, to a problem that you are looking for. That's if you can figure it out.'

'I like this room,' said Charlie.

'Me too. I might pop down here in a bit to see what it can do,' said Amanda.

'What room are you in?' asked Charlie.'

'I'm in 9a, just below you Charlie,' she said cheerfully. The view must be great from our rooms so I'm glad I'm not stuck on the ground floor.'

'Come on, let's go and see our rooms,' said Charlie.
All three of them left the room and proceeded towards the lift. On the way, they noticed another room, so they went to examine it. It was a drawing room, similar, though much larger, than the one he had at his house. It was very posh and there were enough tables for all of them. The books seemed old and you could smell the age of them; they made you feel quite important somehow.

'I like this room,' said Charlie. 'We've got one at the house,' he said.

'Yeah, me too, there are lots of books in here and there are even more in the main school library. I saw it in the summer when I came with mum and dad,' said Tom.

They spent a few more minutes looking around the room and Charlie was impressed with the self-working executive toys that moved by themselves. There was a globe of the earth and the rest of the planets that rotated, hovering in one corner of the room.

A few more minutes had passed and they left the room. They walked into the lift.

'Floor nine and floor ten please,' said Tom.

Amanda got off first, and then Charlie and Tom got off on their floor.

'I'm busting for the toilet,' said Tom. 'See you in a bit.'

Tom ran towards his room clutching himself. He said his name and ran in once the door opened. Charlie walked quickly to his room, said his name, and entered. Charlie suddenly realised that he finally had his own space. He had never slept in a room by himself, let alone had an entire room to do as he wanted. 'This isn't going to be as bad as I thought,' he said to himself again.

The things he had brought with him from his old house greeted him and he went over to examine them. He took out his favourite sports poster and stuck it to the wall. He felt comforted that he had something to remember the old world by.

He couldn't be bothered to unpack the rest of his things but ran and jumped onto the double bed. 'Grow,' he said to himself. Nothing happened. 'Rubbish...' he shouted out. The expanding bed was a luxury that he'd have to wait for in his new house in Wondle.

Charlie lay there momentarily when he heard a noise: it was a whooshing sound followed by a thud. He turned to his left and he saw he had a Scroll-Porter with its own pigeonhole underneath. There was a scroll.

Charlie flung himself out of bed and he remembered what Tom did earlier. He said his magickal name and the scroll flew at him. Surrounding the middle was the same seal. It said, *Magick Mail Postal Service*, and then the seal vanished without trace.

Hello son, mummy here. Charlie's eyes widened and he felt excited that he had heard from his mum so soon. *Randle showed me how to use this thing and I must say, it is rather more impressive and quicker than the postal service back home. Anyway, all is good here and I now have my magickal name. It took me four attempts before it would accept it and poor Mr Campbell was at it for nearly an hour for his. We're settling in fine and if I were you, have a read of 'Invoking Family Helpers'. Mini the Brownie is really nice and a great help. Best read about them before you go around invoking them. Randle is helping us out quite a bit, which is great; otherwise, it would have taken us ages to get everything sorted. We're heading to the local later for something to eat. Andrew insisted as he wants to try the local ales.*

Anyway, best of luck to you sweetheart. Your sisters say hi and I've sent a letter to your brother also.

Write soon — lots of love Mum

Charlie saw some Parchment paper left on the side with some instructions on how to use them by Reginald Gimbus, Head of Postal Service for Plainlanders.

Charlie was about to use his first spell in the magick world; he was very excited by the prospect. *What if this doesn't work?* He thought. He started to panic. What if his magick was rubbish and he'd look stupid in class!

Charlie picked up some spare letter parchment and said, 'Speak.' The parchment gave a little vibration.

Hi mum! Said Charlie as the words began to appear on the paper. Charlie went all goose pimply as he did so. *Everything is going better than expected and I have met a new friend called Tom who's been very helpful. I am living on the top floor, room 10a, next to Tom, and Amanda's room is just below mine. The bed doesn't expand like the one at home, though I am sure there are plenty of exciting things to discover.*

Write to you soon.
Love Charlie

Charlie quickly checked his instructions and said, 'Finished.' The scroll rolled up and he placed it vertically in the Scroll-Porter. Charlie was about to say his first incantation, but he felt a little nervous in doing so. 'Ascedo Mum,' he said loudly. As soon as he said it, the scroll dematerialised right in front of him and that was that. Charlie felt really proud that he had used magick.

'It works,' he shouted. Even after all that he had seen he was still somewhat sceptical, but in using magick, it was confirmation to him that he had officially arrived in the magick world.

Buoyed up by his experience, Charlie sent messages to his brother, Amanda and Tom. It was the most amazing thing that he had done and he wanted to learn more about magick.

He received a letter from his brother saying that he should examine the shower, so Charlie ran into the bathroom. The bathroom was large and had a cosy feel about it. An unusual looking shower cubical dominated the right hand corner of the room. Posted on the right hand side was another set of instructions. 'Marvellous,' Charlie said to himself as began to read. Charlie's eyes lit up, but, before he could finish, there was a knock at the door.

'What you up to Charlie?' shouted Tom.

'Come in,' said Charlie.

The door opened and Tom came in.

'Does this shower really do all this?' asked Charlie.

'Yeah, though some are better than others. These are deluxe models; we are quite lucky you know,' said Tom.

'I've never seen anything like it,' enthused Charlie.

'Blimey, I guess you have nothing like this in the Plainlands?' said Tom.

'Not quite,' said Charlie. 'I understand now why you call it the Plainlands.'

'Anyway, are you heading down to the Common Room? Amanda has already made her way down as she's hungry,' said Tom.

'I'm starving too,' said Charlie as his stomach began to churn. They left the room and headed towards the Common Room.

'Hey Tom, hey Charlie,' said Amanda waving and shouting at the same time. Tom and Charlie walked over to her table. She was reading the magick book by Dr GT Spellbinder entitled, *Beginners Guide to Spells and Incantations.*'

'I sent my first Scroll,' said Charlie all excited.

'Aye, me too,' said Amanda. 'I had this feeling that it wasn't going to work, but... but it did. Incredible!' she said beaming.

'Just look at the timetable and we've got *Introduction to Meditation*, then, *Basic Spells and Incantations*, then we've got *Magical Tools, and The History and Magickal Practices of Magick*.'

'Where did you get the time table from,' asked Charlie.

'They're in the school bags,' said Amanda. 'I guess that you haven't looked yet?' she chuckled.

'Crikey, I forgot all about it. I'll check it later on.'

Charlie headed to the fridge and thought of a bacon sandwich. He opened it and it was there. *Wicked*, he thought to himself, 'but it's cold!' he said aloud. He immediately saw a sign saying that "hot food can only be obtained in the main canteen." He gave a small sigh, and went to sit down to eat his food. What impressed Charlie the most were the Re-Fillable Cups that gave you the choice of just about any drink, apart from a Percy and any alcoholic ones. He then picked up the cup and said, 'Tea, white and no sugar.' Sure enough, the tea filled up from bottom upwards creating the perfect cup of tea. Something then caught Charlie's attention: a child vanished from sight.

'Tom! Where has that girl gone?' he said panicking.

'They're playing Wizopoly.'

'Wiz what?'

'Wizopoly. It's a game. You go around buying famous magickal places with fake money. But sometimes you have to go and barter for a property,' he said casually.

'Oooh, that sounds similar to a game we have in the Plainlands. Why do people keep disappearing,' asked Charlie.

'Well, how else are people going to have their turn,' said Tom looking as confused as Charlie.

'What do you mean?' asked Charlie.

'When it is your go, you go into the game. It is a lot of fun, even sitting in the dungeon is a lot of fun.'

'Incredible. So let me get this right. The game somehow shrinks you, and you end up in the game.'

'Yes,' said Tom. 'This looks as if it is the latest version: the buildings are brilliantly enchanted. They look just like the real thing as do the people.' Charlie and Amanda just looked at each other impressed and then ate their food quietly.

The rest of the afternoon and evening went quickly and they all explored the campus. There wasn't much to do as the Orberon and societies weren't open until the weekend.

Afterwards, they spent some time in each other's rooms. All of them were slightly different from each other, somehow reflecting the characteristics of its tenants.

Night fall came, and they were all very tired. Charlie had asked Sebastian if he could wake them up early, which he courteously agreed.

Having felt the weight of the day, they all went to their respective rooms and collapsed in their beds. The first day was over, the lessons were about to begin.

Chapter 14

HISTORY OF LEGENDS

The night had passed quietly. Charlie snored the night away in the privacy of his own room. The night was peaceful and the stars in the sky shone magnificently; Charlie failed to notice this as he was so tired. The air was so clean and fresh, it was intoxicating and the freshly cut grass enhanced the texture of the air. Time in the night moved very slowly but it couldn't hold back the dawning of the new day.

As morning broke, Charlie received a surprise wakeup call: the curtains in his room flung back with the sun's piercing rays hitting Charlie in the face. Then, some ancient sounding horn blew loudly taking Charlie completely by surprise.

'AHHHHHHHHHHH,' screamed Charlie. He launched himself out of bed, instantly landing in some martial arts pose. Heart still pounding, he slowly began to compose himself.

'Crikey,' he shouted. 'That was the wakeup call? I need to have words with Sebastian,' he said letting out a sigh and a laugh, before taking steady breaths.

Despite the shock alarm, Charlie acknowledged to himself that the wakeup call had done its job, and proceeded to the bathroom.

He suddenly remembered the note from his brother about exploring the shower. He took off his Dragonstone pyjamas and placed them on the rail close by. Charlie walked into the odd-looking shower cubical and closed the door.

'Shower,' he said aloud, following the instructions. Water came rushing out from all directions, moving, circling, caressing, tickling; it had a life of its own. A jet came from above, stimulating his head, and he grabbed some *Leprechaun Soap* and then some *Leprechaun Shampoo*. It was an amazing experience; his old shower seemed to be like a hose pipe in a sewer by comparison.

'Slightly warmer,' he said and the shower responded to his

command. 'Much better,' he said. Charlie then prepared himself. 'POWER SHOWER,' he shouted, wondering what marvel was going to happen next. The water now gushed in from all directions, cleaning and refreshing him; it somehow suspended him two inches off the ground before it gradually slowed down.

'Stop,' said Charlie, and the shower again responded.

'WOW, that was amazing,' he blurted out to himself.

'Oh yes, dry,' he said, issuing out his final instruction. In came a warm yet powerful air flow. Seconds later, he was dry. He heard a scroll arriving.

Charlie quickly put on his Dragonstone robe and headed into the room to read the scroll. It was from Tom.

Hey Charlie, heading down for breakfast soon, are you coming? Charlie quickly responded.

Ten minutes later, Charlie had managed to put his uniform on, though he still hadn't managed to work out how to knot a tie properly. He wished, at that point, he had one of the dwarves with him.

Breakfast consisted of cereal called Gobby Brisks, which didn't sound too appealing to Charlie or Amanda; it tasted good however. By the end of it, they all decided the next day they would head to the main canteen to treat themselves to a full English breakfast comprising of egg, bacon, tomatoes, beans, toast and a nice cup of tea.

Time was ticking and they knew that they had to head up to class. They collected their things and put their bags on their backs, then left. Hundreds of students were rushing around, looking at their timetables; some were fumbling as they looked.

'I wonder why we are doing meditation?' asked Tom.

'Aye,' said Amanda. 'At least it is not a too strenuous start to the day,' she smiled.

'Sounds good to me, too,' Charlie said. 'My old Kickboxing teacher said that some martial artists use meditation to help you focus better. It makes sense, I suppose,' said Charlie replying to Tom's query.

'How long have you done that for?' Tom asked.

'Oh, since I was four,' said Charlie confidently. 'My dad took me and my brother before the divorce,' he said. 'Yeah, I really enjoyed kickboxing, so I hope they do it here. I've not practiced for days,' concluded Charlie.

'You seem pretty good from what I've seen,' said Amanda referring to the Felicity incident.

'Ha-ha thanks. I got into a fight at the end of term at my old school with a bully called Vinnie, and his stupid thicko gang. I told Amanda about it yesterday.'

'What happened?' asked Tom.

'Well, they avoided me until the end of term,' said Charlie.

'Ha-ha. You must have really scared them.' said Tom.

'I hope so,' said Charlie smiling.

Moments later, they arrived at the top of the sloping hill, heading towards the rear side of main building.

'What class are we in?' asked Charlie.

'Er, let me have a look,' replied Amanda.

She pulled out her timetable, which was neatly printed on some parchment paper. On one side of the paper, she had a list of all the lessons. On the other side, was a compass arrow that had changed from black to yellow, indicating the way. There were other useful details and a sketch of the building also appeared. It was an amazing piece of magickal invention.

The first lesson of the day was meditation with a kind old teacher, Master Sidhara, Buddhist Mage, master of meditation, visualisation and second sight. The mage was teaching them the importance of meditation and visualisation. The two where different, but meditation was a way of being able to relax down so you could visualise or image properly. He explained that 'to image' was an advanced form of visualisation as you use all your senses: smell, taste, touch as well as sight. He explained that it was important, as it is one of the keys to be able to perform all levels of magick. It helped to increase the power and efficiency of the spell or incantation. With the meditation he said that "Stillness, quietness, reflection, observation, focus, clarity, answers, sharpness, bliss, knowing, enlightenment; these are just some of the many benefits. In time, I hope you see and feel the benefits of doing such a practice," and they would understand this, in time.

Then, Mage Sidhara made several items materialise in front of all the students. Seconds later, the objects started to levitate in

116

front of them, rotating very slowly. When the objects vanished, they had to write down what they remembered... the greater the detail, the better. Afterwards, he took them through an exercise to meditate on the breath, so everything else was blanked out. Mage Sidhara then told them to write down that what they remembered, regarding the objects in the first task and, much to their surprise, they remembered considerably more detail about each object. Of course, many struggled to keep their focus, many snored, but he wisely told them not to force the exercise and just allow any distracting thoughts to pass through, don't fight them, and above all, *relax*.

After the first session, Charlie, Amanda and Tom had something to eat, but their break overran slightly. They quickly gathered their things and left.

'You're going to be late, you're going to be late,' teased the Un-Potted Plants.

Amanda got out her timetable, which said, *'This way'* in a quirky voice, much to Amanda's surprise. They moved as quickly as they could to the Earth element block and, there waiting, was the rest of the class and another teacher.

'Sorry we're late sir,' said Charlie. 'We were eating and we forgot the time,' he said feeling rather embarrassed.

'Not a problem, don't panic. However, as you have missed the introductions, I am Astrophos, Mage of Scrolls and Technology.

'Oh, you're the guy who designs all the cool things,' blurted Tom.

'In a manner of speaking, yes,' said Astrophos. 'Hum, interesting,' he said looking at Amanda. 'Amanda, could you please see me after class?' he said rubbing his beard, as if working over and idea.

'Er, me? Well... OK, sir,' she said, sounding uncomfortable.

'Good, we must get on now,' said Astrophos.

'This is great,' said Tom.

'Let's make haste. This way, much to do,' said Astrophos.

'Sir, where are we going?' asked Timothy Morden.

117

'Into the Great Wood of course…exciting place you know,' said Astrophos.

'Why?' asked Timothy.

'You'll see,' said Astrophos, leading the way at some pace. They walked beyond the assembly area, across a field, and into the woods. There were a variety of trees, some unique with amazing, exotic blossoms. These blossoms delivered the most breathtaking fragrances.

The sky was still and cloudless whilst the sun got slightly hotter during the remarkable Indian summer that had graced them.

'What are those… and those… and those,' Charlie looked eagerly at strange creatures that darted in and out of the area.

'They're elementals of the woodland,' said Tom. 'They help look after the woods.'

Amanda got very excited and shouted, 'Look over there, is that a gnome?' she asked.

'It certainly is,' said Astrophos. 'It is a tree gnome which lives inside the trees. They're generally friendlier to humans than most of the elementals, you see, and they like to see what's what, especially when new visitors arrive.'

'Look, he's waving,' said Amanda, as she waved back to the gnome who was smoking a pipe, which emitted yellow smoke.'

'SIDNEY!' shouted another voice.

'What is it Matilda my sweet?'

'Don't you Matilda sweet me! Where on *earth*, have you been? Been with Rumbus again, drinking no doubt,' she said, whilst she clouted her husband with a rolling pin. The students laughed as they continued further along a pathway.

'Now students please do not tread or venture onto here.' Astrophos was pointing to an area with withered and frightening looking trees, surrounded by lots of grass that seemed inconspicuous.

'This is Carnivorous Grass,' said Astrophos. 'Some old Warlock put a curse here. It's a long story,' he said, shaking his head. All the students looked rather frightened and, slowly, they walked carefully past. Minutes later, they walked through a dense woodland of trees and then into a clear area. Standing majestically in the middle was a very unusual tree: it was a giant one that

118

seemed to have other trees for branches. It was like a miniature woodland in itself, a confusion of many trees.

'This is the lord of trees, The Eternal Tree. It was the first tree that shaped the woodland and forest, beyond. It must be approached with the highest respect.'

'This is amazing,' said Charlie, as some wood-elves entered and left the Eternal Tree.

'Why are we here, sir?' asked Steven Coldwell.

'A good question. You are all probably wondering what does this have to do with Magickal Tools, yes?'

'Yes sir,' some replied, whilst others nodded.
Astrophos raised his Staff and spoke.

'What is this?' asked Astrophos.

'A staff sir,' said Tom.

'Precisely. What else can you tell me about it?' asked Astrophos.

'Er, it's used in magick,' said Parveena.

'Yes. What else?'

'It is made of wood,' said Charlie bluntly.

'Where do you get wood from?' said Astrophos.

'Trees,' said Heinz.

'Yes, so we need to get our wood from that tree sir,' said Charlie.

'Very good,' said Astrophos.

At that point, the students began to look nervous. Their nervousness was heightened when a scurrying wind whistled through the branches creating a haunting sound.

'One by one, you all need to approach the tree and do so respectfully and cautiously please. The wood-elves are very protective of the tree. Once there, you must say your magick name and the tree will provide you with the right branches so you can create your staff and wand.'

Charlie remembered reading that some elementals can change form and can appear any size they choose. Elves were one of these elementals though, at this time, they appeared quite small, with a faint glow around them.

'There is one more important instruction. You must ask the tree if it is OK to take the wood from it. If it agrees then it will

119

release it to you. If you show the maximum respect, there will be no problem. Don't forget to bow and say thank you.' One by one they all nervously approached the tree. All manner of elemental creatures were looking at them as they did so.

Charlie suddenly saw the mysterious shadow creature make an unexpected appearance when it was his turn to approach. 'Here we go again,' Charlie said to himself. He approached the tree courteously and Charlie said his magickal name. The shadowy creature went into the tree. As it did so, the tree opened up and Charlie walked inside. The tree closed.

'Charlie! Where has he gone sir?' shouted Amanda.

'Sir, what is going off,' said Tom. 'What's happened to Charlie?'

Felicity just sniggered as if to say good riddance, whilst David looked panic-stricken.

Astrophos just watched, and said, 'Wait… all is well.' The tree opened and Charlie walked out with his branches.

'Are you alright?' asked a worried Amanda.

'Well, that was really strange,' he said, literally looking as if he'd been dragged through a hedge.

Astrophos took Charlie to one side and asked him what had happened.

'Well, I walked in and somehow I got pulled forward and… well… I did as you said, sir. One of the elves, a gnome, and some other elemental creatures came forward and gave me these.'

'Fascinating,' said Astrophos.

'The next thing I knew, I was heading out.'

Astrophos did as Cosmolos often did. He rubbed his brown beard in ponderous fashion.

'You've been given an ancient bark from the Arterious tree, very rare and very old; a great privilege indeed.'

After a short walk, they arrived back at the school and headed towards the workshops. The walk wasn't without gossip and conversation. Astrophos distracted the conversations by pointing out the various plumages around the school ground.

The students then went to a workshop to mould and shape their staffs and wands from the newly acquired wood. Astrophos relayed to the class the importance of making their equipment themselves by putting their 'being,' 'spirit' and 'heart' into creating their own magickal tools. 'It is this, which gives it special magickal energy and power,' he said.

The machines clunked away to help smooth and shape the wood with help of some dwarves. Hand tools were also used to add some personal touches. Astrophos also said that in time they could add to their designs as they'll acquire more knowledge about magickal workings and symbols, but for now it was done. All they had to do was take their wands back to their rooms to activate them using special power words whilst holding the wand aloft.

The Arterious wood that made Charlie's wand was deep red, tinged with black, and a ruby tip securely embedded into the top and bottom of the wood. For now, he made one simple engraving: the symbol of the elemental sign of air; a triangle pointing upwards with horizontal line connecting the upper part of it.

Afterwards, Charlie told his friends what had really happened in the wood, and Astrophos cancelled his meeting with Amanda as he had an important meeting in the Great City.

Next on the agenda were Basic Spells and Incantations with Guildus Grey. Having made their way over to the classroom, they waited outside.

'Come in,' said a voice sharply. The door swung open and they entered.

'Sit down,' said the teacher abruptly.

'I am Guildus Grey, Mage of Spell Casting and Incantations. You must listen carefully to your instructions and I expect you all to do well; but only some make the grade. Astrophos has told me you are all in the process of making your magickal tools. You will learn that you won't need staffs and wands to perform all magick. In time you might not need them at all. For now pay attention, and please stop nattering at the back whilst I'm talking! I hope you will learn more about manners in your Etiquette class,' he said to Felicity who was discussing joining the Cheer Leaders' squad. She wasn't happy at Guildus for showing her up, though Charlie found it most amusing, as did Amanda and Tom.

'Open your Spell book to the first Chapter entitled, Sending and Calling Objects, otherwise known as the lazy spell. These are the most basic of what we call Non-Personal or Level One Spells, but we'll go into that at some other point,' he said mechanically.

Guildus stood at the top of the class, and his clothes matched his name: grey. He didn't wear robes like all the other teachers, but instead wore an old fashioned suit with a thick grey cape and a strange looking hat, which looked similar to a beret. In fact, if he'd worn brighter clothes, he'd look rather like an obscure artist.

'Now let's start with the less dangerous activity of the two spells we are doing today, calling an object to you. On the paper in front of you is the name of the spell that you are going to be using to summon. Make your intensions clear and your voice loud, and the object should come to you.'

'Where are the objects sir?' asked Charlie.

Guildus ignored him to begin with. Like his first session, a group of items appeared at distant locations within the class room.

'These are the objects, Stuart,' he said abruptly. 'Now the spell we are using is derived from the Latin meaning to come. Everyone looked at the word "Venio". 'It is pronounced as it reads, by the way. In addition, it is important to use the techniques you learnt with Master Sidhara.

'Sir,' Charlie interrupted. 'Why do we have to use visualisations with our spells and incantations?'

'A good question, Stuart. The whole point of using words and images is that they are used to focus the energy and generate power to the task at hand. You will learn more as we move on Stuart.'

'OK, Sir, I understand,' he said whilst looking at his instruction sheet. Charlie was to call a ruler to him, Amanda a small cushion and Tom, an eraser.

'Now take a deep breath, see the object, say the incantation with some meaning and summon,' said Guildus.

'Venio ruler,' said Charlie. Nothing happened.

'VEnio ruler,' the ruler twitched forward.

'Come on,' said Guildus 'Give it a bit more umpf!'

'VenIo ruler' he said more purposely. It came hovering and stuttering in the air and then crashed down on the desk in front of him.

'FANTASTIC!' screamed Charlie.

Amanda managed about the same as Charlie. For some reason Tom's did a loop de loop as it came over. David Moarns was summoning a piece of chalk. It flew three feet, landed on the floor, and then made its way really, really slowly over to him. With most of the class watching, the chalk drew a line as it etched its way along. Guildus just shook his head with great trepidation.

'I think it will be easier for you to go and pick it up. On the other hand maybe I should make a cup of tea.' he said sarcastically. 'Well, at least yours is moving, unlike *some* people.'

Felicity was screaming loudly but her small ball seemed somehow defiant in making the journey.

'Probably scared to go near her,' laughed Charlie.

She wasn't the only one. Raphael Guseppi and Timothy Morden's objects were just levitating and swirling, and Steven Coldwell's was ping ponging its way across.

'May the gods help us,' said Guildus. 'I see plenty of practice is required. Dare I take us on to the next activity? Oh well, better get this one over and done with.'

Guildus raised his ornately crafted staff made from Silver Birch and made the objects that hadn't quite made their way land on their desks.

'Now, I might be tempted to put protection or even a deflection spell up, for this one. We are now going to send the objects back to whence they came. First thing is to see it in your mind's eye. Then you need to send the object using the following incantation, Reverto. Again, it is derived from the Latin, *Revertor*, meaning to go back; in this case, we want the object to be sent back where it came from. In an advanced form of this spell, you can actually send back someone else's spell. Especially useful if someone is casting a curse at you. Alternatively, you can use Reverto Scorpus as it can add more focus. Scorpus, is also derived from the Latin *Scopus*, meaning target. It helps to take deep breaths. Just close your eyes. See the place you want to send it to and then say the short incantation. One, two, three, go!' Disaster! All the objects flew at speed in all kinds of directions, either hitting each other, slamming into the walls, flying out of the windows and, if it wasn't for the teacher's mastery in stopping the objects, they would have all hit him.

'Shambles, shambles, where did they get you lot from?' he said thinking aloud. 'Dear oh dear. Try again, calling it to you and then sending it,' he said to the surprise of the students. 'You're going to need the practice.'

Charlie couldn't quite work Guilds Grey out. One minute he seemed quite insulting, the next he seems to be encouraging them. Suffice it to say, he was right, more practice was required.

The session finished having made a tiny bit of progress, but everyone seemed worn out by the experience.

After a short break and drinking some *Percy Pick-Up Juice*, they went to their final session, The History and Magickal Practices of Magick. Amanda got out her timetable to see where the final lesson of the day was going to be.

'Oh, we're in the Earth Elemental block, fantastic,' said Amanda.

'I wonder what it's going to be like in there,' said Tom.

'Do you know who is taking us for that lesson?' asked Charlie.

'You guys should really get out your timetables you know…er, let me have a look. Apparently, it is Mage Brimstone-Greenback. Oh, hang on, it's changing. It's Guildus Grey,' said Amanda.

'Oh no, not that miserable git,' said Tom.

'It says that he is just covering as the main teacher is poorly.'

'Good, as long as we don't have him every lesson. I think he'd do my head in,' said Tom.

'I quite like him,' said Charlie. Tom looked surprised by Charlie's remark and continued to moan about Guildus as they proceeded to the earth block.

Upon arrival, there was a group of students waiting to head in.

'State your name,' the door said sharply, making some of the students jump in the process. Each student gave their name,

124

but for some reason the building didn't seem to like some of the students.

You could easily tell why it was called the Earth block as it was a cross between the main entrance to the school and the earth corridors they went to give their magickal names.

Vines and root-looking objects moved and wiggled around, with small and unusual insects going about their business; everything seemed to pulsate. It was dark, so each student moved tentatively through the strange corridor. Some obscure looking thing came towards them: it was a Mud Sprite. It stopped and looked at the students with its strange wide eyes. It scratched its crooked nose that protruded magnificently out of its large head, accompanied by a large bulging forehead. It then beckoned them by lifting its short arms. Its hands only had three fingers and it said nothing, waving slowly to follow him.

They walked along the corridor keeping well away from the cold damp walls. Charlie looked up and he could swear that he could see large still faces on the mud ceiling above; they looked almost statuesque.

Having walked by three rooms, they arrived at a fourth. The door opened and they entered. Much to their surprise the room looked rather ordinary: it had plain wooden tables and chairs made from light wood. However, there were no windows but the room was nicely lit up with old-fashioned gas lighting.

'Sit down please,' Guildus said unenthusiastically. 'For anyone who bothered to look at their timetable parchments, Mage Brimstone-Greenback has been feeling rather unwell after his holiday, so Headmistress has asked me to cover this lesson. As I was informed at the last minute, I have no lesson plan. Is there anything that you would like to discuss or learn about?'

Charlie flung his arm up quickly, much to the surprise of his classmates.

'Ah Stuart, one of the students lost in the Plainlands, what a shame. I'd imagine you wouldn't have any idea about magickal history. Remember, I haven't got all day to explain everything,' he said sarcastically. Charlie ignored his taunt.

'Sir, could you please tell me more about the Half Prophecy and the times of Lord Mortus and Prince Zordemon.'

125

'Well, well Stuart, there is hope for you yet. Does anyone object to this?'

No objections came from the rest of his classmates.

'Very well,' said Guildus. He walked over to the main bookstand and rubbed his hands along the spines of the books, looking for the correct one. Guildus muttered something under his breath and the book popped out.

'Ah, here we are,' he said pulling the book off the shelf. He took it to the front of the class and put it on the desk. He looked at the index, touched the page at the relevant point and the book automatically opened at the appropriate page.

'Projectum,' he said. To the class's amazement, a large 3D projection of the prophecy appeared before them. Impressively, the projection floated around the room, hovering over the desks for the students to see, and then moved through the students like a ghost though a wall, going to the next student to peruse.

After all the students had had a good look, the projection then moved to front of the class where it remained. Charlie had a good look at the scroll.

'I see,' said Charlie. The scroll wasn't just an ordinary bit of parchment folded up. A wooden handle was fixed to the end part of the it to keep it secure. It would have rolled up to meet the other half in the middle. There was a neat tear down the edge, with a perfect square piece of parchment sticking out. This would have slotted into the other half of the prophecy to connect them.

'There are questions raised about the so called Half Prophecy because there is such a precise cut along the middle. It is said that the Half Prophecy was deliberately separated and the other half-hidden elsewhere. However, do you see the fold that comes out? Some say that the prophecy isn't split and the fold simply seals that part of the scroll. Of course the text tends to indicate otherwise.'

'What does the text say?' asked Charlie.

'The prophecy, in essence, is also an agreement created by Lord Mortus to say that Plainlands and magick would be separated, thus respecting the free choice of men. However, Lord Mortus, like Merlin before him, possessed the gift of foresight and prophecy. He said that the Plainlanders would struggle by

126

themselves and that their world would descend into chaos. The prophecy suggests that there will be a "man born of dragon," that will help bridge the gap between the Plainlanders and the magick world. The scroll says that this man could intervene if the Plainlanders could not rule sufficiently without magick. There are several problems with this, one of which is how can man be born of a Dragon? It is impossible. The second part of the prophecy suggests revealing more about this person. People have searched high and low for this object and no one has ever found it. There is much speculation about what the other half of the prophecy contains. Because it is enchanted, some say it will bring unique powers back to the world. As for what powers, if any, nobody knows. One thing's for sure, the Plainlanders could never rule properly and through ignorance and fear, they have fought many wars and disrespected the planet greatly. Nothing has happened to say this will change. In fact, no one really cares anymore, only obsessives about finding the prophecy. Our worlds are pretty much set now and the Plainlanders cannot affect our world. This is another reason why magick folk do not care what happens to Plainlanders.'

All the class listened intently and you could tell by Guildus' voice that he was interested in that period of history.

'What about Prince Zordemon?' Charlie asked.

'Well as you can imagine, Prince Zordemon being heir to the throne, wasn't particularly happy at Lord Gideon's plans as it would mean that he'd miss out in ruling the kingdom. King Rebus agreed it had to be done as it respected free choice of men. Also, humanity had something to learn from their decision.'

The lights began to dim as Guildus continued to speak.

'It was said that Zordemon was furious and set about to disrupt proceedings. Stories say that he was a highly intelligent man, kind, but may the gods be merciful if you decided to cross him. You see, Zordemon was renowned for his knowledge and use of the deadliest form of dark magick known as Black-Fire. Nothing much is known about it, but it was one of the foulest and most devious forms of magick there is. The scripts, which exist today, were embalmed with some evil protective magick that prevents them from being destroyed. As such, they are kept hidden

127

in secret and guarded by the most skilled Magickal Knights there are.

'Sounds scary sir,' said David.

'Oh yes, very,' said Guildus. David froze on the spot as some of the first years caught their breath.

'What happened to them all?' asked Helen, speaking for the first time.'

'Well, maybe this could explain it.'

Guildus used some magick to summon another book; it launched itself from the shelf and landed in his outstretched hand. Guildus pulled out a thin red looking wand, which was still showing the marks of the original tree carvings; it had a dark blue crystal pointing out of the end of it. He pointed down at the book and it immediately flicked to the page he wanted and said, 'Projectum Megalus.'

Before the students could catch their breath, the room transformed itself into a re-creation of the times of Zordemon. Simultaneously, the students seemed to glide into the background of the room.

'Wow, this is fantastic,' said Helen getting all excited.

The scene started with Zordemon killing his father. He was standing over him with a cold, chilling smile that oozed naturally from his perfectly formed mouth. He was then joined by his followers known as Dark Keepers because they are renowned for their knowledge of dark magick. The most expert of these were known as the Lordos. They were all comprised of men and women of prominence and nobility.

There was fighting on a grand scale between the forces of the Prince and Gideon Mortus. Blood and guts were spilled by blade and spell alike, making some of the children's stomach churn.

Thank goodness, mum isn't seeing this, Charlie thought; they obviously have never heard of eighteen rating certificates. Guildus then spoke again.

'In the end, reports by the last known powerful wizard, Ferdore, stated that there was an explosion so powerful that everyone was obliterated within the area.'

Charlie immediately conjured images of some kind of magickal nuclear explosion. The final scene showed the prophecy /

agreement being signed by Ferdore and the newly appointed King William I, whom is known in the Plainland's history books.'

As soon as it finished, the class returned to its normal condition.

'You'd be interested to know that the original prophecy, well half of it, will be displayed in the museum in the Great City later this year.

'Really, I'd like to see that,' said Charlie.

'It is more a historical artefact now, but still draws many people. It moves from city to city; it never has a home, as such. The Great City Museum has petitioned for years that the scroll to remain there,' said Guildus.

'Right, I believe this is the end of your lesson and day. You may leave and please don't be late for your next spell session with me,' he said as if it was an inevitability.

Chapter 15

KNIGHT FEVER

Wednesday seemed to have come around quickly. Charlie, Tom and Amanda had spent some time practicing spells, using their completed and charged staffs and wands, to reasonable effect. They seemed to be level pegging in terms of ability but Charlie, who had a promising start, seemed to struggle. However, they ended up being quite competitive in a playful sort of way.

On the Tuesday, they had taken lessons in etiquette about the benefits of being civil to each other and how no matter what you gave out it would eventually return.

Ancient languages seemed interesting as they discussed how the ancient languages had a power in the writing. The final lesson fascinated them all as they were learning about their own signs and the types of skills and natural abilities that could come with being born in that sign.

The first lesson of the day was with Cosmolos, the new House Master of the Air House of Paralda. There was some discussion about the Kings and Lords of the Watch Towers, before learning some of the founding qualities of being an Air sign. Charlie loved the fact that his Aquarian sign were renowned for being forward thinkers and that they have a great potential to be a creative genius. However, his sign indicated that they can have their heads in dream land most of the time; this he could understand. Charlie did not fully understand what gregarious and humanitarian meant, which typified his sign, though he made a point of reading up on their meaning at some future date.

Cosmolos made the point of encouraging them to seek a society that would help them develop their talents in different ways, as "it opens up the creative centres", he kept saying.

In the accommodation block, there were a few arguments about using the Wizopoly as it was being hogged by Giuseppe, David, Helen and Melay. Charlie had skilfully managed to devise some rotation to use the board, despite the occasional moans and groans. Besides, neither he nor Amanda had ever been shrunk and put in a game before, so they wanted to try. As it happened, the timing couldn't have been more perfect as it was Charlie, Tom and Amanda's turn Wednesday evening, between 7 and 8pm.

Knight Training was to be the most popular subject of the day. You could hear students pretending to be knights the night before. Amanda, however, didn't see the point of it and decided to attend an alternative lesson.

'Where are you heading to for Healing Arts Amanda?' asked Charlie.

'Oh, it's in main block,' replied Amanda. 'Where do you go for knight training?' asked Amanda curiously.

'Yeah, we've got to head right down past the arena, over the bridge and beyond the trees. There is a special place for knight training.'

'Fabulous,' said Amanda.

Charlie instantly thought back to Sherwood Forest where he helped make a sword and wished that he lived there during medieval times. Well, it looked like that he was going to get his wish.

'Oh, Astrophos said that he definitely wanted to see me after class. I have no idea why, though I hope I am not in trouble,' she said sounding slightly concerned. 'Maybe they think I am not good enough or something.'

'I'm sure you will be fine,' said Tom reassuringly.

'I hope you are right,' said Amanda.

It would be the first time that Amanda was going to be separated from her new friends, though she didn't seem to mind.

'Well, good luck and if you break a leg, maybe I can fix you up,' she laughed.

'Thanks Amanda, though I'll do my best to avoid that,' he said, laughing back.

'OK, I'll catch you in a bit,' said Charlie.

'Yeah, good luck, Amanda,' said Tom.

'Thanks,' said Amanda, looking through her bag. 'Oh no,' she said 'I've forgotten my book on chakras... I'll quickly head back to get it. You guys go, and I'll see you both for lunch.'

'OK, I'm looking forward to having fish and chips,' said Charlie.

Charlie and Tom went through the archway and disappeared down towards the training area. Amanda wheeled herself back humming cheerfully in the warm breeze. However, something was going to happen that was about to change her day...

'Oi Wheelie, by yourself are you?' said a familiar, unkind voice. Amanda's heart seemed to stop and turned around in the hope that Charlie was going to be there.

'Why are you doing this to me?' asked Amanda calmly. 'If it was for running over your foot, I did say sorry. It was an accident,' she defended her self.

Neither Felicity nor Annabel said anything. No matter what Amanda said, it wasn't going to change anything.

Felicity's cunning smirk was replaced with a cold evil stare through her steely blue eyes. They circled Amanda like birds of prey and Felicity struck the top of her head with a pronounced slap.

'Ow! Leave me alone,' begged Amanda.
Annabel struck out at Amanda though Amanda, this time, lifted her hand to protect herself.

'How dare you raise your hand to me you freak,' said Annabel cruelly.

Felicity and Annabel were about to strike again when Felicity screamed out. Annabel froze and Amanda turned her head to see what had happened. There was another girl standing behind her with her hands firmly on her hips. She was a slender girl, pretty, with long brownish hair.

'If you want to fight someone, try me for size,' said the girl.

'Who are you?' said Annabel, as Felicity was still holding her head.

'Her friend,' the girl quickly responded.

Amanda had recognised her from class, though the girl always kept herself to herself. At this point, she was just grateful for her help.

'Now what are you going to do about it,' the girl reiterated. Felicity's other friends arrived as back up; they were clearly outnumbered.

132

'Now let's see,' said Felicity. 'There are five of us against you and wheelie.'

'I'm surprised that you can count that high,' said Amanda's saviour, sarcastically.

'Now you're going to see what we are going to do,' said Felicity sounding victorious.

'What, you and those pathetic no brain thicko friends of yours?' the girl said winding them up further.

'We'll see who's the thicko at the end,' Felicity retorted.

There was a momentary Mexican standoff, standing still, watching who was going to make the first move. As predicted, Felicity put one foot forward.

'Oi,' shouted a voice. Everyone looked round to see where the voice was coming from.

'Up 'ere,' shouted the voice. 'Starting on my little sister again, eh?' said Bruce, with Emmanuel right next to him. 'Touch her, and you'll be eating your lunch through a Percy straw. I suggest you move away quickly or I'll be down before you can say Cosmolos,' said Bruce. 'I've never hit a girl, but….' He just stopped the conversation there.

Felicity was really angry, but there was nothing she could do so she backed away defeated; her friends followed. Minutes later they had disappeared onto the main grounds and Bruce and Emmanuel had made their way down.

'Thanks for sticking up for my sister,' said Bruce.

'No problem,' said the girl.

'Yes, thanks so much. She's really got it in for me,' said Amanda.

'Yeah, I saw what happened on the first day. I was going to jump in then, but, you were in good company,' said the girl.

'What's your name?' asked Emmanuel.

'Imogen. Imogen Braithwaite. And your name…?'

'I'm Amanda as you know, well Amanda Campbell. This is my brother Bruce and this is Bruce's friend, Emmanuel Stuart, who is also Charlie's brother.'

'Nice to meet you all,' Imogen said feeling more relaxed.

'Where is my brother?' queried Emmanuel.

133

'Oh, he and Tom have gone for knight training. It's the first years first thing on Wednesday. I'm not really interested as I'm looking at doing the healing arts instead.'

'I was heading up to Knight Training, though I was going to go to the next session of Healing Arts after the first Knight Training class,' said Imogen. 'I enjoy all the fighting stuff and was heading down to the knight arena just now. Growing up with a knight dad and two brothers kinda rubs off on you. I tell you what, I might as well come with you to Healing Arts now and then head to the next knight's session,' said Imogen.

'Well then,' said Amanda, 'next week, all four of us will head to knight training, though I'll probably just watch and then we can head to the second Healing Arts session afterwards. You never know, Charlie and Tom might be interested in the healing arts.'

'Sounds like a plan,' said Imogen. 'Crikey, look at the time we're late, so let's go.'

Amanda and Imogen split off to head to class, whilst Bruce and Emmanuel enjoyed their free period not doing much.

***

Tom, Charlie and dozens of other students were waiting in a special area designated for knight training. It was medieval looking with huts and buildings made out of solid wood. There were stables and a blacksmith area where swords and armour were being made.

'Hello there again,' said a voice.

'It's you from the forest; the blacksmith….'

'Yes, well remembered,' said the blacksmith. 'I don't believe I introduced myself. I am Sir Barnaby, chief blacksmith, swordsmith and Magickal Knight of the Realm. Well nowadays, I prefer to focus my skills on fashioning the greatest blades and armour that I can. I prefer working here than in the Great City; the open air and fields are inspirational in forging new blades.'

'Fascinating,' said Charlie.

The students spent a few minutes getting changed into their sports gear. They were all wearing shorts with matching house tee-shirts or sporting vests.

'RIGHT YOU BUNCH OF DUNG WORMS! Let us see what you have got.' All students came out of the changing area to see Sedrick.

Sedrick and his massive frame came into the area. No students cared about the way he spoke as most were in awe of him. After all, he was a hero in the Magicklands.

'Oh, he's big,' said Michael Thorpe.

'He sure is,' said Felicity Rhoads.

'I am told that Dragonstone produces some of the finest warriors and I'm here at my friend Barnaby's request. After all, he does produce the best armour and weaponry around. You will be learning some of the greatest methods developed over centuries and some of my knight associates will be coming to show you some of their tricks. The aim is to keep you fit, focus the mind, learn great skills and, above all, find the ones who have the potential to make the magickal knight grade. Any messing around or bad behaviour I'll stick you in the dungeons myself. Do I make myself clear!?'

'Yes, sir,'

'I can't hear YOU!'

'YES, SIR!' All the students shouted in unison.

'Like the Greeks say, "In a healthy mind, lives a healthy body." Right follow me, we need to warm up those muscles of yours,' said Sedrick.

Sedrick lead them around a made up course and the group found it hard to keep up with him. Huffing and puffing, they followed Sedrick around. His blond hair flowed behind him and his beard swayed from side to side in front of him. It was only a few minutes before everyone was out of breath, apart from Charlie, who was used to physical exercise through his kickboxing endeavours. Some grasped their hips, some doubled over, whilst others complained about getting a stitch.

'By Odin, I've never seen such a sight. By the end of the year you'll be able to run to the Great City and back.'

They then spent a few moments stretching and Charlie was impressed by the flexibility of Sedrick as he was so big.

'Now, go and get your weapons. We will start with the swords.' Barnaby came out pushing a large trolley full of wooden swords.

'Wood?' said David looking confused.'

'So, you want to yield steel on the first, day eh? I'm afraid you can't yield steel until you become competent with wood. No, no, definitely not. I want no deaths or limb-lopping on the first day, thank you.'

All the students picked up some wooden swords and started swinging them around.

'Ouch!' shouted Chris, as he was accidently hit on the leg by his friend Oliver.

'Sorry mate,' said Oliver.

'And you wanted real blades?' said Sedrick, laughing away with his deep voice. He did make his point, however.

'Now give yourselves plenty of space, though make sure you can see me.'

Sedrick demonstrated a series of lunging, striking and defensive manoeuvres, which they all copied...well at least they tried to.

'You keep that arm high,' he shouted to one pupil.

'You! What on earth, was that? You couldn't squash an ant with that hit,' he said to another.

'No, no, no, no,' Sedrick sighed again.

They spent half an hour, practicing, moving swishing and slashing. They were all getting quite tired, apart from Charlie.

'Flippin 'eck, you're fit,' said Tom.

'Ah, this is nothing. You should see what we do in our kick boxing class. I have to admit, I haven't done any training for a couple of weeks, though trying to learn about this place has been exercise enough,' said Charlie.

'Now I would like a volunteer to come a sword spar with me,' said Sedrick.

'Don't we need armour or something sir?' said Felicity Rhoads.

'Don't worry, I'll not be hacking off your head with an axe, or be on the end of my two spears,' he laughed. 'No armour yet, it will help keep you on your toes being without it. Now, who wants a go?' No one responded.

'You go Charlie,' whispered Tom.

'Me? Look at him, he's huge,' giggled Charlie.

'Ah, I see I have found one,' said Sedrick looking straight at Charlie. 'Well, you seemed to find something amusing, maybe you were laughing at me,' said Sedrick to a stunned Charlie.

Charlie gulped and realised that everyone was deadly silent out of fear.

Charlie, just looked at his sword and then at the grinning Sedrick. But before he could do anything, Sedrick lunged with his sword. Charlie turned to the side to avoid the hit. Sedrick raised his brow.

Charlie, despite all his training was still petrified; he wasn't sure what to do. He lifted his sword up to strike, but Sedrick casually deflected his hit. Sedrick somehow moved forward, clipping his leg, but instead of falling over, he cartwheeled to the side.

Sedrick maintained his grin and composure as Charlie spun round with his sword to hit Sedrick.

'Trying to be clever,' said Sedrick as he lunged forward at the same time as Charlie, though Charlie got clipped on the arm this time.

'Come on Charlie,' cheered some the crowd finding their voice. 'Charlie, Charlie!'

Sedrick lunged forward, though Charlie used a roundhouse manoeuvre, hitting Sedrick's sword quite forcefully, making it move to the side. The children just gasped, seeing the manoeuvre as some form of contempt, but Sedrick just said approvingly. 'Good. I see we have a warrior among us.'

Seconds later, Sedrick, lunged, twisted, spun at Charlie who tried to keep up. In a flash, Charlie was on the floor with Sedrick's wooden blade point at his chest, with his own sword lying four feet away.

'You move like a warrior, but you have no skill with a blade. We will change this. Well done!' said Sedrick. The cheering stopped.

The rest of the class practiced and you could hear various screams as wood and flesh collided.

'You did really well Charlie,' said Tom. 'I think you took him by surprise with that spin kick thing you did. You could tell by his face.'

'I was really nervous,' said Charlie.

'Well, you never showed it,' said Tom.

'Right!' shouted Sedrick. 'Your first lesson is over… now, for your cool-down.' Sedrick took them through a series of stretches before they went to the showers.

Gossip was spreading amongst the first years how well Charlie did against Sedrick, even though they knew there was only going to be one winner.

'Nice one Charlie,' said David Moarns, who had bruises on his right arm and legs.

'Hi Charlie,' waved a smiling Felicity Rhoads. *Well she's nothing like the other Felicity,* Charlie thought to himself as he waved back at her.

Most students congratulated Charlie and that made him feel more welcomed and settled at the school; Charlie loved this session and he couldn't wait to come again.

'What time is it?' asked Tom.

'Oh crikey, we're running late. We need to meet up with Amanda. She's probably by herself,' said Charlie.

They hurriedly gathered their things and made their way as quickly as they could towards the canteen. There was a bit of commotion in the canteen and there seemed to be a few people surrounding Amanda.

'Hey Amanda,' shouted Charlie.

'Hey Charlie, hey Tom, look at this,' said Amanda.

'What's happened to your…?' asked Charlie.

'Eh?' said Tom.

'Astrophos,' said Amanda beaming.

'Well that makes sense,' said Charlie.

'Good, isn't it?' winked Amanda.

'How long did it take him to do it?' Charlie asked.

'Not long at all,' said Amanda. 'He was amazing.'

Astrophos had magically altered Amanda's chair. There were crystals embedded in the sides as well as a controller and some buttons. She even had her House emblem imprinted on her seat.

'It is brilliant,' she said. 'I can get around so much easier. It even has some special features that I'll show you later,' she said.

'Oh by the way, this is Imogen Braithwaite, a new friend,' said Amanda proudly.

'Fantastic! Hi Imogen,' said Charlie.

'Hello Imogen, pleased to meet you,' said Tom. 'Fire House, I see.' he said observing the red emblem on her blazer.

'Oh yes, a Leo,' said Imogen playfully boasting.

After shaking each other's hands, Amanda told Charlie and Tom about her encounter with Felicity Phelps and, how Imogen, her brother and Emmanuel came to her rescue. Charlie seemed mortified, but relieved that there were people around to help. The conversation reminded Charlie to contact his brother to see how he was progressing and if he enjoyed the knight training with Sedrick.

Tom then told Amanda and Imogen about what had happened at the knight training session. Amanda was really pleased and Imogen was very impressed that he'd lasted that long with Sedrick. She explained that her father was also a knight who had encountered Sedrick often in the Great City.

Eating dinner seemed a joyous occasion, as the dinner comprised of roast chicken, Yorkshire puddings, mixed vegetables and Lord Quimbus Finest Roast Potatoes, covered with delicious gravy.

Mutterings could be heard from first years, telling other first years about Charlie's encounter with Sedrick; Charlie simply ignored all the fuss. He looked over to Amanda and Imogen who were laughing and talking. He was really pleased that Amanda had found a good friend so that they could go off to do girl things together.

With the afternoon upon them, Amanda got out her timetable to see what wonders lay in store for them next. It was to be an afternoon of fun and frolics. The usual timetable disappeared and was replaced with a map, and list of all the societies, so they decided to go and see first-hand what was on offer.

Chapter 16

THE DOOR OF MYSTERY

After receiving some carefully crafted insults from Un-Potted Plants, they walked to the rear of the school where hundreds of tents and marquees were erected. They had never been there previously. Students and teachers alike were beckoning them to join their society. Enchanted signage such as speaking levitating heads, glowing signs and special fireworks advertised each group to encourage new members. Each tent had something to represent their society and some of the stalls actually looked like the society, for instance, the Painting Society's tent was a very large painting easel, with a giant brush stuck in the ground, flying the society banner.

Charlie, Amanda, Tom and Imogen had never seen such a sight and were getting excited by what they were seeing.

Amanda now had the freedom of her magickally enchanted crystal-powered wheelchair, which had various settings including: walk, run and spin quickly to change direction, to name a few.

'WOW!' said Tom. 'Look over there! What society is that? Let's go and look,' he continued excitedly. He had observed three people around various canvases, drawing pictures without the aid of brushes.'

'How are they doing that?' asked Charlie.

'They're psychic artists: they use the power of their minds to create the pictures,' said Tom. 'I've heard of them but not really seen any before.'

'Look,' said Amanda they have their eyes closed. That's even more amazing,' she said, as they got closer.

'They're not just closed,' said Imogen, 'they're blind.'

'BLIND!' shouted Charlie, stopping the artists and everyone else in their tracks.

'Sshhhh,' everyone else said. The lady artist turned around and her face looked as if it had just been burned. She just smiled

140

and turned to the canvas and a picture was developing on the canvass.

'What?' said Charlie. 'How… ? Why…? Impossible!'

'What is it?' said Imogen.

'It is my old house in the Plainlands.' Charlie froze on the spot as a shiver went up his spine.

'You're kidding,' said Tom.

'I'm not,' said Charlie, sounding more disconcerted.

'There is more,' said Amanda. 'I've looked on the societies listing and there is no mention of them.'

'Really…so what are they? Eh…where have they gone?' asked Tom. They all faced where the artists were and, sure enough, they'd all disappeared.

'*Really* strange,' said Charlie.

It was an 'add on to the list' of strange experiences that baffled even his Magickland friends.

Imogen brought everyone back down to earth, diverting their attention to the multitude of societies before them. Sure enough, they all mingled in with the rest of the crowds and the maze of tents. The best included the Magick Book Society, Spell Casting Society, Witches for Women Society, Magician Society for Boys, Wizopoly Society, Etiquette Society, Jousting Society, Archery, Martial Art Society, Poser Society, Painting Society, I am the Best Society, Language Society and many, many more. You could even set up your own providing you had ten keen members or more.

It took some time walking around all of the tents and the societies were more than just organisations to join; they were helpful places to learn. It was part of the school's policy to make learning fun and they strongly encouraged these activities to 'maximise learning and creative potential and, by doing so, opening yourself up to greater magick and creativity', whatever, that meant,' said Charlie, who couldn't quite understand the statement.

Charlie was really excited by the prospect of signing up and being a member of some club. There were some tough choices, but he and Tom chose to join the Extra Knight Training and Martial Arts (including Kick Boxing) and Spells. Charlie remembered what Cosmolos said in trying something different, so he thought that painting seemed quite interesting after seeing the artists, whilst Tom thought the Woodland Society seemed interesting. Amanda and Imogen decided to try the martial arts, and Spell casting as well as joining the Healing Arts and Magick Book Club.

The Orberon was slightly different as nearly everyone entered a magickal team to gain extra magickal credit. Charlie wanted to see a little more about the mysterious Orberon. As it happened, there was going to be some demonstration to launch the opening of it.

Having popped their names down, they spent a short while looking around the society buildings that were located beyond the trees to the far right of the Orberon. All events were starting the following week.

After a couple of hours on the tour, they headed back towards the canteen to have a little snack. The temperature suddenly dropped and there was a smell of rain in the air. Charlie looked up when a familiar apparition appeared before him: it was the shadowy entity. Charlie froze on the spot, observing what was happening. He had come to understand that whenever this entity appeared it was there to help him.

'You OK?' Amanda asked Charlie.

'It's back. The entity that has been following me and helping me,' he said.

'Really?' said a surprised Amanda.

'Eh?' said Tom whilst Imogen just looked confused.

'I'll explain later,' he said, '…this way!' He began to run.

'What are we doing? Where are we going?' demanded Imogen.

'No time to explain,' said Amanda. They quickly followed the entity that only Charlie could see. The entity glided along, always maintaining a reasonable distance between them. They crossed the courtyard, brushing past Reginald Bloom.

'Slow down, do you hear? And don't you dare tread on those Poppylop flowers,' said a very angry Reginald. Having completely ignored Reginald, they ran out of the courtyard and past the Earth tunnel, past the Elemental Fire tower and along a pathway leading to some small woodland area.

142

'Where are we going?' demanded Imogen. With the entity on his mind, Charlie just ignored her.

The soil and loose twigs just crunched beneath them and they eventually approached some ruined stonewalls and trees. Weaving in between them, Charlie began to slow down. Charlie stopped and the rest of the gang followed. The woodland and stone walls prevented them from seeing any part of the school and the dark sky made the whole area look very creepy. It was like a graveyard without the gravestones. Charlie and his friends made their way through some overgrown bushes.

'What is this place?' asked Amanda.

'I have no idea,' said Charlie.

'Are you going to tell us what this is all about?' asked Imogen, impatiently.

'I will,' said Charlie. 'Later I promise,' he reassured them.

'Of course! Don't you remember what Hecate said on the visit?' said Tom. 'The School is built upon an old fortress that used to be here. This must be part of it.'

'Yes, Randle the Tracker said that the main entrance to the school was part of the old Castle,' said Charlie.

About fifty yards in front of them was a perfectly preserved door with a couple of stone obelisks located just in front of the doorframe.

There was a dirty, stony pathway leading up to the door with a pathway cutting across the middle forming a cross. In each quarter section were some bushes and grass that blended with the open landscape.

'Ah, I think I know what this is,' said Imogen.

'What is it?' asked Tom, enthusiastically.

'There was something Hecate said in assembly that there are old enchanted places that we should avoid at all costs. This must be the Door of Mystery. My dad says that people have disappeared in there,' said Imogen.

'Really?' said Amanda. 'I think we should do what Hecate says,' she continued.

'So why isn't it guarded or boarded up?' asked Tom.

'I have no idea,' said Imogen. 'Maybe they are too afraid to go near it.'

143

'Charlie, what are you doing?' asked Amanda as Charlie approached the doorway.

'Stay away,' said Tom sounding very concerned.

'You're crazy,' said Imogen.

Charlie ignored them all and proceeded towards the door. With the dull grey gravel crackling beneath him, he stepped over the threshold of the cross pathway. A chilling wind passed through the area making everyone shiver. Everyone froze and you could almost hear everyone's heartbeat.

Unexpectedly, a clicking and grinding noise came from the door with an accompanying scream. Both Imogen and Tom grasped Amanda who sat in the chair in front of them.

Charlie stretched out his arm and, with a shaking hand, he reached for the iron door handle and turned it slowly.

The door took it upon itself to open fully and there, appearing before him, was a multitude of rooms and images, spinning and contorting so quickly that it made Charlie feel very nauseous.

Suddenly, the door started pulling him in and he immediately grasped the right-hand obelisk to prevent it doing so. The room seemed to know that he was resisting, so it began to pull harder.

'Help! I'm being pulled in!' screeched Charlie.

'Charlie needs help!' said Amanda, so they all began to run forward to try to prevent Charlie from being sucked in.

'Leave it to me,' said Amanda, as if having thought of some cunning plan. She sped ahead, veering off the main pathway and on to the old garden that was level with the ground.

Charlie, now with body in midair, grasping for his life, turned his head round briefly and with eyes squinting, he looked.

'What...? How...? Why...? Is it...?' he said, but he quickly turned himself back as he was now getting a hideous headache.

'Hang on Charlie,' said Amanda. 'When I come around, grab the back of the chair and I will pull you away.'

'You're crazy,' said Tom. Charlie tried to have one more look, but Amanda arrived. The images were moving so quickly and

144

violently, he felt like he was going to be sick.

Amanda slowed herself down before reaching the entrance and said, 'Grab the back of the chair as I pass. Do it quickly or we will both get dragged in.' Charlie nodded in acknowledgement as he found it now difficult to talk.'

'NOW!' shouted Amanda.

Amanda pulled in front and Charlie, with a struggle, reached out and grabbed the chair. Amanda instantly went to the highest setting and pulled off but the ordeal wasn't over: Amanda's chair got caught in the pull of the door and started it to pull her in. Tom and Imogen ran forward to help.

'Wait there!' yelled Amanda.

Amanda reached underneath the arm and there was a crystal that was only to be pushed in case of emergencies. She quickly twisted it. A bright red light circled the tyres and the chair, boosting them forward, pulling them away from the gravity of the door that was sucking them in like a black hole.

As they pulled away, the door slammed shut and it went deathly quiet, until Charlie emptied the contents of his stomach.

'Are you OK?' asked a worried Amanda.

'Just about,' said Charlie, wiping the remaining sick off his face.

'I thought you were a gonner there,' said Tom.

'Me too,' said Charlie.

'Next time, listen,' said Imogen angrily, but in a concerned sort of way.

As Charlie composed himself, he felt annoyed at what had happened. He felt betrayed and gullible that he should trust in something he knew nothing about and that no-one else could see. Was it some sort of joke or his imagination?

'Thank you,' said Charlie to Amanda.

'That's OK, we're even,' she said, starting to giggle.

'Are you going to tell us what it is all about?' said Imogen sounding very fed up.

'Let's head back. I think I need to freshen up a bit,' he said.

'So what did you see?' asked Tom.

Tom's comments had brought back his memory of what just happened. 'I'll explain that later,' Charlie said feeling perkier.

145

Back in his room, Charlie freshened up with a long shower and he changed back into his usual jeans and tee shirt.

More thoughts started accumulating in his head: should he tell them what he saw or thought he had seen through the door? He knew that he'd have to tell them about the entity because he promised to do so. This didn't matter so much as he knew this phenomenon would be more accepted by Magickland people than Plainland ones.

Charlie spent a few moments replying to a message sent by his mum. He also sent one to his brother saying thank you for looking out for Amanda and that they should meet up soon to catch up.

Charlie put on his new white trainers then headed down to meet Amanda, Tom and Imogen.

Charlie went through the story of the entity and the things it did to help and guide him.

'Well it didn't seem particularly helpful an hour ago. You could have gotten yourself killed!' said Tom.

'I would agree with Tom, apart from, well…er…there is something else that I haven't told you all,' said Charlie.

'What's that?' asked Amanda.

'I think the entity was trying to show me something,' said Charlie.

'What?' asked Imogen, trying to hurry proceedings.

'Well, you might think that I'm crazy,' said Charlie. 'It doesn't make any sense.'

'What doesn't make sense?' asked Tom.

'Spill the beans,' said Amanda.

'Should I get some dinner first?' said Imogen, sarcastically. Charlie took a deep breath and…

'Hey guys…,' said a voice.

'Not now David,' they all said together. David knew he'd interrupted something and promptly turned the other way.

'Where were we?' said Imogen.

'I saw the Half Prophecy,' said Charlie.

'What?' said Tom 'How? It's under lock and key.'

'Do you think the room is some kind of strange TV that shows you things?' asked Amanda.

'How could it?' said Imogen, 'it was trying to suck Charlie in.'

'True. Ok some kind of teleportation device,' said Amanda.

'Maybe it is,' said Tom, 'that would make sense.'

'You don't understand,' said Charlie.

'Understand what?' asked Imogen.

'I saw the Half Prophecy,' he said again.

'We know,' said Amanda looking confused.

'The OTHER half,' said Charlie. 'I'm sure of it.'

Stunned silence hit them and they just looked at him.

'Are you sure?' asked Amanda.

'That's impossible!' said Tom. 'The other half is legend. People have searched for centuries and not found it. Are you sure?' he said sceptically.

'The room was spinning really quickly. Maybe it was a trick of the mind, after all, Guildus, only showed us this the other day,' said Imogen.

'I had thought of that,' said Charlie, 'but don't you think it would be a great place to hide it?' said Charlie. 'After all, it is one of the oldest parts of the school and who would be crazy enough to go in there to find it?' Charlie posed them with some good arguments.

'Are you one hundred percent sure,' said Amanda.

'Pretty sure,' said Charlie. 'But yeah, like you said, it was moving rather quickly and my eyes were half closed as it was making me feel sick - but I'm sure I saw it!'

'OK!' said Tom. 'We need to do some research.'

'I agree,' said Imogen. 'We need to find out when it was built.'

'Hang on. Say that everything checked out, what do we do then? Do well tell the teachers?' asked Tom.

'Much more to the point, how in the Magicklands do we get it out?' said Imogen. 'It would be the greatest find in history. I say tell no-one.'

'I agree,' said Charlie.

'I think we should check the drawing room and the main library as there is bound to be something there.' said Imogen.

Plans were in motion and they were all getting very excited.

147

Helen came over to them carrying an object in her hand; it was the Wizopoly board game.

'Thanks Helen,' said Charlie.

'No problem,' said Helen, walking back to her friends.

'Fantastic!' said Charlie.

'I've been looking forward to this, after all, enchantments don't work in the Plainlands,' said Amanda. 'This is going to be interesting.'

'Sounds quite dull living without magick. Very plain,' said Tom.

'Yeah it does, though it isn't all boring,' he said. 'What do we do?' asked Amanda.

'Well, here are your wallets,' said Tom.

'They're tiny,' said Charlie.

'Not in there they aren't,' replied Tom, quickly.

'But how do we get into the game?' asked Charlie.

'Well, when it is your turn, you role dice to get your number to move around the board. When you have that, you say enter, and then you will end up in the game.

'I get it,' said Charlie and Amanda.

'Let's play!' said Tom, excitedly.

Sure enough, they played for two hours. Charlie and Amanda were fascinated when they entered the game: everything seemed so real and they loved the Magickland money. Amanda liked the miniature horse and carts they could sit in as it moved along to each area but when looked at from the normal size they were like solid metal pieces on a plain board.

The enjoyment of the game had made Charlie, Amanda, Tom and Imogen forget about the Half Prophecy until they all had gotten back to their rooms; it was going to play on their minds well into the night.

Chapter 17

THE ORBERON

The next few days brought some interesting new lectures, including: Signs and Sigils, Nordic Runes, More Spell Practice, Magickal Powders and an Introduction to Spells for Specific Things (ISST). Charlie knew little about spell-work and the Magickland in general. What comforted him was the thought that his Magickland-born friends had a lot to learn too. The ISST session explained there were different levels of magick to do specific things. The first level was learning basic summoning and sending as they had done earlier, but the next level was more complicated and required additional work, whereby magick is used for personal projects that can't be summoned like a book off a shelf.

Witch and Sorceress, Hegarty Blood, was a lovely old Hedge Witch and an expert in forming complicated spells. A typically dressed witch all in black with a pointy hat, she lived by the seaside in a cave, making spells for people as well as making potions and lotions for health. A Hedge Witch, as Charlie soon discovered, were witches who preferred to work by themselves. And like some of the teachers this year, she was new to the school but she never stayed on campus beyond the school day as she liked to return to her cave.

The teacher started what was to be a long speech and lecture into her brand of magick. She explained to the group that to achieve a real success in life, like a good job, relationship or even becoming a first class witch or mage, you needed to do extra work. She also said that you could summon anything and everything, though it depended on how much faith you had in the magick that works in the unseen, your focus, and the amount of attention and dedication you put into your work. She warned that 'you get what you wish for' so be careful what you order. Second level magick is not only about bringing what you desire or need, but it adds energy and vitality where you want it.

You can help others, nature and the world. A simple act of kindness can bring untold fortune, so it isn't always necessary to formulate complicated spells. Finally, you use magick only for good. Never use it to bewitch others or to use it against their will. Remember, what you give will return to you three fold. This does not just apply to magick, but in thought and deed too.

The group looked a little confused by what she said, though she re-assured them that they would understand in time.

The entire group had been given a Moonometer that was placed in their school bags when they first collected them. It was like a watch but had a larger face on it, with the moon surrounded by various astrological symbols. Charlie looked at Hegarty and put his hand up.

'Yes young man and you are?' For the first time, he'd met someone who didn't know who he was.

'Charlie Stuart, Madam,' he said.

'How can I help you?' she said smiling at him.

'What does a Moonometer do?' asked Charlie.

'It tells you the phase of the moon and the position of the planetary influences,' she responded swiftly.

'Why is the moon important to magick?' asked Charlie.

'A good question. You see; the planet and the universe flow in cycles, just like the seasons. The moon has a massive influence on the planet, including controlling the tides and even emotion. Did you know most crimes are committed during the full moon?'

'Really?' said Amanda.

'And your name young lady?' asked Hegarty.

'Amanda Campbell,' she replied.

'Hello Amanda and yes, it is true. In fact, the influences of the moon are much more extensive than you think,' the teacher said. 'Like the changing of the seasons, the moon has its own cycle. The moon goes from nothingness into fullness and from fullness into nothingness. Let me explain. When the moon is heading into fullness, it is called the Waxing Phase of the moon and when it reduces to its smallest element, it is called the Waning Phase. In simple terms, if you want to bring things into your life, like a new job, or money, or relationship, or gift, the best time to work on this is on the waxing moon as the energy works to pull and bring things into your life. If your spell requires power, then the best time to do it is on the full moon. If you want to get rid or banish non-useful things in your life, like a bad habit you might have, it is best to work on the waning phase as the moon's power shifts things out of your life. Remember never banish people from your life as what you give out will return. If someone is annoying you then there are more intelligent ways of handling them, see me first,' she said. 'Lastly, the best advice I can give you is to work from your heart and not out of hate. This achieves the best results and increases your power threshold.'

The session continued and the class asked lots of questions about what she had said; it was very confusing to them. She told them not to panic as they had a lifetime to learn magick.

The session finished by Hegarty asking them to think of a spell that they would like to work on. Charlie wanted to do a spell about finding out more about the shadowy entity, so he spent some time with Hegarty formulating a simple Revealing spell for this.

Much to the relief of the class, the next session wasn't as mind boggling as the last: it was Magickal Powders. The teacher, Professor Lambert Snuffle, was from the Magickal Powder Institute. He was quite large and looked like a typical mad scientist with crazy, big hair and a white lab coat. The lesson was great fun as they could create powders that could do just about anything, from vanishing people, providing quick getaways such as teleportation, make you faster, make your opposition slower; a great level one magickal aid. The possibilities were endless. It involved the mixing of herbs, woods, metals, and crystals to name a few. Professor Snuffle was an eccentric person who was very passionate and spoke so loudly you could never fall asleep in his class.

He discussed the history of magickal powders and demonstrated with some of them. The first powder he took moved him from one part of the class to another at great speed. The lesson's finale involved him walking on the ceiling and down the walls.

The students got very excited by this and mischief was on the back of everyone's mind. Unfortunately, it was impossible, even

151

with the magick powders, to escape the school grounds, to which there were a few groans and moans by the students.

The first thing Professor Snuffle got them to do was to try to create a defensive shield powder that protects the Magician or objects against all kinds of magick and weapons for a few minutes 'great in emergency situations,' said the Professor.

So they all set about the lab which was full of test tubes, liquids and ingredients. The session was set into two as ingredients had to be set before being ground into a powder not too dissimilar to sand, though jet black in colour. The students did the best they could, but only the following week would reveal the truth of their endeavours.

Nothing else brought more joy than the opportunity to study freely in their societies. Charlie took it upon himself to teach Tom some kick boxing moves and, to his surprise; he was picking up the basics quite quickly. However, Charlie was way ahead of the others as he had years of experience. The head of the martial arts club, Sensei Lee, was most impressed with Charlie and he was considering pairing him up with some of the older students.

Spell-casting was something new to Charlie, though he was determined to learn. He, Tom, Amanda and Imogen joined in this session and worked hard to send and call objects. The practice went quite well, though Charlie still had problems sending objects to a specific place, often hitting other people, which frustrated him and annoyed the others, especially David Moarns. Tom had problems calling objects to himself, which either moved far too slowly, or so quickly that he hit himself regularly with the small ball he was using. The girls seemed to do far better, though there was a lot of work to be done for everybody.

'Relax Charlie,' said Imogen, 'you're concentrating too hard so it won't work,' she told him.

Afterwards, Charlie loved the knight practice, learning from one of the older pupils, Robert Ambrose, a few defensive and offensive moves.

This was the perfect build up for the next big event: the launch of the Orberon over the weekend.

With being so busy, the one thing they didn't do was to research further the Half Prophecy, and it was beginning to play on Charlie's mind.

Time passed quickly and it was nearly seven o'clock on Saturday evening. Charlie, Amanda, Tom and Imogen were waiting in the canteen, drinking hot chocolate out of the refillable cups.

'So what happens at the Orberon?' Charlie asked Tom.

'Well, I can't believe that you have not heard of the Orberon, it is the coolest thing ever. I think you need to see it to believe it,' said Tom.

'I agree,' said Imogen. 'My dad was really good at it. I hear that Sedrick is going to be part of the launch also.'

'Really!' said Tom excitedly. 'I've only seen him on TV. Well, I've never actually been to an Orberon before.'

'Really, wow! My dad used to take me all of the time. He is part of the Black Dragon League of Knights, you know.'

'That is so cool,' said Tom.

Charlie and Amanda just looked at each other as if to say, 'what on earth they are talking about?'

The temperature dropped slightly outside, as the sun lowered in the distance. Charlie put his Dragonstone leather jacket on and zipped it up, tucking his scarf into his jacket and putting his matching gloves and hat on. Amanda, Tom and Imogen also proudly wore their own house clothes.

They left the building and followed the multitude of students heading down to the arena. The area was clear, apart from large flags representing the School, The Orberon, The Great City, and one flag representing all the elements and magick that blew imperiously in the air.

As they walked down the field, you could see students heading down passageways to the arena.

'The ticket says we need to go to the west entrance to get our seat,' said Amanda, so they did as she said.

Down, down and down they all went until they reached the entrance to the inner arena. Charlie had never seen the arena properly before and he certainly wasn't going to be disappointed. They were at the lowest level below ground, on a level with the participants. A special place was set, for Amanda, which was the

153

reason they got a terrific view. Charlie's mouth dropped and he couldn't believe the vastness of the gigantic stadium.

'This is amazing,' he said, feeling excited like the first time he entered the magick world.

'It certainly is. I can't believe a thing of this size is underground,' said Amanda.

The stadium filled up slowly and there were various levels of entrances to make it easier for students, teachers and visitors to find their seats.

The lights were bright as the sun had practically set. Mumbles, rumbles and mutterings were rife, all filled with excitement and expectancy.

'What time does it start?' asked Charlie.

'Oh, about 8.15pm,' said Tom.

The lights dimmed slightly. A familiar figure entered the scene. It was Sedrick, wearing unfamiliar smart clothing. His hair washed and tied back and his beard trimmed.

'Ladies and gentleman, students and teachers alike, I Sedrick, three-time winner of the Orberon with the Black Dragon League, say in traditional magickal voice, Hail and Welcome,' he said speaking through some magickally adjusted microphone.

'HAIL AND WELCOME,' shouted the crowd.

'We have a treat for you tonight. Coming together we have the best duellers, jousters and fighters of Magick to entertain you.'

'Fantastic,' said Charlie, as did most of the children.

The lights dimmed further with deep interchange of red and blue lights filling the stadium, making it difficult to see. The lights dimmed further until it went dark. Suddenly, the lights came on again making everyone either squint or shut their eyes completely. Leading from the four entrances, coming from the lower changing areas of the arena, the knights came storming in on horseback. A jousting partition had mysteriously appeared when the lights dimmed. Without further ado, the knights went straight into action. The knight with red markings came galloping towards the knight with blue markings, striking each other on the chest and knocking each other backwards with every hit; the crowd roared as they did so. 'Get him!' the Fire House cheered for the knight in red who obviously belonged to fire element sign.

'Put his fire out,' teased the Water House, supporting their man in blue.

The knights turned to make another run and the horses galloped as fast as their legs could carry them. Smash! The red knight blocked the blue knight's lance and knocked him off his horse. The whole stadium erupted with another roar.

'One to zero to the reds,' shouted Sedrick as it flashed up on the main board.

'We've got this in the Plainlands,' shouted Charlie over the noise of the crowd.

'Just watch this,' shouted Tom.

The blue knight quickly got up, minus his horse that had ran back down the entrance. The knight in red went bearing down onto his opponent, when he remarkably jumped over the thrusting lance of the oncoming red rider like a high jumper would over the pole bar. Immediately, he got his sword out, landed on his feet, and struck the red knight off his steed.

'One all,' said Sedrick. 'Who is going to be the mightiest today?' he bellowed.

'WOW! How did he do that?' asked Charlie.

'That's a Magickal Knight,' said Tom.

Then something happened, which surprised Charlie further.

The red knight took out his sword and shot a large magickal red pulse that went straight towards the blue knight. The blue knight raised his shield and blocked it. The man in blue reciprocated, this time sending a spread of blue pulses, just like an old Gatling gun. However, his opponent blocked some with his shield and deflected the rest with the sword. Suddenly, the red knight sneakily put something into his armour and, at great speed; he zoomed towards the blue knight knocking him to the ground. The crowd roared once more.

'Two one to the reds,' said Sedrick.

'Roast him!' shouted the Fire House, so he obliged.

'That's curious,' said Imogen whispering something to Amanda.

The knight swung his sword up and around. His sword glowed red and caught fire and its flame was directed towards the

155

knight on the ground. Within seconds, he was in flames; the crowd gasped.

The knight on the ground grasped his sword pointed it upwards above his head, magickally dragging himself along the ground.

'So you have this on the Plainlands?' asked Tom.

'Er, not quite like this,' said Charlie laughing. 'This is so much better,' he said grinning like a Cheshire cat.

Imogen was cheering away and Amanda, completely nonplussed by the whole experience, still she managed to scream very loudly at various points.

The knight picked himself up quickly and, after that, followed a series of close combat manoeuvres: the large swords moved effortlessly, speedily, clashing and sparking up different colours of energy, whilst simultaneously producing a strange kind of magick involving attack and defence, trying to defeat each other; it was breathtaking.

Everyone sat on the edge of their seats observing the combat spectacle, when all of a sudden; the knight with the blue markings caught the red knight in some kind of magickal net. The knight grasped his fist and the blue knight made a flinging gesture, sending the red knight crashing to the ground.

'Two all! The one who strikes the next point, wins the match.'

Combat resumed. Bludgeoning maces were swinging, striking each other's shields and armour. Shots of red energy balls the size of the mace heads went shooting towards each other and each were as skilful as the other, clanging and clashing, sparks flying everywhere. Some were even hitting the side of the arena much to the nervousness of the children.

Then suddenly, the knight with the red markings produced a cunning move: whilst avoiding the blows from the blue knight, he twisted on the spot and took out a dagger and, like a wand, he pointed at his lance that was on the floor behind the blue knight. The lance came hurtling towards the man in blue. He was totally unaware of the lance spinning towards him like a helicopter blade and, within seconds, the lance took the blue knights legs out and he landed on his back.

'Three two to the Reds, he's the winner!!'

Roars from the crowd came as Sedrick made his announcement. Charlie looked round and Water House looked rather disappointed. The Fire House held up signs saying, "Your Fired," "Fire Rules," "Your water has evaporated," "Let off some steam," to name a few. The only remaining blue sign left up was from one of the older children saying, "You need cooling off."

The blue knight looked dejected, though he got up, bowed to his opponent, bowed to Sedrick and then bowed to the crowd. Everyone just applauded, including Charlie, who had never seen such a thing before.

It wasn't over. Sedrick spoke again, 'Now for the task! Release the Lionoth.' A peculiar looking creature appeared from nowhere. Like the name implied, it looked like a lion, though it was at least ten times bigger than a normal lion.

It sat there on its back legs and its claws started to stick out. Further and further, they came and it became clear these were no ordinary claws. They looked like huge needle spikes that were about three feet long. Along the body, armour appeared, and the tail became like a spiked club.

'That's an Apparition Enchantment,' said Tom.

'You're kidding,' said Charlie.

'But it looks so real,' said Amanda.

'The killing of beasts for recreational purposes was outlawed two centuries ago for being barbaric and against the natural laws. They can only be killed if your life is in danger or if they're a danger to anyone else, including other animals. My dad told me,' said Imogen.

'That's brilliant,' said Amanda.

'Yeah, the enchantment is very real and the more advanced you become, the more dangerous the enchantments. They can do serious damage though, as far as I know, no one has ever died before,' said Tom.

'Well that's good to hear,' laughed Charlie.

Two other knights joined the fray. The first knight had yellow markings indicating that he was an air sign and the second knight bore green markings indicating he was an earth sign. All four knights were on their horses circling around the beast that sat right in the middle of the arena. The beast, sensing the danger, began to roar loudly and it started walking around signalling that he meant business. Some of the children panicked and screamed as he did this.

Its claws remained remarkably straight and then Charlie noticed that some mercury type substance started oozing out of its claws.

'What's that?' said Charlie.

'Not sure,' replied Tom.

'Ooh, poison is now coming out of the Lionoth's claws, the knights better watch out,' said Sedrick.

'Without warning, the beast lunged towards the blue knight, who by the skin of his teeth, got out of the way. As it did so, the red and yellow knights thrust their lances onto the beast from behind, having no effect. In fact, the Lionoth swished his tail knocking the lance of the yellow knight onto the ground.

'Come on Air!' shouted Charlie.

The Lionoth swung round and its javelin-like claws slashed into the armour of the red knight.

'What? That is magickal armour,' exclaimed Tom. 'I thought it was supposed to be impervious to everything.'

'Not everything,' said Imogen, frowning again.

'Ooh, the beasts poison can get through the armour,' said Sedrick softly. The red knight scarpered very quickly and the other knights kept their distance.

The red knight got out his sword. The flame that nearly roasted the blue knight earlier came hurtling out, hitting the beast fully in the face. The Lionoth raged as it stood on its legs and lunged towards the red knight. Thankfully, the yellow knight, being of air, sent a strong wind, pushing the knight out of the way and the Lionoth skidded on the surface missing him. This time the blue knight yielded his mace, swinging it round furiously and the head frosted over with a large spike sticking out of the top. He threw it at the creature and the yellow knight accelerated the rate at which the mace flew, using a miniature hurricane as a propulsion mechanism. It stuck in the beast's forehead. The wounded creature became angrier and started chasing everyone wildly and the knights went in different directions to confuse it.

158

It focussed on the green knight and the others regrouped around. Out of the blue, another person entered the arena holding a spear in each arm.

'It's Sedrick,' shouted a student. 'WOW.' Charlie was now on the edge of his seat, as was most of the arena.

He came in with each spear above each shoulder. He was going to perform a double spear throw. 'Articus,' said Sedrick as he released the spears and the heads frosted over as he threw them. They moved with such force that the spears penetrated the natural body armour of the Lionoth and into its heart. The beast roared its final breath and the magickal apparition enchantment vanished into thin air.

Roars and cheers erupted from the audience as Sedrick raised his arms in triumph, roaring like the Lionoth had previously. It tuned out that the Lionoth's weakness was ice as well as steel to penetrate its armour.

'That was scary,' said Charlie.

'Sedrick's the best,' shouted David who was sat a couple of rows above them.

The red knight, on his horse, came towards where Charlie and his gang were sitting. He was then right in front of them and took his helmet off.

Charlie, Amanda and Tom didn't know what to say as they were in shock. Imogen just looked at the knight and said, 'Hello dad.'

'Hello Imogen, didn't quite get the beasty this time eh? I must brush up on my ice, what, what,' he said chirpily.

'Yes father,' said Imogen looking rather embarrassed.

'Don't forget to send your mother a message. She's sent you three scrolls already this week,' he said.

He put his helmet on and trotted off to meet Sedrick and the other knights.

'Your father is the red knight,' said Tom in disbelief.

'Yeah,' she said simply. 'I wasn't sure to begin with, though when he summoned the lance that laid out the blue knight, I knew it was him,' she said coolly.

'How cool. Of course, he's Sir Michael Braithwaite. Brilliant!' said Tom. 'Just flippin' brilliant!'

Imogen just became embarrassed as some of the other students started chatting about her.

'Thank you for coming,' said Sedrick, now wearing his full Viking gear. 'The Orberon is now officially open at Dragonstone and you can now put your teams together. Get plenty of practice in now.'

'Give us more,' shouted the students. 'More… more… more… more… more…' Sedrick was unmoved and the event finished shortly afterwards.

Back at the accommodation, they sat in Imogen's room and, sure enough, there were three scrolls waiting for her like her father mentioned. In fact, a fourth one appeared.

'I guess I better reply,' she said.

'Yeah, you don't want to worry her,' said Amanda.

They sat discussing the Orberon and maybe they should get some kind of team together, after all they all belonged to different elemental houses, so it was perfect for them, even though you couldn't participate properly until the second year.

Charlie and Amanda wanted more clarification on the Orberon, so Imogen spoke: 'Well, it works like this. Each team that enters has four members in it and they compete against another team. Normally, you have one member who does the duelling, though everyone can duel. Some teams change and rotate so that each member has a go each week. However, you will mainly find that the rest are there as stand-ins, just in case one team member is ill or injured. During the game, you heard Sedrick keep score on how often the knight hit the ground, well, that's what happens. Three hits to the ground and you are out with points gained to the other team. At the end of it there is a 'Task' to complete, like the knights having to slay the Lionoth. This normally involves all team members coming together to help. In the league, there is a panel that scores points in other areas, such as effort, co-operation, courage and ingenuity. The first team to complete the task in the fastest time gets a ten point bonus; it is awarded at the end of the week. The Orberon tests your individual skill as well as being able to work as a team. It is really good because it keeps you on your toes and makes work for your team and house. It also makes you spend a lot of time studying magick. In many ways, it is like the societies: it helps to make learning fun.'

'Well, how does it work for your house?' asked Charlie.

'Well each score from each team member goes to your elemental house score. The house with the most points wins. So in the end, you end up having a team and house score,' said Imogen. 'Oh, the knight with the most individual points becomes knight of the year. Also, there is a duel off between the top knights to become ultimate champion.'

'So why don't you group everyone from one house together?' asked Amanda.

'Well, they say it is important to work with other houses to achieve things and it is also important to see the value of all the elements working, as they are all needed,' said Imogen. 'Of course we can all use all the elements ourselves, though the element we are born with is our strongest. Some of the great magicians and wizards learn to use all elements equally, though, this takes years of practice and learning,' said Imogen.

'I think I get it,' said Charlie. 'I can't wait to start!' he said with a sparkle in his eye.

Chapter 18

A MUM'S TALE

The alarm went off early and the bed returned to its original size. Victoria Stuart opened her eyes gently and smiled. Slowly, she sat up and there was a pile of books on the table next to her. She picked up her long lightly varnished oak wand and said, 'Aperio window', and the window opened. The sapphire glistened at the end of her wand. It looked like there was a world of its own in its shiny body.

The fresh morning air wafted in bringing the scent of fresh flowers, perfuming the room. 'I love it,' said Victoria loudly as she so often said. It seemed that magick was something that came very easily to Victoria. She was as excited and as enthusiastic about magick and spent as much of her time as possible reading about it. A few weeks had passed and she was definitely enjoying heading back to school again, especially as they had to wear uniforms. 'You're never too old to learn,' said Corbus Strong, the headmaster, on her first day. He strongly believed in etiquette and keeping high standards, as well as dressing appropriately, so he got on superbly with Victoria.

Victoria got out of bed and had a look outside. The garden was bustling with faeries, gnomes and other elementals going about their business. It was like the garden was a great city and they all had jobs to do. She spent some time studying the elemental kingdom and never realised that each species of elementals had their own quirks and personalities. Some elementals were enthusiastic to work with humans and others cared less about them. Their main focus was looking after the planet and the environment whilst their agenda for living was quite different from human kind; it was something that remained a mystery for most humans. If you get on the right side of them they could be your greatest ally. Get on the wrong side of them and they could be your worst enemy. It was hard to imagine that these creatures are forged from the very essence of nature. They are, to a certain degree, masters of certain aspects of nature and can lend a very helpful hand in magick, assisting you with spell-work. They can be summoned, though they won't necessarily choose to work or help you; all you can do is ask.

It took a while for Victoria to adjust to the quirkiness of Mini, the family brownie. Brownies are very helpful elementals that generally love children and are amazing at getting the house tidy. However, according to the books, thanking a brownie or even giving them a gift is deemed to be quite insulting to them and they could leave. However, just being polite, a friend and leaving out some delicious pastry or something with butter on it, is the best way of saying 'thanks for your help'. They get on with magick folk much easier than Plainlanders. Victoria was very happy to see a kobold knocking around the garden, as they are a rarity. It happened that when the elemental appeared by chance, Victoria did the right thing: she didn't ignore it and then offered it some food. This one loved sausages. Consequently, her rose bush grew quite suddenly. This kobold, called Raymond, was three foot tall and wore brown knee-length cord trousers, a blue and green chequered shirt as well as a bright red felt hat. He looked quite old and had a peculiar and funny looking face, covered in wrinkles.

Unlike magick folk, elementals carry a lot of influence in the Plainlands and get rather upset when Plainlanders destroy their habitat, but they like to get their own back by creating bad weather and other natural phenomenon, using their unique brand of magick.

It took a few moments before Victoria got herself out of bed and headed to wake Lucy and Olivia. Amazingly, they were still fast asleep, but they were usually the ones jumping up and down on the bed waking her up.

Olivia loved Dragon Tots. The nursery was teaming with faeries and other pleasant elemental creatures. She loved the teddy bears that came and cuddled you when you were upset; Moonie, the nursery brownie, who soothed you with her enchanting voice; and the pushchairs that automatically pushed you around to get you to sleep. The other children were nice too, apart from Toby who liked

163

to pull your hair and bite you when you thought it was safe. However, Mrs Hibbit, the carer, was a natural with the children and could dissolve any bad behaviour without raising her voice. After all, tranquillity spells are an advantage in any tense situation. Olivia loved playing with Lottie Campbell and they seemed to be the best of friends.

Similarly, Lucy and Martha got on well at Dragonstone Juniors. It was a bit of a strange time as they learned about magick, though their powers would not develop fully until they got their magick name, much to the annoyance of them both. However, they enjoyed the school they went to and the teachers did not seem too bad, apart from Mr Calderdale, the history teacher, who tended to snigger when you got something wrong.

The family finished some Wizard Pops that crackled different sounds every time they popped. This included a foghorn and a chimpanzee sound amongst many more. Without warning, there was another noise… a knock at the door.

'Good Morning Victoria,' said Andrew.

'Coming,' shouted Victoria. 'Come on my dear lovelies, its time to go,' she shouted to the children.

The door kindly obliged by opening up and Michael, the door, bid everyone hello as well as a good bye.

Victoria was about to leave, when a scroll appeared in the Scroll-Porter.

'It's Charlie,' said Victoria sounding ecstatic.

She opened the letter and read how he was enjoying school, his new friends, and most of all his lessons, and how they had gotten a team together for the Orberon, even though they couldn't compete until next year. He was that busy, that there wasn't enough time in the day to do everything, but he'd have it no other way. He said that he did miss everyone and that he met up with his brother who had also had some new friends. It wouldn't be long until they'd be meeting up again. He couldn't wait to taste her cooking and sleep in that amazing bed of his. He gave his love to everyone and the letter finished with a flurry of kisses and the scent of fresh flowers.

A tear came down her cheek when Mrs Campbell spoke.

'You missing them too?'

'Yes, though I am happy that they are happy. I can't wait to see them,' said Victoria.

'Me neither,' said Mrs Campbell.

'A fine Indian Summer we seem to be having,' said Andrew changing the subject.

'It's lovely here,' said Victoria. 'Life is so different.'

'We'd better get on or we will be late,' she said adjusting her tie.

'They walked along the cobbled street into the main town centre, walking past the ironmongers, blacksmith, apothecary, and of course, *The Warted Witch Tavern* and its opposite rival, *The Warlock's Wand Inn*.

Walking further into the village, they crossed a humped river bridge, turned, and walked down another road. Ten minutes later they dropped off the children and headed to the Dragonstone School for Adults.

Immaculately dressed in their uniforms, they met up with other new friends including Cynthia and Arthur Reynolds, Joshua Horn, Mickey and Paula Brown, Antoinette Price and Rupert Binks. They were all new additions from the Plainlands, so they had much in common.

'Hello there,' said a voice they hadn't heard in a while: it was Randle.

'Hi Randle,' they all enthused.

'Just seeing how you are all getting along in your new homes,' said Randle.

'It is of supreme quality,' said Rupert.

'I love it,' said Antoinette.

'The Great City is beyond what I could imagine,' said Cynthia, shaking her red hair in the warm breeze.

They spent a few minutes discussing the marvellous experiences they had and the places they were intending on seeing.

Randle was invited as a guest speaker to discuss the role of druids in the magick world and how they had changed over the centuries due to the influx of many magickal practices from the different cultures.

Meditation practice was no different to that of Charlie's school in that it was quite a struggle to still the mind. Andrew found this especially hard, grunting angrily every time a thought went by.

They were all now equipped with wands and staffs. They were now learning the function of a cauldron and athame, a symbolic ritual dagger, to add to their magickal armoury. Athames were banned in schools after an unfortunate incident some years ago; they are still used in home magick.

Charlie's mum was top of the class in spell-work and Cosmolos made several appearances to teach them about spells and the levels of magick. They were even societies providing the same opportunities to study and have fun as in the main school.

The School itself was large and impressive, though smaller than the main Dragonstone School. It was an old Mansion house, rectangular in design, with a courtyard separating the buildings.

It was also home to many academics who taught there, as well as having their own lessons in Advanced Magick.

All teachers were called by their titles: Mr, Madam, Professor, and Mage to name a few, so it was literally like being back at school in the Plainlands; Victoria loved it. Being there brought back so many memories of when they were at school. Repeating the experience made them all feel youthful and playful - even getting up to mischief from time to time. It was a fascinating process as parents and children could learn together. Victoria couldn't wait to show off her newly formed powers to her children. Victoria was a Piscean, a water sign, and was highly sensitive and loving to her family. Victoria Campbell was a Capricorn, an Earth Sign, whilst Andrew, unsurprisingly, was a Leo, a Fire sign, always ready for action and to show off.

Having marvelled at the Great City, they were now heading to the Lakes of Colour for their next excursion organised after the Samhien festival.

In all, life was looking pretty rosy for its new arrivals, but for now, they were heading off to learn the Scandinavian Futhark Runes.

Chapter 19

THE GREAT CITY

It was a morning that the first years didn't want to miss: the trip to the Great City. Charlie had even asked Sebastian, the door, to wake him up so he wouldn't miss out. The trip had been postponed a few times for various reasons, including damage to the river flume. Even Eric, who could operate the flume, had crashed due to mysterious crocodiles that happened to get in there.

It had been a few weeks since he'd sent his letter to his mother and he was pleased to get a response back. He was just happy to be in his room when he read it, so that his friends couldn't see the giant pair of enchanted red lips that flew out, giving him a great smacking kiss to his forehead.

Everything seemed to be progressing nicely, though Charlie still struggled to send objects; he was lagging behind the others. They had now progressed to using the Opening and Closing spells, and Charlie was even struggling with that; he was most frustrated.

Guildus Grey seemed to be getting quite frustrated with some of the class. Conversely, Sidhara got more patient as the weeks trundled on.

October 31st was the festival of Samhain. Charlie had recently learned that this festival was the original name of Halloween, which was part of something called: A Greater Sabbatt. It was one of the main festivals of western witches that was generally celebrated through most magickal practitioners in the Magicklands. It was quite a different celebration to the one he'd come to know in the Plainlands, though, he couldn't wait to celebrate it.

Researching the Half Prophecy was becoming a bit of a chore, but one important fact they did find out was that the oldest parts of the school was around when the prophecy was made, so it was possible that the prophecy could have been hidden in the

167

school grounds somewhere. In fact, the more he thought about it, the more he was convinced that he had actually seen it. There remained a fundamental problem but what could they do about it? How could they access the room without being sucked into oblivion? They researched as much as they could, but they couldn't find a piece of magickal text that mentioned that type of magick, but they weren't giving up.

Another question that was annoying Charlie was *why me?* After all, he was just some lost child from the Plainlands. Why did the shadowy thing take him there? Also, why wasn't the second level spell that he created to confirm who the creature was, working? *Maybe, I'm bad at both level one and two magick,* he thought. Most importantly, what would it mean if he did retrieve it? He'd wanted to ask Cosmolos, though something told him not to just in case he thought he was crazy; his friends all agreed with his decision. What concerned him most was that he might get told off for going somewhere he shouldn't have gone. The last thing he wanted was to get detention or worse, banished back to the Plainlands.

Charlie was now realising that he still knew nothing of the Great City or why it was so great. He was so busy that he never bothered to ask. His mother had told him, 'You've got to see it to believe it.'

In general, his lessons had been fascinating. Charlie and his friends had been through all the elemental blocks for their lessons and they were all amazing; each block was constructed with clear representations of their elements. They were now encouraged to call their houses by their proper names; Charlie was in Paralda, so he was a Paraldian, Amanda was in Necksa, so a Necksonion, Tom was in Ghob, a so Ghobdinian, and Imogen was in Djin, so a Djinzarian. The Necksa Building was like walking into a strange aquarium. Instead of normal walls there was glass all around containing water and all manner of sea life, and the occasional flashes of water elementals. They saw water faeries, which are also good for healing magick as well as taking care of a variety of water plants. Tom thought it was interesting that they could travel about on dragonflies to get from place to place. Amanda managed to see a water nymph. They generally prefer to stay anonymous to most

168

folk, especially in the Plainlands. They also like to live by springs, pools and fountains. They are supposed to be able help you in healing and prophecy too. How they did this, is unknown, but they could.

There were so many creatures and elementals to learn, it was fascinating, and the block was perfect for learning all about them. There were rooms dedicated to the seas, oceans, rivers, lakes, ponds, streams to name a few. The least favourite were water bogs and swamps as they were very smelly to be in. The ice and snow rooms didn't go down too well, though snowballing was fun. The seas were the most popular as you could wear the Dragonstone swimming outfits for class. Charlie thought the fourth floor was brilliant, as you had to row your own boat to get to the classrooms. Archimedes' office was located at the bottom of the first floor. It was easily recognisable as there was a water fall covering the door leading into his office.

The Paralda building was just as fascinating. You were greeted with a gentle refreshing breeze that made you relax as soon as you walked in. The main corridor was long and the walls were made up of old rock. With the air being clear and pure to the naked eye, layers of mist slithered down the edges of the rocks, their movement being a demonstration of the movement of the air. The ceiling looked like the clear blue sky, with soft white clouds moving below that resembled cotton wool. It was a very surreal block, with some of the classes seemingly having no floors and with desks hovering in mid-air. Despite the nervousness of the students in entering this room, there was a relief that no one was going to fall through this enchanted sky. Some classes made you feel very drifty, sleepy or very relaxed whilst other rooms weren't as pleasant as the winds became more violent and stormy. Amongst all this, there were birds flying through as well as other air elementals. The ones that caught their eye were the sylphs and zephyrs that made regular appearances. The sylphs looked like beautiful women, forming into glowing, bubble-like people, gracious, and happy, unless angered and they entered into a storm-like frenzy. They were beautiful in appearance but drastically change appearance when angered. Zephyrs were male. They command the winds and playfully flit through the air with the sylphs, gracefully riding the currents of the air. Like their female counterparts, they could change appearance when annoyed, becoming vicious looking with huge frowns instead of their usual handsome appearance. This was Charlie's domain as he was an air sign, and he also looked forward to having lessons with Cosmolos. Charlie tried to visit the building as often as he could in his spare time as he found the building inspiring. After all, inspiration was one of primary strengths of the air element.

The last of the Elemental Buildings was the Djin Building. As Cosmolos told Charlie whilst on the magick carpet, it was named after King Djin, the King of Fire and its elementals. King Djin had been demonised by some for centuries, as fire had always been seen as the domain of hell. Of course, fire can burn and can get out of control, but the other elements can get out of control too. Without fire, things wouldn't grow, motivation wouldn't happen, and neither would a warm heart exist. 'A duality' as Cosmolos explained the nature of the elements, just like people.

All students knew about the firedrakes, as they could regularly be seen lighting and relaxing in the flames as this was their favourite pastime. Like in all the other environments, even fire has its own faeries. Like firedrakes, they love to be near flames and love to bask and dance in them. However, unlike firedrakes, they can't easily be spotted. They have pale orange hair, pasty looking skin and bright eyes; it is this that gives them away. They stand a few inches tall. They do have their magickal uses, mainly all used in level two magick and some used in level one magick for wish gaining, divination and shape morphing.

The one thing that Cosmolos kept repeating is that elementals are independent entities that can be summoned but not controlled. You can request their help and they will either accept or deny your request depending on the worthiness of the task. However, they are known to change their minds. Finally, Cosmolos said that elementals cannot be deceived, try so at your peril, but the more devious elementals can be banished.

Of course, fire was Imogen's sign, just like her father at the Orberon. All the signs seemed important, but what was apparent was that it was more complicated than what they thought to begin with.

***

There was an announcement through the internal post that all students were about to receive a new addition to the uniforms: brand new wizard robes to be used for ritual celebrations and magickal work like spell-casting. The students loved the fact that they could dress in magician's robes.

In the weeks that passed, Felicity Phelps and her crew had a few more attempts at having a go at Amanda, but failed. Her adapted wheelchair made it easier for her to get away from them. She quite enjoyed circling around them running over their toes.

It would be a late October morning that was to be the icing on the cake for Charlie. He thought he was confident in having seen everything to do with the magick world - he was wrong.

It was getting close to the time to head to the Great City. Charlie, Amanda, Tom and Imogen were sitting in the main canteen waiting to transport there by Flume Rail. From what Charlie could gather from Tom's description, a Flume Rail was a bit like the London Underground on water.

Charlie was finishing the bacon on his plate. He dipped into the yolk of his egg and put it into his mouth. Charlie loved egg and bacon. It reminded him of being at home with his mother. Then he spoke.

'Where do we leave from?' asked Charlie.

'Oh, the Flume Rail port is right down at the bottom of school near the river,' said Tom.

Amanda pulled out her timetable and a map appeared showing the way.

'Look, it's right down here,' said Amanda.

'How come I'd never seen this before?'

'Well, dad said the Flume network had broken down. Crocodiles weren't the only thing found in there. Someone had mysteriously placed some water trolls and some gremlins to disrupt the tube. No-one knows why. It took ages to clear them out and that's why it has taken us so long to get to the Great City,' said Imogen.

Twenty minutes later and the four of them left the canteen.

'Oooooh, going to the Great City, think we are great then do we..?' said Neil, the insulting Un-Potted Plant, whilst opening his mouth wide with his fingers, sticking tongue out. They learned not to engage in conversation with him, so they promptly moved along the newly gravelled surface.

'Fancy a lift?' asked Amanda.

As she spoke, two boards came out from the sides of the wheel chair, with a foot-stand at the rear.

'Brilliant,' said Charlie, 'Let's go!' he said enthusiastically.

'Ha-ha-ha, sure beats walking,' said Tom.

Charlie hopped on the back, Imogen to the left and Tom sat on the right. Off they went down towards the Flume Rail, honking an old fashioned horn so students could get out of the way. It was autumn. The summer plumages had all but disappeared. There were a few evergreens and everoranges that stayed the same throughout the year as well as a few plants that enjoyed the autumn and winter months. The air was crisper than it had been recently, so they all wore their winter overcoats, hats, scarves and gloves.

There were bouts of laughter as they went down the hill, especially going over the lumps and bumps in the earth, occasionally falling off.

They went past the Orberon, past the knight's training school and society buildings and eventually they could hear some running water.

'Over there,' said Charlie, seeing some form of port platform. They stood there waiting for the arrival of the flume; he couldn't wait to see it.

After standing in the cold wind for a while, the platform filled with first years. Without warning, there was a crack in the air and a flume arrived out of nothingness. It was very long, pulling several carriages. Each carriage was similarly designed to the Dragonstone bus coach: red with a wide and round, bellied, body. The inside was different, as there were many more seats, but no luxury perks like a mini bar.

The door opened, and a voice sounded as a man exited.

'Hello Charlie,' said Randle.

'Hey Randle, great to see you,' replied Charlie.

'Hello Amanda, lovely to see you too,' said Randle.

'Hello Randle,' smiled Amanda. 'Are you taking us to the Great City?' she said.

172

'Yes, there is no one better to show you around,' he announced proudly. 'Just a shame the pathway was clogged up full of - well, all kinds of things. Water trolls are so stubborn and dangerous if you don't watch it. I have to admit this is the first time someone has done this. By the gods, I have no idea why,' he said sounding very annoyed.

Randle began introducing himself to the other students, when another voice sounded.

'Bloomin' hurry up,' said Eric.

'Oh no, not Eric?' said Charlie and Amanda, laughing together.

'I'm afraid so,' said Randle smiling.

'Who's Eric?' Tom asked.

'He was the driver who brought us here. He's quite miserable, though quite funny,' said Charlie.

'You'll see,' said Amanda.

Randle managed to finish what he was saying and they all got on.

'About bloomin' time,' whinged Eric. 'If they move any quicker, they'd stop' he continued.

'Right, I'm only going to say this once,' announced Eric over the tannoy, 'No litter, no fighting or no stupid anything. I'll chuck you out mid journey, or worse, leave you stranded in the Plainlands. I can do that you know.'

The doors shut immediately and all the school pupils waited in anticipation.

The Flume pulled off slowly, picking up speed as it approached the tunnel. There was a slight lift of the Flume and there was a crackle in the air. The flume entered a watery vortex, moving quickly as it travelled along.

'We'll be arriving in one hour,' said Randle.

'That's too long with this lot,' muttered Eric under his breath.

The journey seemed shorter than an hour, though in that time, they made sure that they checked their bags, as well as checking their money. Charlie's mum sent him some money through the post and he was pleased to see that he had the equivalent of one hundred Pounds or what is known in the magick world as a Grundle. A

173

Grundle was made up of one hundred Groans, which, in turn, were made up of one hundred Onks.

'Brilliant, you've got a Grundle,' said Tom. 'I've got ninety groans,' he said cheerfully. What have you guys got?' he asked Amanda and Imogen.

'Eighty Groans,' said Amanda.

'Two Grundles' said Imogen

'Wow! Two Grundles! Drinks on you Imogen,' said Charlie playfully.

The journey was largely uneventful but it seemed to pass quickly.

'Well be arriving any second now and there might be some turbulence,' said Eric smiling by himself. 'Three, two, one'…There was a rumble, a sharp shake and a crack. The Flume had arrived at the Warlock's Port-Side. Students were shaken. Some fell off their seats and some looked rather green.

'That miserable git,' said Helen. 'Look at him laughing,' she said looking angrily at Eric.

From the outside of the Flume, all you could see was the windows all clotted up with young faces scrambling to see outside. They were in the equivalent a bus and rail station with Flumes of all colours and sizes from all over the place. The Flume moored up with the help of some Water-rail dockworkers; the student's quickly exited. Moments after they left, there was another crack and the flume disappeared from site.

On leaving the station, they could see a wider port area with all kinds of boats and ships moored up. There was a strong smell of fish. Most of the students held their noses in disgust.

'This way,' said Randle.

Moving through a wide alley, they arrived onto a main street called Percival Way.

'Hurry now, we have a lot to do,' said Randle.

Quickly the children hurried along and approached a gate in the city wall.

'Ah Randle old chap, great to see you,' said the gateman. He was a guard unlike anything Charlie had seen so far. He looked like one of the queen's guards at the palace, though the uniform looked very old as though from a few hundred years back. He was holding up a large pole with a spear pointing elegantly out of the top it as well as spear head that protruded like a hook off the side of the pole.

'Ah, Roderick, lovely to see you again, it has been far too long,' said Randle.

'Send me a scroll and we'll meet up at the Siren Inn for some whisky,' said Roderick.

'Will do,' replied Randle.

'I see you have the first years again. Come through, you can pass,' said Roderick.

Roderick cheerfully greeted all of them as they passed through the gate; it made a pleasant change to Eric's miserable whinging.

Inside, the city was teaming with all kinds of people.

'But – what, eh?' said Charlie scratching his head.

Charlie noticed some Romans and English Knights drinking out of horns, cheering and singing songs.

'TO JARV!,' said the knights and Romans together, toasting and laughing.

'You wait until medieval night,' said the large drunken knight to the Roman.

Amanda looked gobsmacked and even Tom looked a little put out, not to mention the other students. Imogen just smiled.

'I don't get it,' said Charlie. 'They are…'

'Yes,' said Randle and he began to explain.

'The Great City is the most unique City in the world. It is forged no only from the different magickal cultures across the world, but they live how they choose to, from the different time periods of history in all its architectural glory, clothing and everything. Most of the trading and work exists in the centre, but when it is all done, they go home to live in their parts of the city known as Quarters, though obviously different to the elemental quarters. There are the Greeks, Romans, Chinese, Egyptian, Native American, Indian, English, Japanese and other countries. There are other nations who come to trade and hope to be part of this community. They bring the best of each culture and, importantly, magickal knowledge. All nations take their turn to take guard of the key areas and to take lead of the council, located in the centre.

175

This part is based on ancient Greece, as they were the founders of democracy. It might seem complicated, though while each nation co-operates and trades with each other, it was important under the founding agreement that each nation preserved the best from each period in time. The Great Council also ensures that laws are formed and dissolved, and that power is shared, but the internal affairs are kept with each Royal House of that ruling nation. It is an interesting system, but one that has worked for centuries and peace has been kept as a result.'

'So is this why people are dressed differently, because they live in a place that, well, a time where people wore those types of clothes?' asked Amanda.

'Well, yes and no. When you go to the medieval part of the English Quarter, you aren't literally stepping back in time, but into the best of that time that is preserved. You can move to a different quarter if you choose to. For example the Mordens recently moved into the Renaissance sector. In general, people wear and dress what they feel comfortable in. It is quite remarkable. Remember at the Orberon, you had a Viking and Knights; both of these are from different periods of time, but both worked together. Here you see Romans and Knights, and next you might see some Greeks and Tudors, etcetera. It is a fascinating reality and it is a place like no other in the world, Plainland or Magickal.

They continued to walk around, and sure enough, they started seeing people from just about every period that there has been. Each was either talking, trading, drinking or laughing. It was the most incredible sight that anyone had ever set their eyes upon.

They were on the outskirts of the central political centre, which was made up of a confusion of architecture, though it all fitted.

'What's that?' said Tom, pointing to a huge grey circular brick building in the middle of a large market square.

'That's the Witches' Coven. They are a mystery even to the magick world, though no one interferes as they do nothing wrong. They chose to remain secret, so it is respected.' Charlie and his friends walked round and round, spotting all different kinds of buildings and people.

'Ah yes, over there is the museum, if it can be called that. In some respects, the whole city is a perfectly preserved museum, but in there exists objects from hundreds and thousands of years ago. It is here that the Half Prophecy will live for a while before it moves on again. It is the most intriguing historical object, simply because this place wouldn't exist without that. Remember, the prophecy is also a binding contract and the key to creating this city, or so it is rumoured.' Charlie, Amanda, Tom and Imogen all looked with huge interest at this statement.

Charlie and the rest of the first years explored the city in all its glory. Not only were there different buildings and peoples, but there were magickal enchantments from various stalls advertising their products. One Arabian market had a young lad who fired three-dimensional holographic enchantments out of the store, advertising its products as they floated down the street. To Charlie's amazement, some of the enchantments were heading back to the store with people in tow.

'How clever!' Amanda exclaimed.

'It sure is,' said Charlie.

There were witches on old broomsticks flying through the air, as well as people on magick carpets. There was a multi-story magick parking area that people could lock away their brooms and carpets and there were Scroll-Porters that were put inside what looked like old fashioned phone boxes. You could see many streets with stores and bazaars, selling food and tourist trinkets, and banks with cash machines at the side; they worked by using your magick name to withdraw your money.

There were apothecaries, blacksmiths, food stores, restaurants and just about anything you could imagine. Down one of the streets there was a man making and selling magick carpets, shouting, 'Carpets starting from Fifteen Grundles.'

'Fifteen Grundles, for that? What a rip off,' said Tom, disapproving of a tatty carpet he was trying to sell.

'Hey look,' said Amanda, 'there's a Magickal Powders store.' 'Get your powders here. We sell rare ingredients for those special powders,' shouted the Asian Indian store seller.

They'd spent hours looking around when Charlie and his gang received another surprise. One of the statues came alive, calling himself Napoleon and telling everyone to be on guard as they were going to be attacked. He was then followed by the great mathematician, Archimedes, who was offering help with any mathematical problems.

'They are special enchanted statues,' said Imogen. 'These statues channel the essence or spirit of the greatest historical figures. My dad loves talking to Achilles about his conquests. Of course, not all spirits come through, however, but some do. It uses some special form of er...I can't remember what the concrete is called,' said Imogen.

'Well that is just amazing,' said Amanda, when a posh piece of parchment flew over carrying the details of *Maisie's Magickal Jewels*, saying they'd been 'mined from the finest mines around, perfect for wands, staff's, work and home.' There was another message: "Follow the paper to my stall, or keep for later."

'Keep,' said Amanda. The paper folded itself into an envelope and lay dormant in her hand.

'Terrific,' said Amanda.

'Look at that,' said Tom.

The all turned around and saw a bright blue light circling into the sky, before it disappeared.

'What was that?' asked Helen.

'That was the Witches' Coven,' said Randle. 'They send out different spells into the world.'

'Why?' asked Charlie, as a large beautiful green light circled round and shot into the air.

'No one knows exactly, though they did help out during the Beltane festival by bringing out some sunshine when torrential rain threatened the celebrations,' said Randle appreciatively. Charlie remembered from his history class that Beltane was the May Day festival. He remembered celebrating at his old school, though it was quite different. In the Plainlands, most have no idea of its magickal origins; even the May Pole itself has a magickal meaning. Around and around they looked, and it seemed that the city would never end.

'I'd love to come back here,' said Charlie.

'And you will.' said Randle. 'There is much to learn here,' he continued. 'We'll also get to see the Half Prophecy when it arrives next year,' said Randle.

'When is that?' asked Charlie.

'Oh, I'm not too sure, possibly around the Ostara spring equinox celebration or the next Beltane festival.'

'When is Ostara?' Charlie asked Randle.

'Oh yes, you are just learning all this. It is around the twenty first of March.'

'I can't wait for it,' said Charlie.

'OK FIRST YEARS, GATHER ROUND,' shouted Randle to get their attention. It took a few minutes for them to gather. He then changed the pitch of his voice. You could tell that he wasn't comfortable in raising his voice.

'There will be plenty of opportunity to explore the shops, the centre, and the museum. However, for now we are going to explore, quickly one of the sections in the quarters. Follow me,' said Randle.

The group walked westwards and it took about twenty minutes to get there.

They walked along a dusty pathway until they reached another large wall and then another gate. This time, there was another guard: he was a Roman.

'Greetings Randle,' said the Guard.

'Greetings Brutus,' said Randle. 'I see the Romans have taken over the guard.'

'Yes. I see you have the young ones again, this must be the fifteenth year in a row now?'

'Has it really been fifteen years? I lose track you know.'

'That's Junii Brutus, Magickal Knight and Champion of the Roman Orberon. A great warrior,' said Tom.

'Cool, I never realised they had their own league,' said Charlie.

'Oh yes, all the communities and schools have their own, and there is a show down of the Champions at the end.'

'I bet that's a sight,' said Charlie.

'One of the best,' said Tom.

179

It just dawned on Charlie that he had just entered the most amazing world ever and it was much greater than the one he had entered at the school. After all, that was impressive enough.

Brutus stood up, and he was massive and nearly as tall as Sedrick.

'Wow, he's bigger in real life,' said David.

Randle and Brutus discussed the coming tournament and, after a few minutes, the guard let them pass.

'Good luck first years,' said Brutus, waving his large hand then giving them a typical Roman salute.

As they passed the gate they entered Medieval England. There was a castle at the top of the hill, with a town beneath it. Unlike the Plainland medieval towns, which lived in squalor, this place was very clean and looked immaculate. They seemed to have a shining edge to everything, almost like a faerie tale, though it seemed more real.

Randle waved his hand at someone in the distance and the couple waved back.

'Who's that?' Amanda asked.

'Ah, that is Mr and Mrs Bimble. They run the local orphanage. A lovely couple taking on all those children,' he said approvingly.

'That's a nice thing to do,' said Amanda.

'It sure is. For some reason, the orphans that he cares for have experienced severe trauma and it affects their magick,' said Randle.

'Really?!' Imogen seemed surprised. 'How?'

'Well, those who have suffered some form of trauma, either struggle to do magick, or can't do any magick at all.'

'That's horrible,' said Amanda.

'Yes. So they take it upon themselves to educate and magickally train them as best they can. Some do become completely healed then lead normal lives.'

Charlie and some of the pupils looked and waved at them and the couple waved back. There were a few children outside helping in the garden. They looked at the first years and waved. Moments later, they were taken inside, with Mrs Bimble gently carrying the youngest.

They looked around the village and they stopped in a local inn to eat and drink before departing for another quarter.

The size of the city was so large that it would take weeks or even months to explore everything. It didn't matter, as being part of the magick world they had all the time to explore.

'Is everything this nice in the magick world?' asked Charlie. 'Well, apart from those poor souls I mean.'

'Well, a good portion of it certainly is,' said Randle. 'There are some who elect not to get involved with the mainstream of society. They are called Squirms.'

'That doesn't sound nice,' said Amanda disapprovingly. Helen agreed with her.

'That is because they aren't very nice people. They are quite an angry crowd, who involve themselves with all kinds of craftiness. Some go and live there because they have no one, or they have run away from home. They are taken in and they are soon taught, well, how to go about life in a less honourable way. Squirms live in all sectors and communities, but they have their own areas where normal folk dare not tread. This is why it is important that we have the knight guards to ensure they don't get out of hand.'

After they had finished their hog roast and non-alcoholic mead that tasted like strawberry, they moved on to visit the Roman Quarter. It was as amazing and interesting as the medieval city. It was beautifully made out of marble, with gold embedded in the structures. Again, the area seemed to have a magickal shine to it. Some folk were paying respects to the gods at small temples dotted around the place. Some were performing magick rituals in the open and you could see bright colours emanating from their beautifully crafted staffs and wands. It was amazing to see how magick and everyday living came together as one and not separate from each other.

Exploring the towns is all they had time for. The others would have to wait. However, there was one more thing that Randle had promised to show them in the Great City before they headed back. Like everything else that Randle had promised, it was something that wouldn't disappoint.

Back in the centre of the Great City, they headed in the opposite direction to which they had walked, whilst the Witches' Tower had fallen quiet of spell-working.

They walked down a couple of side streets past some shops where a Victorian man was buying some meat from an African seller. Charlie found it hard to process what he was seeing, but he found it intriguing.

Charlie was quite thirsty. He cracked open a can of *Percy Thirst-Quencher* that turned a cola type colour.

The temperature changed wherever they went, so they were continually changing various clothing items. The centre of the Great City was chilly with fresh clear skies. They could smell and hear the different aromas and sounds wherever they went. Enchantments were everywhere, either stationary or floating around, trying to draw customers in with their latest offers.

'I know where we are heading,' Imogen smiled.

'Where?' Tom asked.

'You'll see,' she said teasingly.

Turning another corner came into view a brilliant sight.

'WOW', said Tom.

'What is it?' Charlie asked.

'That is the main stadium for the Orberon,' said Tom excitedly.

'Yeah, I've been here quite a few times with my dad,' said Imogen.

'You're so lucky,' said Tom.

Randle had lead them to the entrance of the arena, which looked a bit like the Colosseum in Italy, but, like everything in the Magicklands, there was a slight quirkiness to everything, making it every bit as breathtaking.

They passed a Musketeer guard who coincidently, happened to be called Athos, and was recognised by both Randle and Imogen. Entering a side tunnel, they reached the seating area of the arena.

Charlie's mouth dropped open at what he was seeing. There were Romans, Greeks, English, Scottish, French, Egyptian, Dutch, Scandinavian and many more combatants working out, training together; it was a warriors dream.

'This is just practice,' said Imogen.

'This is flippin' brilliant,' said Charlie, as did most of the first years.

'You see, over the centuries, all the warriors came together to learn from each other, learning about the different techniques from each culture and finding what works best for each warrior. It is quite amazing,' said Randle.

They just sat there transfixed, as Roman was instructing Viking, English Knight instructing the Japanese Samurai; the combinations were endless and they looked highly skilled.

An hour passed as they observed the training, and then the students were allowed to go and collect autographs.

On the way home, there were excited conversations all the way to the Flume Rail. Completely exhausted by their experience, most fell asleep on the Flume. David was actually sleep walking, or to be accurate, *sleep fighting*, much to the amusement of the ones who stayed awake, teasing him as he waved an imaginary sword.

It was done. The day had finished more than satisfactorily for them all. It was something that would remain with Charlie for a very long time.

Chapter 20

SAMHAIN

The week had gone swiftly and now all eyes were set on the main weekend event: Samhain - the witches' New Year. It is a custom now adopted and celebrated by many magickal traditions. In the Plainlands, as Charlie had previously read, Samhain eventually came to be known as Halloween. The meaning of Halloween has vastly been misinterpreted and it's been used to inject fear into Plainlanders. The Plainers see it as a time where only nasty ghosts, ghouls and demons come out to scare everybody. The energy of fear is reinforced with watching terrifying films about these malevolent beings, with blood and gore in them. In reality, this is about as inaccurate a description about the festival as is gets. Mage Brimstone-Greenback explained in the History of Magick class that, Samhain was a very powerful time for most magick folk. It is where the veil between those who have been and those who remain was at its closest. In other words, the worlds between Spirit and the living was at its thinnest, so, in some cases, it would be possible to see those who have died, such as your guardians, relatives or pets to name a few; this is why it is also known as the Festival of the Dead. He further explained that it was a time to honour and pay respects to our ancestors, a point that was emphasised by White Eagle, during another session. White Eagle also said it was a time of 'reflection, contemplation and honour.' He also said the spirit world is as very much alive as this one. However, there would be a celebration afterwards, as it is the Magickal New Year, after all.

For this celebration, all students were to receive a plain black robe with a long hood and large sleeves as a mark of respect for the occasion. Also, students were required to bring either their staffs, wands, or both. Finally, as a mark of respect, everyone was supposed to bring a photo of someone that had passed to the spirit realms. As it happened, Charlie and his friends didn't know any close family members or friends who had passed on so there was no need to take one. The ritual was to take place at the Orberon as it was big enough to include everyone.

The evening approached quickly. It was cold and stars came out to watch the evening's proceedings. Charlie, Amanda, Tom and Imogen put on their new robes. It was a simple throw-over gown with long wide sleeves covering their arms and hands. They put their hoods up and spoke.

'This is great – loving these robes,' said Charlie.

'Yeah, it makes you feel all mysterious,' said Amanda.

'We need to head off soon,' said Tom lifting his staff, pretending to be Cosmolos.

'But it's early,' said Imogen.

'I know, but I want to get a seat at the bottom so I can see,' said Tom enthusiastically.

'But it's freezing,' Imogen responded.

'We'll be fine in the Orberon,' Tom reposted.

'I think we'll be fine,' said Charlie, defending Tom. 'Besides, I've never seen anything like this before, so I want to get a good seat.'

'Oh, OK,' said Imogen, conceding.

'We'll be fine Imogen,' said Tom. 'I love Samhain. I hear they've had to adapt the ceremony as they are doing something really new.' Charlie started feeling the excitement.

They had a quick drink and gathered the things they needed for the ceremony. They left Charlie's room and headed down in the lift.

There was an icy chill in the air but there was no frost; you could almost feel the presence of the ancestors.

They walked past the courtyard and headed towards the Orberon. The Un-Potted Plants that had insulted them over the term had migrated to the greenhouse. Charlie found this quite funny as he saw them leave with scarves around their necks, with little suitcases clutched to their little-stick like hands made from the roots.

The ground was lit with a parade of tall torch posts that were fuelled by the tiny firedrakes that graced the magick world so readily. The heat from the torches provided some comfort from the cold; Imogen particularly enjoyed this.

185

Most students had the same idea in getting there early and some had already entered the arena. Something new was added to the arena: there were four chimney towers at the four corners of the stadium.

No-one dared speak. The evening possessed its own power, which brought about a special stillness and humility.

Charlie took one more look at the sky as he was impressed by the lack of pollution in the atmosphere. The stars looked like small moons dotted all over the place; you could see the natural range of colours that emanated from them so grandly.

A buzz of excitement could be heard as they entered the arena. To their surprise, the arena was approximately a quarter full with plenty of time to spare. There was a sea of black robes looking down at the arena. This powerful sight would normally look threatening but for the words of Hegarty, who loved to wear traditional witch clothing. She explained that wearing black was not an evil thing as some Plainlanders had portrayed it to be, 'Bar the stars, space is black,' she said. "Is that evil? Nonsense, pure nonsense,' she uttered under her breath, whilst getting angry. 'Yes, black is used by magick folk who follow both light and dark ways. What's different is the person underneath. There is a majesty in black, a power, an aura; it is like silk,' she said with eyes gleaming.

It wouldn't be long until the stadium was filled to capacity. Everyone was looking round and at each other. Many had brought pictures of family, friends, and even pets that had died.

Many of the women teachers who didn't usually wear traditional witch clothing did so out of respect. Cosmolos and many of the male teachers also wore black robes.

Cosmolos banged his staff on the ground three times for the few who where muttering, and all went quiet.

'Welcome,' boomed Cosmolos. 'We have a special evening for you; a ceremony with a difference. It has the blessing of all the High Priestesses of the Coven of Witches from the Great City.'

The few conversations that existed in the stadium fell quiet as Hecate banged her staff on the floor three times. Hecate, Cosmolos, White Eagle, Artuk Ra, Archimedes, Guildus Grey and Sedrick, all stood in and around the centre altar table. The centre table had various objects on it, including: four candles, an Athame, a wand, a chalice, a cauldron, a book and an incense burner that burned impressively providing a mist, adding to the mystery of the ritual. Also, there were several pots, containing different coloured powders.

Hegarty picked up a besom, a witches broom, and started to make sweeping gestures, whilst uttering some words as she went around. On the upward sweeping stroke of the broom, it shuddered, and thunderous sparks could be seen and heard escaping from the bottom. As it did so, a wave of energy was created, which could only be seen by the distortion of the atmosphere. The wave went out and upwards, piercing through the crowd, sending shivers and tingling sensations amongst all the pupils.

The temperature suddenly dropped. A terrible phantom screech could be heard then a murky white apparition flew out of the stadium, making several people jump out of their skin.

Silence fell once more in the arena in anticipation of what was to come next. White Eagle approached the table and picked up one of the pots that contained a green salt-like substance, throwing the powder outwards as he walked quickly in clockwise direction known as deiseal around the arena. As he did so, an earthy smell was apparent. On completion of the circle, there was a zip and crack and some previously unseen energy shot through the top of the arena, flying into the sky.

Artuk Ra, who, for most of the year had remained pretty anonymous, was present for the ritual. He moved forward to the altar and picked up a red powder from one of the containers. Similar to White Eagle, he threw the powder, walking around, deiseal. As the powder was released, it transformed into a giant wave of a fire ball, expanding outwards. Many of the students panicked, jumping out of their seats as it hurtled towards them. Remarkably, the fire passed through them, causing no harm. They were relieved to see it head upwards and out of the stadium.

Cosmolos was next. He picked up a container filled with sky blue powder. Following the same procedure, Cosmolos threw the powder outward, which turned into a wind. This time, the wind was made apparent as the pupil's hair and robes flapped

187

about, before heading out of the stadium, creating a haunting sound as it did so.

Archimedes was the last. He picked up a dark blue powder and threw the powder outwards; it turned into ocean water. Just like the fire, it passed through and around everyone, amazingly, leaving everyone dry. It flowed upwards and out of the stadium.

Sedrick came forward with a sword. This sword different to his fighting one as it was long and thin. It was a ceremonial sword with a star embedded into the centre of the handle and there were various engravings marked down the blade.

Sedrick raised it above his head then outwards in front of him in the east direction. He muttered some words in Swedish as he turned round in a clockwise direction. He circled three times. There was a mass of invisible energy that penetrated the arena, which made everyone feel very light. The energy in the arena had seemed remarkably calm, yet energetic.

One by one, the house masters approached each corner to summon the energy of each quarter.

Cosmolos started in the east.

> *'Guardian of the Watchtower, Lord Aldebaran,*
> *King Paralda, Syphs, Zephyrs, Gargoyles and*
> *Pegasus. We summon you to come forward to*
> *Guard our circle and witness our rites –*
> *Hail and Welcome'*

The entire arena replied, 'Hail and welcome.'

By sheer force, the tower that had been placed, leading out of the top of the stadium, came alive like the main east tower of the school. There was a crack of thunder as it reached its peak. Charlie could swear that he could see all the things he summoned in the almost liquid air.

Artuk Raa, went to the South Corner and said,

> *Guardian of the Watchtower, Lord Regulas,*
> *King Djin, Dragons, Alsvidr, Arvakar and*
> *Slamanders. We summon you to come forward*
> *to guard our circle, and witness our rights.*

Hail and Welcome.'

Again, the arena responded with, 'Hail and Welcome.'
As soon as the words were spoken, the tower came alive with fire, burning ferociously showing the power of its flame, burning proudly.

Next, Archimedes walked forward to the west corner and said,

> *'Guardian of the east watch tower, Lord Antares,*
> *King Necksa, Nymphs, Tritons and Merfolk. We*
> *Summon you forward to witness our rights*
> *And guard our circle.*
> *Hail and Welcome.'*

'Hail and welcome,' the students and teachers responded. Suddenly, the tower came alive as the water circled upwards, gushing outwards, majestically.

Last was White Eagle, who said a few words in Native American, before saying,

> *'Guardian of the North, Lord Formalhaut,*
> *King Ghob, Dwarves, Elves, Gnomes and*
> *Faeries. We summon, you to come*
> *Forward to guard out circle and*
> *Witness our rights.*
> *Hail and Welcome.'*

Everyone responded the same, again.
This time, the tower burst into soil, vines and branches, as they wrapped tightly around the tower; the stadium vibrated.

Once the fourth quarter was called, an amazing sight transpired. Each element somehow fed into each other, forming a giant pentagram. It vibrated and pulsated. It was the ultimate mark of protection.

Hecate then went in front of the altar, and said:

'I call upon the source of all things,
The great spirit of all,
The universal power to which all
have been created, to guard or circle
and witness our rights.
Hail and Welcome.'

'Hail and Welcome,' they all repeated.

As she did so, there was a glowing orb around the stadium that encompassed everything, keeping the elemental forces contained.

Charlie realised that there was so much to magick. It was an amazing ritual and one that was similar to the one in the forest.

All of a sudden, voices could be heard humming. The sound reverberated all around them, gradually getting louder and louder. Mage Sidhara came from one of the entrances, where the Orberon sporting contestants come out to compete. Dozens of other Buddhists chanting deeply and powerfully followed him. As they chanted, all the photos that everyone had brought with them lifted and levitated towards the floor of the arena, near to the centre altar table. Everyone looked amazed.

'This is amazing! How cool!' said another student.

As the pictures floated down like snowflakes, more chanting could be heard. This time, White Eagle, who had made his way out of the arena, came back with dozens of his tribe folk, singing and chanting a Native American song. It was beautiful and amazing, as there was a harmony between the Native American Indian's and the Buddhists.

The chanting subsided and Hecate spoke, 'Welcome all to this most sacred and revered festivals in the Magickal calendar. It is a time for reflection and honouring those who had come before but who are always there with us, watching us, guarding us encouraging us and guiding us; may they never be forgotten Blessed Be – So mote it be.'

'SO MOTE IT BE,' repeated the crowed.

The chanting progressively got louder again and everyone shut their eyes, their mind's transported by the mesmerising tones.

Charlie shut his eyes. He was amazingly relaxed and was drifting to what seemed a far off place. He felt comforted like he'd never felt before, though the air was becoming very cold and tingly.

Minutes had passed and Charlie was in a very quiet place. He heard a voice. 'Charlie.' His heart kick-started suddenly, beating quickly; he dare not open his eyes.

'Your name Charlie, use it,' said the voice.

Charlie couldn't contain himself and he opened his eyes.

In a flash, something vanished.

Was that the shadowy thing? he asked himself. *It couldn't be as there was some green and silver to it*, he concluded. He was completely confused by the whole thing. First, there was a shadow following him, but now there was this other entity. Charlie, closed his eyes, but couldn't get back to the state he first went into.

More time passed and then the chanting naturally subsided, gently bringing them out of their trance-like state. Typically, some had gone to sleep and were snoring. David was one of them and Tom had unwittingly decided to join him. After a little encouragement, the ones that had fallen asleep woke up. The teachers and house masters who worked the ritual reversed the summoning spells by respectfully saying 'Hail and Fair Well' to all they had called. Sedrick went widdershins (counter clockwise) with sword pointing forwards and slightly downwards and the stadium returned to its normal state.

'Now go and enjoy your party,' said Hecate. 'Feast, celebrate and, above all, come midnight - a Happy New Year to you all.'

'HAPPY NEW YEAR HEADMISTRESS,' they all shouted.

Charlie led Amanda, Tom and Imogen down one of the passageways to tell them about what he'd experienced.

'You're kidding,' said Tom.

'I'm not,' said Charlie.

'Not again,' said Amanda.

'Use your name for what?' quizzed Imogen.

'I have no idea,' said Charlie.

'Well, as long as it doesn't mean getting into trouble again and me rescuing you,' said Amanda.

191

'Do you think it means my name or my magickal name,' asked Charlie. 'I suppose I'll find out at some point.'

'HEY CHARLIE!' shouted a voice.

Charlie's head instantly turned. It was Emmanuel and Bruce.

'Hey, guys,' Charlie said cheerfully.

'Hey Bruce,' said Amanda.

'Hello again,' said Emmanuel to Imogen.

Charlie introduced Tom to Emmanuel and Bruce.

They spent a few minutes talking about the ceremony, the Great City and many of the other things that had happened.

'Hey, come and look at this,' said Bruce after disappearing back into the stadium. They all hurried back in and, amazingly, the room had been transformed into a disco. But first there was a live performance of Duran Duran - he couldn't believe it. "The Reflex..." sounded out. It was his mum's favourite group, but looked to be popular here with everyone.

'I didn't know they were magick,' he said to himself.

There were two stages where people were serving drinks, and two more where food was served to the ravenous students. Charlie had to laugh to himself as it reminded him of the end of term party at his old school, though this was on a much bigger scale.

Up above and floating in the centre, there was an unusual disco ball. Light came off forming all kinds of colours that created many shapes. Instead of the light just reflecting off the surfaces, some of the light hovered in the air and danced in rhythm to the music before fading. The lights even danced around students. They were brilliant and of varying degrees of intensity and hues. Charlie couldn't help but stare as he was sure that he saw colours that never actually existed.

The night was moving fantastically; every one ate, drank and danced the night away. Winston was one of the main teachers on duty that night and he spent some time undoing some magick powders that'd been thrown at some of the other children. This included Bruce, who concocted a powder that made people dance frantically in mid-air and another that made you stoop over and dance like a monkey in slow motion. Other powders included stink

192

bombs of every nasty smell you could think of, including Goblin Breath and Bog Monster Dung.

It was getting close to midnight and the party was still in full swing. Charlie and his friends went out for a breath of fresh air and the night was about to take another eventful twist.

'Five, four, three, two, one – HAPPY NEW YEAR TO YOU ALL,' echoed a voice loudly from the inside, as a roar followed the announcement. 'Fireworks were lit, hurtling towards the sky, making the most unusual patterns, shapes and spirals. Everyone shook hands and gave a friendly hug. Charlie was giving Imogen a hug when he saw the shadowy entity.

'Look,' said Charlie, 'It's back,' he exclaimed, '…the shadowy thing,' he said excitedly.

'Just when I thought the evening was going so well,' said Tom.

'Please don't follow it,' implored Amanda.

It was too late. Charlie was off like a horse running out of the starting gates at a race. Galloping away, Amanda, Tom and Imogen all chased after him.

'Charlie, wait!' yelled Amanda.

Back up the hill towards the school they went, then changed direction suddenly, heading past the earth tunnel, the fire block, and then back along the wooded area towards the door of mystery.

Charlie stopped. He panted, catching his breath and the others turned up moments later.

'You can't be serious,' said Imogen. 'Remember what happened the *last time.*'

'Yes, I do,' Charlie said, 'though it's different this time…I feel it.'

'If you don't watch it, you'll be feeling the inside of that room. You could even be killed,' said Tom dramatically.

'Aye, how is it different?' quizzed Amanda.

'I don't know,' he said, 'but we are supposed to be here.' Remember I saw the other half of the prophecy,' said Charlie.

'You mean, you thought you saw the Half Prophecy,' said Tom, bluntly. 'It could have been a trick of the mind.'

'I know, but everything that has happened has led to here, to this point. It has got to mean something,' said Charlie.

'Well, what are you going to do? There aren't any spells or powders that work to keep the room open. What are you going to do that is different?' asked Tom.

'I'm not sure…there has got to be some sort of solution,' said Charlie.

'Mages, Wizards and most magick folk have tried and you're telling me that you can get into the room safely?' said Imogen, trying to be realistic.

'Well, no-one else has had a shadowy thing showing them the way to here. No-one else has seen the Half Prophecy,' said Charlie, defensively.

'Or so you think?' said Amanda.

'It could be a trick. The shadowy thing could be some sort of enchantment sent to trick you,' said Imogen.

'I'd thought of that, though it can't be. I first saw it in my bedroom in my old house. It was there before I knew anything about magick or the magick world for that matter. Why would someone do such a thing?' Charlie asked.

No one could answer. Charlie was convinced that he had to be here and he wasn't about to leave.

The door stood silent like before. The leaves on the tress had fallen and their remains lay on the floor beneath them.

Charlie started pacing around, trying to think what to do, when he suddenly noticed something on the floor that glimmered slightly, before the intersection of the pathway. Charlie approached.

'Where are you going?' said Amanda, in a concerned manner.

'Wait…I can see something,' he said.

As he approached, the thing that glimmered became clear: some tiny rocks had formed in a circle that splelt: *Remember before you enter.*

'Remember what?' asked Imogen who was stood behind him.

'I don't know,' said Charlie.

They all tried to think what it was that Charlie was supposed to remember, when Imogen smiled, and said, 'I think I know what you're supposed to remember.'

194

'Really,' said Tom.

'Remember what happened tonight at the ritual. The message you got about your name,' said Imogen.

'That's right,' said Tom getting excited.

'You could be right,' said Amanda. 'I'd completely forgotten about it.'

Charlie smiled also as the hairs on the back of his neck stood up. Without giving it much thought, Charlie promptly approached the door of mystery, and, just as it did before, it started to activate again, clunking with strange sounds coming from within and light penetrating the doors.

Charlie took a deep breath and said his name. Nothing happened. He then used his magickal name. With a clunk and a bang, everything went still.

Charlie's heart was pounding frantically. Both Imogen and Tom grabbed hold of Amanda's chair, breathing quickly wondering what was going to happen next.

Charlie took another deep breath and walked a few more feet until he stood in front of the door. He put his hand on the round handle and slowly began to pull down. He was ready to leap onto the post like he did last time, just in case it decided to suck him in.

Slowly the door opened. Charlie just stood there with his mouth aghast, not because the room wasn't spinning anymore, but at what he was seeing. He was right: it was the Half Prophecy, perched on a marble reading plinth.

'Look!' said Charlie. 'I was right. Come and have a look,' he said excitedly.

Amanda, Tom and Imogen came quickly to have a look.

'I don't believe it,' said Tom with his mouth wide open. 'I can't believe it,' said Imogen. 'My dad has told me all kinds of stories about this place. I never thought, this…' she paused, completely transfixed by what she was seeing.

'Aye! What does this mean?' said Amanda.

'I don't know, but I know it is the most important discovery. It is supposed to tell us what is going to happen,' said Charlie.

'Let's get it quick before the room changes its mind and starts spinning again,' said Tom.

Tom began to walk forward, when Imogen suddenly grabbed him.

'Ah, what you doing?' said Tom aggressively.

'Think about it,' said Imogen. 'Enchanted objects that use magickal names are for that person only. Why is this any different?' she said logically.

'She's right,' said Amanda. 'This is for you,' she concluded, comprehensively.

'Yes, this is for you Charlie. For whatever the reason, you have to enter. It wants you to go in...' said Imogen.

Charlie agreed and prepared himself to enter. He looked at the Half Prophecy, neatly rolled up with a glowing golden counterpart, like a phantom limb, making it look complete. It sat at least 40 yards on the other side of a strange looking room which looked like some old medieval ruins. Charlie took another step forward, then....

'Help,' he shouted.

'Oh no! Charlie!' shouted Amanda.

The entire floor had disappeared, and there was now a giant chasm left in its place. Charlie had fallen through, holding on for dear life on the top of what looked like a never-ending stalagmite several feet below them.

'Charlie...hold *on*...,' said Tom.

'I'm trying, but its slippery...hurry... do something!'

Imogen and Tom looked at Amanda if her wheel chair could do anything.

'Sorry, I don't think this can do anything,' she said regretfully.

'Hurry please, *I'm slipping*,' said Charlie, desperately.

Charlie couldn't cling on any further and slipped.

Amanda instinctively grabbed her Purplewood wand and said 'Venio Charlie,' Charlie froze in mid-air, but he still wasn't coming back up. 'Not sure how long I can keep him,' she said sounding strained. Tom held up his staff and said, 'Venio Charlie'. Charlie began to rise, though there was still a struggle.

'Venio Charlie,' screamed Imogen. Underneath him, a golden cloud had formed, lifting him out of the bottomless pit. A he reached the top, he flew out, landing before them. They were all in shock, shaking and sweating.

'Are you OK?' asked Tom gently.

'That was close,' he said restoring what composure he could. 'I'm alive,' he said.

'Don't you ever...' said Amanda

'I didn't know that was going to happen,' he said defensively.

'It is well protected,' said Imogen. 'Whoever put that in there has gone to great lengths to protect it.'

'You are right,' said Charlie. 'We just need to figure out what to do next,' he said.

'Figure out!' exclaimed Tom. 'You must be crazy if you want to go back in there.'

'Don't you see; it *wants* to be found. There must be a way!' Charlie was determined to get to the root of all this and he really wanted to figure out how to get the prophecy.

Before they closed the door, they all tried a summoning charm to fetch the Half Prophecy; there was no luck. Charlie took one more look, shook his head then closed the door.

All four of them went back to the concert that was still going on. "Wild Boys", followed by "Being Followed" blurted out. Everyone was singing as Charlie laughed since he was 'being followed' by the shadow entity.'

They all had a drink, though the mood had clearly changed. After, they spent hours discussing the night, including the mysterious golden cloud that suddenly appeared below him. The mystery was set to continue...

Chapter 21

YULE

After the excitement of Samhain, the rest of the term remained relatively quiet. There was no reappearance of the shadowy creature and there were no more strange voices offering guidance. This disappointed Charlie somewhat as he was comforted by the thought of adventure. It was as if the magick he was learning wasn't enough, craving the thrill and excitement of the mystery that was thrust upon him.

Charlie was developing a fine hand at swordsmanship, which was more than he could say about his magick: he was starting to lag behind the rest of his friends and he couldn't figure out why. Maybe he was meant to be more of a knight than a magickal person or maybe the fact he was born in the Plainlands somehow disadvantaged him in someway. *How could it though?* he thought. Amanda was storming ahead in spell-casting and she came from the same place as him. *Maybe magick works best for Scottish people,* he thought, trying to find someway of explaining what was happening to him.

Tom was doing well, even matching Charlie with some of the swordsmanship, but Charlie's kickboxing endeavours made him more agile and instinctual with his movements.

Amanda was in love with the whole magickal world. She loved the healing arts, learning about the energy centres of the body, as well as the energy field. Once or twice, she could see a range of colours around people, but these were momentary glimpses. Amanda also saw the same group of ghostly people at the front of the school on her the first day and couldn't figure out who they were. They seemed different to the ghosts she had seen before, more vibrant. She also joined in with the knight training and found she could do more than she thought.

Imogen was certainly a character, very passionate and knowledgeable about the magick world, mainly to do with her privileged upbringing and the endless tales of adventure that her father had told her. Her magick was good, and she was more than a match for anyone in knight training thanks to her father and growing up with two older brothers that she never mentioned.

Teacher and Mage Artuk Ra, who was absent for most of the year, finally began to teach. He seemed a powerful man, always wearing his favoured gold threaded clothing and carrying a long golden staff which held a diamond at the top. He was very clever but rarely showed any emotion. His knowledge of astrology rivalled that of Cosmolos and Astrophos. He was a champion of levitation and a master of mathematics. He explained to the first years how the pyramids were really built, using some form of advanced levitation techniques to move the giant bricks. He demonstrated this by using tiny blocks to form a miniature version of a pyramid. Then, he rearranged the class to how he wanted it, moving all of the pupils and its furniture with great ease! The students were astounded!

***

It was the end of term and winter had settled in nicely. It was time for everyone to head home to their families. Charlie was very excited about seeing his mum, brother and sisters. Of course, this holiday would have extra meaning for Charlie as he would be heading back to the Plainlands to see his grandfather. So much had happened to him during the term that he had almost forgotten the Plainlands.

Cosmolos had made an appearance to take Charlie, Emmanuel, Amanda and Bruce back to Wondle using his magick carpet and Portus spell. Charlie and Amanda said good-bye to Tom and Imogen.

'Well Charlie, Amanda, see you after the holidays then,' said Tom.

'Yeah guys, I can't believe Cosmolos is taking you back… you lucky things,' said Imogen.

'Cosmolos only wants to see us all together, just to see how we are getting on in the Magicklands,' said Charlie.

'Oh right,' said Tom. 'We have to go by Flume Rail to the Great City. I'm meeting mum, dad and my little brother Edward. We are going shopping and then head back home to the City of

Elderick. I'm going to help dad out in his shop over Yule. Imogen's lucky of course as she lives in the Great City.'

'What does your dad do?' asked Amanda.

'Oh, he's a jeweller,' said Tom. 'He's had the business for years and wants me to take over someday. I'm not too sure I want to, but there is plenty of time to figure that one out. Dad would like to move his business to the Great City someday, though there is a lot of competition. He is very good, and it'd be fantastic if he could open a shop there,' he said wishfully.

Cosmolos had arrived and it was time to go. After saying their goodbyes, they set off on his magick carpet.

Seconds later, they arrived.

'Charlieee!' shouted Victoria, as she came running over, giving him and Emmanuel a hug. Charlie and Emmanuel both gave their sisters a hug and everyone got very excited at being reunited again.

They spent a few days getting reacquainted. Charlie loved his bed, expanding it out and using it as a trampoline much to the annoyance of his mother. Hours were spent discussing stories and demonstrating spells. Charlie and Emmanuel were amazed at how good their mum was at spell-casting. Charlie was feeling some frustration at this, as even his brother was very proficient at magick.

Victoria wasn't too sure about their knight training lessons and thought it was dangerous. *Dangerous*, Charlie thought! She had no idea of the real danger he'd been in and he daren't tell her the little adventure he'd experienced.

Victoria explained about how Andrew joined the Scottish Highland Knight Division of the Orberon. He showed them the multitude of bruises he had gotten in practice and he was very proud of them. He was even more amazed when he heard that Scotland still had its Royal House representing them.

As for the Orberon, it would be a year before Charlie could enter the school league, though Emmanuel, who was old enough, joined a team called the Warlock Bandits - they were doing quite well.

The introduction of Minnie the family Brownie came as a bit of surprise. Not to mention the little elemental helpers that also assisted Minnie with the chores. Nonetheless, he was happy to hear that Minnie could assist the family no matter where they were staying and made a note to summon her to school at some point in the future. He found it unusual that you shouldn't thank a brownie as they find this to be quite offensive. He was even more impressed at all the elementals tending to the garden, though Victoria explained that she still wasn't too sure about using elementals in magickal workings. The head of school told them to wait and not to use them, yet – 'don't run before you can walk,' the headmaster would say.

The visit of Cosmolos was a pleasant one. He was ecstatic with the way they had settled in, but it was time to return to the Plainlands.

In the Magicklands, the equivalent of Christmastime was called Yule, which was celebrated on the 21st of December. Christmas had adopted some of the older Yule traditions including the Yule log, the colours of red and gold and more. There was much more to the festival that fascinated Charlie.

Having made the journey back to the school, Eric was waiting eagerly to take them back as it meant he could start his holiday. Eric and the old guard knight gave each other evil looks, grunting, snorting and grumbling at each other, much to the amusement of Charlie and Emmanuel.

'I wonder what that is about,' said Charlie.

'No idea, but they definitely do not like each other,' chuckled Emmanuel.

'Right, before we leave, I must warn you of something we call, Dimension Lag,' said Randle.

'Dimension Lag?' said Victoria sounding worried.

'Yes. Well you see, you have integrated and have had full exposure to our world. Without sounding too condescending, our world is a big step up on the energy ladder. You'll find the Plainlands quite a different proposition now and, unfortunately, you will definitely feel the difference,' he said regrettably.

'How?' asked Charlie.

'You'll soon see,' said Randle, loosening his tie; you could tell he didn't enjoy wearing Plainland clothing.

The gate opened. Eric and the guard gave each other some final scowling looks as they left, turning right.

'Get out of the way you stupid Plainer,' said Eric, taking the frustrations he had with the guard onto the oncoming driver.

'What's that smell mummy?' asked Lucy whilst trying to cup her nose.

'That's the Plainlands,' said Randle. 'It is both the physical and mental pollution that ravages the atmosphere,' he said coldly. 'You are all used to the clean and clear air back in the Magicklands. It comes as quite of a shock I'm afraid.'

Eric drove them back to their old house and there was a strong dislike to what they were seeing and smelling.

Many of the neighbours came out to see and greet them, asking all kinds of questions, most of which they could not answer.

'I've got a headache,' said Charlie.

'Me too brother,' said Emmanuel, looking pretty fuzzy. In fact, they all had a headache, bouts of dizziness, disorientation and imbalance. This was then followed by sneezing and running noses, to which Randle handed out some tissues and headache tablets. He would have given them a Percy drink, though the magick that made the drink work couldn't, as they were in the Plainlands.

Having unloaded their belongings and frightened off the neighbours saying they had flu, they headed for the front door. At this point the atmosphere was intolerable to them: a suffocating dense pressure that had hit them, just like a diver would experience heading deep down into the water.

Charlie had a look round and there was a sense of deep disgust and shame for having lived in such a world. The place had no vibrancy at all; it was dull, grey, dirty and lifeless. The term Plainlands couldn't have described this part of the world more accurately. Looking depressed and dejected, they went to their old rooms to unpack their things. Charlie and Emmanuel lay down in their old beds wishing the headache's would go away.

'This is rubbish,' said Charlie.

'Yeah, it sure is,' said Emmanuel.

'I'm glad that we don't have to wait long before we head back,' said Charlie. 'I might send a scroll; er I mean telephone Amanda in a bit. I bet we're all feeling the same.'

'I bet,' Emmanuel replied.

Seconds later, they fell asleep to escape the horror that they had witnessed.

Two hours had passed and there was a knock on their door, waking them.

'Are you two OK,' asked Victoria. 'You were both snoring very loudly.'

'Just about,' said Charlie.

'Yeah, the headaches gone,' said Emmanuel.

'I'm just going to get some fish and chips as we have no food,' said Victoria.

'Nice mum, thanks,' said Charlie, cheering up a little. Charlie got out of bed and headed to the bathroom.

'Yuk,' he said seeing the green mould on the walls and on the crack in the window. He quickly freshened up then headed downstairs. Emmanuel followed minutes later.

Victoria had returned from the chip shop, as well as making a small shop in the local supermarket to buy provisions for the house.

The TV was on in the background discussing the coming election and they were all keen to find out what was happening in the world.

'Utterly depressing,' said Victoria. 'I feel sorry for the people who have to live in this,' she said, angrily.

Charlie had learned that his football team had performed dismally and they were likely to have their worst finish in years if they were not careful.

'Mum,' said Charlie. 'How long do we have to stay here?'

'Well, we have to go and see your Grandfather first then we'll see,' said Victoria, instinctively reading Charlie's mind: he wanted to get back to the magickal world. Charlie was at least willing and happy enough to go and see the Granddad he loved so dearly; it was his only real motivation for staying.

Later in the evening, Charlie's old friend, Lee, popped round. He was most definitely pleased to see him but frustrated he couldn't say anything about the school. For the most part he either lied or exaggerated what he did at school. Lee also discussed his new school, saying that he was happy to have avoided Mrs Harrington for any classes and that he had also made some new friends called Steven and Daniel, which Charlie was pleased about. Charlie had told him about how nice Amanda, Tom and Imogen were. It was frustrating for Charlie not to be able to tell him what he was doing, as he knew he would have been jealous if he knew he was training to be a knight.

Emmanuel and Victoria also caught up with old friends. Meeting with old acquaintances really cheered them up no end.

The next day, they all went to the hospital. Their Grandfather had been ecstatic to see them, looking so much better than he had done previously. He was still grumpy, complaining about the hospital, swearing they were doing strange tests on him; it was just his way. The great thing was that colour had returned to his cheeks and he had put on some weight. He explained that he had been home and they had brought him back to do some more tests. However, he would be home for Christmas day.

They had just missed Grandma Maria by half an hour, which annoyed them. Nevertheless, the encounter brought much needed cheer to their miserable return. They were all eager to make Christmas a special day as the whole family would be getting together. Charlie's grandfather said that he was very proud of him and the rest of the family. He gave Charlie some money and a chocolate bar as a treat then gave him a big hug.

After the visit, they all went home. Charlie was feeling rather bored at the same old television programmes they put on at Christmas so he put on his warm Dragonstone coat, scarf and gloves on, and went for a walk. He thought it was a good idea to head for
the local woodland as it reminded him of the school.

Ten minutes had passed when he arrived at the entrance to the woodland. Charlie looked up, smiled and entered. *No cheeky Un-Potted Plants here*, he thought to himself. Charlie could feel the difference as he went in, but it still wasn't quite like the Magicklands.

The air was fresh and crisp. He took some deep breaths, filling his lungs with clear air, which regenerated him. Until now, he had never appreciated the qualities of nature.

As he walked through, Charlie remembered that elementals weren't tied to the agreement made all those centuries ago, so he

204

was hoping to at least catch a glimpse of a wood elf, or gnome smoking his pipe. There was nothing as yet, though he kept his eyes peeled.

Most of the woodland seemed naked as it was winter time, when Charlie noticed something in the distance. 'No, it can't be…' he said to himself. He ran over to something that looked remotely similar to the shadowy entity but, as he arrived, there was nothing there.

'Naa, surely not – not during the holidays,' he said.
Charlie walked forward and he felt a crunch under his feet. He looked down and he couldn't believe what he was seeing. There, scribed deeply into the ground, were both halves of the prophecy drawn, side by side. In addition to this, there were two arrows at the top pointing inwards. *What does that mean?* Charlie thought.
Charlie got out his phone, took a picture of it and sent it to Amanda. Seconds later his phone was ringing. She promptly answered.

'Hey Charlie… great to hear from you. Yeah, it took us a while, it was awful adjusting back. I had a headache for a whole day. Anyway, where did you take the picture?' Charlie explained what happened and asked Amanda if she had any ideas.

'I have no idea, though I will have a think. I've met up with some of my old friends, though I'm missing Imogen and Tom,' said Amanda.

'Yeah me too… Won't be long now though,' said Charlie.

'I know I can't wait to spend some time in the new house. I also want to explore the town,' she said.

'I know, everything here seems boring now. There is too much to see and do back home. When we get back, we should meet up with Imogen and Tom and see whether they have any ideas as to what this means,' said Charlie.

'I agree,' said Amanda.

'Hey Charlie, I have to go, mum has got dinner on the table. She says to say hi, as do the rest of family.'

'Great, say hi back please. Take care Amanda and I'll see you soon – byeee.' Charlie put his phone away and, buoyed by his conversation with Amanda, he left for home. Charlie also enjoyed his unexpected homework in trying to work out another clue to the mystery of the Half Prophecy.

The rest of the holiday went better than expected, though they'd spent longer there than Charlie would have liked.

Chapter 22

AN IMPOSSIBLE MISSION

Going through the School Gates was like being reborn, breathing in the fresh, vibrant and clear air of the Magicklands. Of course it was winter here too, but still, the atmosphere was so, so different, and it wouldn't be long before they were all back in Wondle.

Charlie got out of his bed and looked out of the window. Robert the garden gnome lazily sat on a deck-like chair, wrapped up in winter clothing, smoking his pipe. His eyes kept shutting, though he seemed to be in deep thought about something, whilst the other elementals moved along casually, tending to the winter plants. It was snowing. The fields behind the house seemed to stretch for ever, all blanketed in pure white snow that was untouched.

It was, however, time to head back to school. Sadly, for Charlie, Eric had problems with the coach, as someone decided to set some engine gremlins under the bonnet, wreaking havoc. It took a few days to find them all, clear the problem, and make repairs. Eric was furious and requested the help of a knight guard to protect the coach whilst he wasn't there. Because of the recent events, Charlie and Emmanuel could only spend two days at the house.

It was pointless in unpacking everything, so it didn't take long for Charlie to gather his things for the arrival of Cosmolos, who seemed so keen to ferry them backwards and forwards.

Charlie, Emmanuel, Amanda and Bruce, all said their good byes, and, with a wave of Cosmolos's staff, they were back at the school. About a hundred students had witnessed the arrival of the group much to their astonishment. *Why would such a prominent Mage do such a thing*, they thought? You could only imagine the gossip that followed.

It took a short time for Charlie and his friends to unpack. Charlie looked around his room and realised it was actually quite a mess. He reached for his staff and said the following incantation: 'I call upon the elemental Brownie Minnie, to come forward, and assist me – please.' Within a flash, the elemental appeared in front of him with one of her helpers.

'Hello Minnie, nice to see you again. As you can see I need some help.'

'Hello Charlie, no problem. Glad to be of assistance,' said Minnie. Charlie stopped short of saying thank you as not to offend her. Charlie then pulled out a delicious pastry with butter and sugar topping and placed it on the side. Minnie's eyes widened and shined appreciatively.

'OK Charlie, I know what needs to be done,' said Minnie. Without warning, Minnie vanished into thin air.

A familiar whooshing sound came…it was a scroll.

Hey Charlie, Tom here, are you back.
Send me a reply. Ta – Tom ;0)
PS – Imogen has just arrived also.

Charlie sent an instant reply and they agreed that they would all meet for a snack and to catch up.

Charlie was late getting to the canteen, whilst Amanda, Imogen and Tom all sat laughing, discussing the holidays. Amanda happened to tell both Tom and Imogen about Charlie's experience in the Plainlands and tried to show them the picture. For some strange reason, Amanda couldn't access the pictures on her phone.

'Hey Charlie, whatever is happening, this thing you keep seeing is very persistent,' said Imogen.

'What do you think it means?' asked Tom.

'I don't know. It was the scroll as a whole with two arrows pointing inwards towards the centre – very strange - any idea guys?' said Charlie hoping for some inspiration.

'No,' said Tom and Imogen.

'Ah, but of course,' said Amanda.

'What, you know what it is?' Charlie asked.

'No, but what do we have here that could help us?'

Charlie, Tom and Imogen all looked confused.

'We have the Room of Reflection to help us,' she said.

'Of course!' shouted Charlie, leaping off his chair, catching the attention of everyone in the room.

'That is a fantastic idea Amanda, I can't believe we didn't think of it before,' said Charlie.

'Yeah, I've never used the room before, though my dad swears by it. He's thought of various fighting strategies using it,' said Imogen.

Charlie, Amanda, Tom and Imogen left for the Room.

They walked across the old corridor and entered the room, closing the door behind them. The stained glass was immediately activated. It was remarkable as it shone as if it was daytime in the middle of summer.

The room was surprisingly quiet and soundproofed from the external world.

They all went round and sat down at the designated seating areas. The room instantly transformed into a glowing yellow, which meant that some logic was required to work out the problem. The greatest concentrations of light surround their heads, which intensified as they shut their eyes. With their intentions clear of what they wanted from the room, a sweet scent entered, helping them to relax further. This was needed as Charlie's mind was very excitable. *Help me*, he said in his own mind. Charlie thought it would be a good idea to use Mage Sidhara's breathing technique to help. It worked.

Ten minutes had passed and a gentle music could be heard. The soothing tones were designed to aid their thinking.

All Charlie could see was the image of the whole prophecy with the two arrows he'd seen on his walk in the Plainland woods. The arrows began to move backward and forwards, which confused him.

After an hour of being in there, the lights dimmed, the sweet scent and music vanished. The room went back to normal.

'Well?' said Charlie, did you get anything?

'Not really,' said Tom.

'Me neither,' said Imogen.

'I'm afraid I didn't get much either. I kept seeing it, but the image kept distorting, separating and coming back together,' said Amanda.

209

'Oh well, all that happened in mine were the arrows kept moving backwards and forwards, meeting in the middle,' said Charlie.

'In mine, I saw one arrow pointing inwards,' said Tom.

'Well mine didn't make much sense either; I struggled to keep it together: One part of the prophecy kept floating away, then coming back,' said Imogen.

They went back into the common room to drink some hot chocolate before bedtime. Tom particularly enjoyed this, so he had two glasses.

They continued to discuss what they had seen, trying to make sense of it all, but couldn't. They thought it best to sleep on it then maybe the answer would present itself in the morning.

The next day, Charlie woke up to an alarm by Sebastian.

'Charlie, you're running late,' a voice blasted out. Charlie leapt out of bed and, with heart still pounding, he ran to the bathroom. He could hear a series of horns, shouting and screaming in his accommodation block; everyone had over slept.

Charlie didn't have time for breakfast and headed straight towards his lessons, meeting up with Amanda, Tom and Imogen.

The day's lessons went as normal, with Sidhara teaching them meditation using the flame; Guildus' usual sarcastic reposts, followed by helpful hints, made his teaching style bewildering and confusing to say the least. Even so, Charlie still couldn't understand why he was struggling so much with spell-casting; the sessions made him feel very tired. Even David Moarns was getting the hang of it and Helen was top of the class. Nevertheless, Charlie was determined to persevere in the art of spell-casting, so he made sure that he attended every lesson and society practice.

In the evening, Charlie was enjoying his knight training even more, sparring regularly with Tom. Sedrick was keeping a close eye on Charlie, assisting him whenever he could. 'I see you doing well in the Orberon,' he kept telling Charlie; it motivated him to train harder. However, he needed to address the issue of improving his magick, as you had to be good at both to be Magickal Knight class.

The one thing that Charlie was enjoying with some of the theory aspects in knight training was learning about the code of honour, loyalty, fairness, respect; and using your skills to lead well, helping those who need it. These are some of the signs of real nobility. 'Those nobles who can't live by these rules are not deserving of such titles,' taught Sir Barnaby.

The weekend came quickly. Charlie went to his early morning kickboxing sparring class with his brother for the first time in ages; he really enjoyed Emmanuel's company. Emmanuel was somewhat his equal, regularly scoring points off each other. Tom couldn't go as he said he wasn't feeling too well and Imogen and Amanda were far too tired and wanted to spend the morning in bed.

After enjoying the luxury of a power shower, Charlie headed down to eat a serving of Gobby Brisks, as well as drinking a Percy Refresher-Juice.

On his way out, he turned and saw the Room of Reflection door open and he decided to go inside. The room greeted him with a multispectral light display, which settled down to an amazing purple.

Charlie was the only one in the room, so he went and sat down. He closed his eyes and began to breathe deeply; he could hear his heart beating.

Charlie's thoughts became erratic and wondered all over the place. For some reason, his thoughts went back to the time he saved little Tommy at his old school.

Ten minutes had passed when he saw something he didn't expect: it was the complete Half Prophecy with an image of a lock closing whilst hovering over the top and then a key appeared. The image then faded and the Prophecy came in the form of a jigsaw. Charlie couldn't believe it: the image was so clear it was like watching a film. He went all shivery and cold.

'I'VE GOT IT,' he celebrated. 'I'VE GOT IT,' he said again, thumping the air. Still tingling, he ran out of the room, and up to Amanda, Imogen's and then Tom's room, banging on the doors, telling them to go to his room as soon as possible, it was about the 'You know what,' as he called it so others couldn't understand.

Charlie ran to his room. Pacing up and down: he was feeling agitated that they weren't there. He sent them scrolls, telling them to hurry up and adding animated trumpets, which blurted out, just to emphasise the urgency of his request.

Five minutes had gone and there was a knock at the door.

'Enter,' said Charlie. The door opened.

All three of them entered, though Tom was still in his Dragonstone bath robe, blowing his nose.

'What's the matter Charlie?' asked Imogen.

'I've got a stinking cold,' said Tom.

'Oh, you should come to the healing arts class: we are always in need of volunteers to practice on,' said Amanda.

'Well!' Imogen said, bringing their attention back to why they were there.

'It's the Half Prophecy, said Charlie. 'The two pieces have to be united, but there is more,' he said.

'What do you mean?'

Charlie explained what had happened in the meditation room.

'So why the jigsaw,' quizzed Amanda.

'Well, that's obvious: a jigsaw is something you *put together* if you catch my drift.' said Charlie.

'Of course, how silly of me,' she said half asleep.

'The key?' asked Tom

'Yes, it's something that opens something,' said Charlie.

'Very funny Guildus,' reposted Tom.

'Remember what Sidhara talked about images as being symbolic, meaning, it represents something or a situation,' said Charlie.

'Yes - I get it!' cheered Imogen. 'It represents the scroll. It is the key to get in. Yes! Of course! It must act as trigger to stabilise the room,' she continued.

'Yes,' said Charlie. 'I'm sure of it,' he said convincingly.

'...and the lock must mean, they must be locked together. A bit like the jigsaw coming together I suppose' said Tom. 'Brilliant, this will be the discovery of the entire magickal world... I'm sure of it.'

'Hang on a second,' said Imogen. 'Just one small point - how on earth do we get the other half of the Half Prophecy? It is one of the most protected objects in history! My dad being one of the knights protecting it and, ooh, let me think, Sedrick being another, not to mention Brutus and the many other top class knights,' said Imogen. That was it. Charlie's bubble had been burst. Imogen was right, how on earth could they get to it. Charlie looked deflated, Amanda shook her head and Tom rubbed his head then blew his nose.

'There must be a way,' said Charlie.

'We could just ask the museum,' said Tom.

'Yeah right...hi, I was wondering if I could borrow the Half Prophecy for the afternoon. I'm sure that would go down a treat,' said Imogen sarcastically.

'Ok, lets all take it turns to be Guildus then,' said Tom, slightly irritated by her remarks.

'I think there must be a way,' said Amanda positively, 'but it will need some thinking. I mean, this has all happened for a reason, so there must be a solution to the problem,' she said, thinking logically about the situation.

They all spent some time trying to come up with some ideas, but they all came to a dead end.

'I agree,' said Tom. 'Well maybe we should use the Room of Reflection again and see what happens.'

'Great idea - after all, it is where I found the solution to the Prophecy,' said Charlie. 'We're going to work this out,' he said rousing him and the others.

***

Two weeks had passed and still no solution.

It was Friday. The snow showed some sign of dissipating as it'd gone from five feet high, to four feet high. Trudging through it, they all headed to Magickal Powders class. It was very popular because of all the great things you could do with the powders and also because of the eccentric and very loud Professor Lambert Snuffle.

He was teaching them about powders that make you move quickly, which is ideal for combat situations. He said, 'It is important to add some Mind Quickness Powder, so your mind can coordinate and get up to speed with the body, otherwise you might end up moving so quickly, you might run into a wall, or worse - feel a sword in your gullet,' he said laughing to himself.

'Yeah, really funny,' said Tom, scrunching his face.

213

Amanda had become unusually distracted by looking at the hundreds of powders that existed in an advanced potions book she obtained from the drawing room. Suddenly, she came across something that could help.

'Humm, yes, it could work…but no, there is still a problem,' she muttered to herself.

'What are you talking about?' whispered Charlie.

'Well, I think I might have an idea of how to get the Half Prophecy, I mean the one that's going to be in the museum,' she said whispering excitedly.

'Really – how?' asked Charlie.

'Yes really, but there are a couple problems that need working out first,' she said excitedly.

'Is there something so interesting that it deserves all of out attention,' said Professor Snuffle.

'Sorry sir,' said Amanda.

The professor continued talking about the importance of putting the right blend of ingredients when concocting Dual and Triple Purpose Powders: 'Otherwise it could 'spell' disaster,' he said at the top of his voice and laughing at his own joke; it wasn't funny.

The final lesson ended and they went back to their accommodation to get ready for a society spell-casting session.

'Tell me Amanda,' said Charlie instantly.

'I can't - not yet,' she said.

'What's going off?' asked Imogen.

'Yeah,' said Tom, 'you two have been arguing since we left Powders.'

'Amanda seems to have a plan regarding the, *you know what*, and she's not telling me what it is,' he said grumpily.

'Really!' said Imogen.

'I'll be impressed if you have,' said Tom.

'I've told you, there a couple of things that need working out. I don't *want* to say anything, just in case I am wrong,' she said defensively. 'I don't want to get people's hopes up,' she concluded.

'Well if you tell us, then surely we can put our minds together to figure it out. You know, put ideas together,' said Charlie, but Amanda said nothing. Charlie grunted, as he knew he

214

wasn't going to get anything out of Amanda, but his curiosity was getting even stronger. After all, what kind of plan could she possibly have in trying to obtain the Half Prophecy.

Charlie tried a couple of more times to prise the cunning plan out of her, but she wasn't revealing anything.

They all went back to their rooms to get ready for the evenings Spell-casting Society, followed by some food and a game of Wizopoly.

Charlie was pacing around the room, unable to settle, so he decided to head out again. Meanwhile, Amanda was chasing around like a crazed Werewolf, trying to get her plan together.

Charlie heard Amanda moving around on the floor, below and then she entered Imogen's room. Charlie waited a few moments then headed down to investigate.

'But I can't,' said Imogen, disbelievingly. 'He'll kill me if he finds out,' she said.

'But it's the only way,' said Amanda.

'It's a great idea, but where?' asked Imogen. 'Surely they would realise straight away?' she said.

'Humm, I see your point,' said Amanda disappointed. 'I'll have to give it some more thought. There must be a way, there must be!' said Amanda sounding as determined as Charlie.

Imogen started to move towards the door. Charlie panicked and ran speedily upstairs, back into his room. Tom opened his door to see what all the commotion was about, saw nothing and went back into his room.

'What was that about?' said Charlie to himself. He was left none the wiser and even more frustrated.

Charlie's thoughts were scattered across the universe during society spell practice, to the point of being dangerous. Thankfully, it was Felicity Phelps who was caught straight in the eye by a flying Moonometer Charlie was trying to send to Tom on the other side of the room, giving her a nice black eye. Felicity just scowled at him whilst everyone else laughed.

In the communal room, they were all sitting down, eating their sandwiches, when David came over with the main Wizopoly board.

215

'Here you are,' he said beaming. 'I finally won a game,' he said happily, and then left.

It was Amanda's turn to roll the dice and headed into the game. She was there a bit longer than normal and then came out frowning.

'How rude was he?' she said, describing a stubborn barterer in the game. 'The room was nice, but hey,' she said, 'I've got it - I have a brilliant plan,' she said boastfully.

Chapter 23

HUNT FOR THE PROPHECY

The subsequent months seemed to pass quickly, though the timing which Amanda had thought up for the plan couldn't have come at a better time. This was because there were special powders that had to be mixed up that required the utmost accuracy. They all helped to concoct the powders for the ultimate and most daring mission. What made this difficult was the fact that they couldn't consult Professor Snuffle because he would have certainly become suspicious of the whole thing.

Charlie, Amanda, Tom and Imogen were sitting in the main canteen, devouring their full English breakfasts. Charlie had managed to get some egg yolk on his nose which Tom found amusing, but didn't tell him to begin with. In fact, it took Amanda five minutes to point it out.

'Spoil sport,' Tom said.

'Thanks Amanda,' said Charlie as Tom frowned.

'Not long now,' said Imogen. 'This had better work. I've taken a great risk in getting this,' she said holding a pouch with an object inside.

'I know,' said Amanda. 'I'm amazed you managed to get it,' she said beaming.

'Yeah, thanks,' said Charlie.

'I must be crazy,' said Imogen.

'I agree,' said Tom. 'Totally mad by the way - what's the worst thing that could happen?'

'I have to admit, I thought this moment was never going to happen: the whole trip got delayed for a third time,' said Charlie.

'At least this has given us chance to do a little reconnaissance. Remember, timing is everything,' said Imogen.

An announcement came over the tannoy for all the first years to meet Winston and Randle in the courtyard. They did one final check of their equipment then headed out.

217

'Hello there first years, glad you could make it on this magnificent day,' said Winston with his usual swagger.

'Yes, what a marvellous opportunity this will be to go and see the Half Prophecy. A true part of history, a rare and outstanding opportunity to see such a rare artefact,' said Randle, who was more excited than anyone about the trip.

'Once there, you will have an hour to spare before the rest of the students arrive,' said Winston.

'Yes!' said Charlie, shaking his fist with approval.

Fifteen minutes later, they were all on the Flume Rail, travelling at speed towards the Great City. Nerves of excitement hit the gang after realising what they were about to attempt. Here they were, a bunch of first years with little magickal experience, trying to steal the rarest of magickal items.

'Are you OK Charlie?' asked Imogen.

'Yeah, I've just got a few butterflies in my tummy,' he said.

'Don't worry, I've bought some *Percy Calm* and *Confidence* drinks, which should do the trick,' said Imogen.

'Good thinking,' said Tom, looking a little paler than normal. 'I think I need the toilet,' he said.

Charlie closed his eyes in an attempt to meditate. Before he knew it, the Flume Rail had arrived at the Great City.

'Ok first years,' said Randle as they all stood on the port station platform. 'Please be at the museum in sixty minutes, before we head through to see the artefact.'

'Yes - and please don't be late, otherwise you'll miss an opportunity of a lifetime,' said Winston, as the group dispersed.

'OK you two, you know what to do,' said Charlie to Amanda and Imogen.

'Yeah we certainly do. Good luck to the both of you,' responded, Imogen. They quickly drank their Percy drinks and sped off, hurriedly.

'Imogen hopped on the back of Amanda's chair. In the fastest gear, they rushed off to their destination.

'Oi you - watch it,' said a passer-by, as Amanda nearly knocked him over.

'Sorry,' she shouted back.

Moments later, they had arrived.

'Are you sure about this?' asked Amanda.

'Yes, it took a while, though he told me himself. There will be a change shortly. We must hurry before they get here,' said Imogen. Imogen got out her little pouch and pulled out a key. She opened a gate and they sneaked inside, moving cautiously along a corridor and into a changing room. Inside, it was crammed full of knight armour belonging to the English medieval knights.

'We must hurry,' said Imogen sharply.

Amanda took out her magickal powder and applied it to the armour. Suddenly, there was a patter of footsteps and deep voices passing by the window located on the opposite side of the room to the door. Imogen flung herself to the ground and Amanda hid around a corner.

They were both about as nervous as they could be. Imogen was starting to look a little like what Tom did earlier.

'You finished,' whispered Imogen.

'Just one more, but it is the one by the window.' This was unfortunate as there were two knights discussing the Orberon just outside the window.

Amanda placed some powder on her hands. She retrieved her wand and said 'Reverto Scorpus,' the powder flew off and scattered itself over the appropriate area of the armour.

'That's it!' whispered Amanda.

'Great work - lets go,' said Imogen.
Carefully, they opened the door, exited, and then closed it.

Imogen climbed on the back of Amanda's magickally adapted wheelchair, moving swiftly towards the exit.

Outside, they had gotten a few yards, when...

'Er, excuse me, what are you...'

'Hello Sir Richard,' said Imogen.

'Oh, hello there Imogen,' said Sir Richard.

'Have you seen my father?' asked Imogen coolly.

'No, he's in the Political Quarter my dear. Shouldn't you be at school?' said Sir Richard sounding suspicious.

'We're on a school visit to see the Half Prophecy at the museum,' she said.

'Oh, wonderful - I've seen it before - it is a wonderful item,' he said. 'I'm going to be on guard there very soon,' he said as the two girls just looked at each other with wide eyes.

'Who is this young lady?' he asked.

'Oh, this is Amanda, my best friend,' replied Imogen.

'Hi,' said Amanda, beaming at what Imogen said.

'Hello, there! Pleased to meet you…' said Sir Richard.

'Er, OK, I'll send a scroll to my father later,' said Imogen. 'See you soon,' she said trying to make haste.

'No problem. You sound as if you are in a bit of hurry so I better not keep you any longer. This way,' he said. Sir Richard escorted them out of the gate. He was completely oblivious to what they had done. 'Have a wonderful day,' he concluded.

Amanda sped off with Imogen still onboard, heading back towards the city to rendezvous with Charlie and Tom.

***

'How do you think they have done,' asked Tom.

'Well, I hope,' said Charlie. 'Otherwise we might get into serious trouble,' he added nervously.

Charlie huffed quietly and Tom just let out a nervous sigh, looking at the huge building in front of them. Randle would describe it as a neoclassical look: it had a Greco-Roman influence, though instead of white marble, the building had brownish tinge to it. There were many steps leading up to the main entrance, with large pillars stretched, along the front of the museum.

'Look, the museum is open,' said Tom.

'Do you think they will let us in?' asked Charlie.

'I don't see why not,' said Tom. 'There are other parts that are open to the public.'

Charlie and Tom walked up the steps. They looked up and the building seemed to get bigger the closer they got to it. They walked inside the main archway and there were statues of ancient powerful wizards dominating the area.

'They're big,' said Charlie looking very impressed.

'They sure are,' said Tom. 'That is the great wizard Valdore. He was the one who stayed to oversee the building of the Great City. The other is, Romanus Orberon. I bet you can't guess what he invented,' laughed Tom.

'Humm, now let me think,' said Charlie jokingly.

'Look Charlie,' said Tom. 'The knights have arrived with the scroll in that plain, wooden casket.'

'Crikey,' said Charlie as he and Tom ran into the museum and started to look at the Dwarven tapestry.

The knights came marching in with the casket. It was small enough to be carried by one person.

The museum curator, who looked rather like a funeral director, came to greet them; he was most excited.

'Wonderful, wonderful – at last, it is here, follow me,' he said gleefully.

Charlie's heart stopped.

'Oh no, we didn't think,' he said. They hadn't counted on an extra person being there.

'Oh cripes,' said Tom. 'What are we going to do about him?' he said in a panicked tone.

'Well, we can't stop now. We'll have to blag it,' said Charlie. 'We'll be quick enough to get away from him.' Charlie and Tom followed the knights and the curator down into the museum, keeping their distance from them all. The knights and the curator proceeded to walk down into some lower levels of the museum.

'Hope it's not far,' whispered Charlie to Tom.

'Yeah, it seems a bit creepy down this part,' Tom replied. The corridor was dimly lit, with only a crackle of flames lighting the way. They walked past some strange three-dimensional portraits with scary looking people in them, and then past some ancient weaponry and some very old trinkets. Further along, they came into an area that lit up suddenly, making Charlie and Tom dive behind some hideous looking statues. Charlie and Tom raised their heads slightly to see what was happening. One of the knights placed the casket on a magnificently crafted display.

'Let's have a look,' said the knight wearing golden armour, the likes Charlie had never seen before.

The other knight, wearing traditional silver armour which had strange red markings, opened the casket.

'This is exquisite,' said the knight.

It was dark. Charlie reached into his bag, pulled something out and opening it up.

'What security enchantments are we to use?' asked one of the other knights.

'Oh, just the usual,' said the man in the golden suit.

Charlie grabbed his wand and said, 'Aktivieren.' Within a single breath, the knights had vanished. The curator looked totally confused, panicked and scared. He was about to raise the alarm when Tom raised his hand and said, 'Reverto Scorpus,' pointing at a small piece of marble on the floor. It went hurtling through the air knocking the curator out.

'Brilliant Tom – let's get it,' said Charlie. 'We've only ten minutes left.'

They ran over and grabbed the other half of the Prophecy, placing it securely in Charlie's bag. Adrenaline had taken over, and they ran as fast as they could up the stairs, straight for the museum doors.

'Hey you, slow down!' shouted an old man with glasses.

They ignored him. They arrived at the doors and saw Winston.

'Oh no, it's Winston and Randle with half the year,' said Tom, as they flung themselves behind one of the giant ancient support columns.

'You know what we've got to do,' said Charlie.

Tom opened his bag and pulled out two powder vials. They sprinkled the powders on themselves and moved as fast as lightening. Giuseppe, who was on the edge of the group, had his hair blown around as if it had been in some storm; such was the speed they were moving. 'Mama mia,' he said, whilst his friends looked rather flummoxed.

Within minutes, they had arrived at the Flume Port Station, and the potion they had drunk had worn off. They found themselves
confronted by Amanda and Imogen.

'Have you got it?' Amanda asked.

Charlie just lifted his bag and smiled.

'Brilliant,' said Imogen.

'There were a few scares, but we did it,' said Tom.

That very second, the Dragonstone Flume arrived carrying the second years. They sneaked on, narrowly avoiding Emmanuel and Bruce, who got out of the second carriage.

With a whip and crack, the Flume disappeared and they were off, heading back to school.

'I don't believe it,' said Charlie. 'I can't believe it worked. If this doesn't work, we are going to be in so much trouble,' he said, realising the consequence of their actions.

Chapter 24

NO TURNING BACK!

Pandemonium hit the Great City. Knights from all nations were out on patrol searching and checking the city. Each quarter was on high alert and lockdown whilst everyone and everyplace were being searched. The knights guarding the Prophecy were dazed and confused, but joined in the hunt.

The governors of the Political Quarter were vexed and angry at what had happened; the curator was in floods of tears because the theft happened in his museum. Lord Balfour was particularly concerned and sent his own investigation team. Even Cosmolos was requested to join in the search using his powerful magickal abilities to help track down the thieves.

Nothing like this had ever happened before in the Great City, hence all the shock and outcry. It was as if in that moment the light that encompassed the magickal world went momentarily dim and a strange fear gripped the lands. Charlie, Amanda, Tom and Imogen had since arrived back on campus, hiding out in Charlie's room, shaking and jumping at every single noise. They sat down to a Percy Camomile Special Drink to calm their nerves.

'Put the TV on,' said Tom.

Charlie put the TV on. He pressed 123 on the strange looking control and Magickal World News (MWN), came on.

'Now reporting from outside the Museum is the news award winner and the very popular, Graham Golden.'

'Well, it still isn't looking good. The knights are completely embarrassed and refuse to comment, but this report was taken earlier from the curator.'

'Why, why, would somebody do such a thing? It is a national treasure. Please, please return it, and you will be treated fairly. If not, may Zeus have mercy on you...'

'On the advice of Cosmolos - the help of the High Inquisitor, Philbus has been drafted in to lead the investigation.

The likes of an inquisitor hasn't been used since those dreadful murders several years ago. This is what he had to say earlier:

'I am deeply saddened at what has happened. However, it is my duty to find the culprits who have done this. If you hand over the object today you will be fairly treated, if not, you will incur the wrath of the inquisitorial team; it won't be pleasant.'

Tom turned off the TV and they all gulped.

'This is serious,' said Imogen. 'I've heard of Philbus before; my dad mentioned him. He is not a nice man at all.'

'Why would Cosmolos use or know such a man?' Charlie asked.

'I don't know, but he was around when the murders happened years ago. Dad never told the whole story.'

Charlie seemed worried that a nice mage would have anything to do with the likes of Philbus. He was now glad that he remained silent, saying nothing to him about the prophecy.

'What shall we do?' Amanda said in a shaky voice.

'Well, we've come this far. We'll have to see it through, there is no turning back,' said Charlie.

'Let us hope that Philbus doesn't catch up with us,' said Tom.

The afternoon had passed quickly and it was nearly dark. Charlie looked out of the window and saw the sun had set.

'Right guys, it's time.' 'We need to go now before it is too late,' said Charlie sounding prophetic.

The news then reported that school children were seen running out of the museum. It was a matter of time before they figure out what had happened and catch up with them.

Charlie opened his door quietly, listening for other students. Some doors could be heard shutting whilst the majority of rooms had the TVs on with the news full blast.

Practically tip toeing out of the building; they made their way towards the Door of Mystery. Charlie clung on tightly to his bag. They made their way back through the small woodland until the frightening door faced them. Charlie and his friends walked towards it, cautiously.

They crossed the threshold. The door began making its usual groaning and clanging noise, which seemed to get more

225

frightening each time they visited. Charlie said his magickal name and a massive thud made their hearts stop; it pulsated faster than it had earlier in the day.

A thunderous crack shouted at them from the sky making them all scream and lightening filled the heavens. The rain began and the winds picked up rapidly.

'Hurry Charlie,' said Imogen.

Charlie then opened the door and saw the room as he had previously seen it; the prophecy glistened just ahead of him. He opened his bag and took out the other half of it.

Other lights had now filled the sky: balls of magickal energy filled the air. Philbus had arrived.

Charlie held out the Prophecy in his hands and took a step into the room. The chasm that nearly swallowed him up did not appear, much to the relief of everyone. Charlie walked forward and Amanda, Tom and Imogen followed. As Tom took a step forward, he got trapped by some invisible force field.

'We can't come in. We're stuck,' said Tom, outshouting the storm.

'Charlie, use the powder!' shouted Amanda.

Charlie took out some golden looking powder out of a velvet pouch and sprinkled it on the Prophecy.

'Put it on...,' shouted Imogen, but out of the blue, the room suddenly transformed in to a very, very long corridor and Charlie didn't hear what she was saying.

The corridor had twisted. There were many levels and pathways that forked upwards, downwards and to the sides. There were corridors in the four corners of this massive and impressive enclosure. There were seemingly impossible structures with staircases that folded and twisted, each being impossible to walk on. Each stairwell led into different rooms.

Charlie then saw a glowing light coming from the top left room and said loudly, 'How am I supposed to get up there?' As he moved forward to walk towards it, the light shifted to another part of the room and kept moving again and again. Charlie looked dejected. It was like some cruel torture that Philbus had set up. No matter where he tried to walk, he just ended up chasing lights. H either ended back where he started from, or finished up at some cruel dead end.

'I need some help,' said Charlie out of frustration. The shadow entity appeared out of nowhere and stood ten feet away from him. It looked at him, staring intensely. Charlie was getting flash backs to the first day he saw the school: when he was in Hecate's office, through the doorway that shouldn't have been there, to Cyril the door. He then remembered something else: Cosmolos had said something, a spell to see them into the magick world. Tingling went down his spine, when he remembered it - but was he good enough to use it?

Charlie, who was armed with his staff, lifted it as Cosmolos did and said loudly, 'Apocalypton!'

The Prophecy began to glow and the light filled the room instantly, transforming it into something more recognisable. He was now outside another room. He began to walk in when something horrible happened: the paralysing pain he'd previously had, had come back with greater intensity.

Charlie shrieked with pain beyond toleration. He felt sick and stumbled into the room trying to reach the other half of the prophecy.

As if matters couldn't get any worse, a horrible chill entered the room. A shriek filled the room that would give any person nightmares. Terrible phantom-looking people flew into the room, wearing black and blood-red cloaks. They all landed and surrounded Charlie. Their eyes lacked any compassion and a suffocating stench seemed to emanate from them. They had a translucent look but otherwise human in appearance.

Charlie really wished he wasn't there. One of the creatures approached Charlie. It held up a twisted, evil, staff and Charlie then rolled in immense pain, before heading into a deep paralysis. Charlie saw one of the creatures move to pick up the prophecy and the creature received a violent shock, whilst simultaneously, the prophecy was catapulted closer towards the other half. The creature was furious, sending a shock through Charlie.

Charlie suddenly remembered what Mage Sidhara has said during his first class: relax and don't try too hard. He took a deep breath to relax his mind and, amazingly, his binds didn't seem as bad, but he still couldn't move.

He'd fallen, loosely gripping his staff. He opened his left eye and he was now breathing calmly.

The creature was about to use a summoning spell, when, with one last effort, Charlie whispered, 'Reverto Scorpus.' His visualisation was clearer than he'd ever seen before and the prophecy flew to its counterpart. Two of the creatures flew after it, but it was too late, the prophecy landed, united once more.

In the background a silvery white light began to form when a man moved forward, wearing white robes. He had long white hair, a large beard and deep green eyes. He looked powerful and had a serious look on his face.

The phantom creatures' deathly faces raced towards the man.

'In Lucium Sophere Porforno,' A large white and silver sphere appeared over the right shoulder of this wizard. Sparks flew out of it and was waiting for a command by its master.

Foul black energy zipped towards the wizard to kill him, but he sent out some golden energy that ate up the dark mass.

A battle then commenced. All the creatures were flying and sending all manner of foul energies towards the wizard. One of the creatures vanished in mid-air. It appeared seconds later behind the wizard holding some hellish dagger and then went to stab him. The ball of light that sat above him was suddenly alerted. Beams of energy reached out and grabbed the creature, shaking it violently, sending electric shocks through it. The creature screamed and managed to escape the orb's grip.

Another dark creature released some vicious etheric entities, designed to eat a magician's energy field. The magician cringed, then instantly sent a powerful jet of water and an electric charge through his staff, which automatically sent them scurrying back.

The entities then gathered, circling around the wizard, faster and faster; another mass of black energy began to surround the wizard like a blanket of death, when he shouted, 'THURISAZ!' An immense light, circled around the magician and, in combination with the silver white ball, dispersed the energy, like a nuclear blast,

228

cutting through the death blanket and forcefully flinging the creatures back, slamming them, against the sides of the room.

The creatures' attention was now focused on Charlie. One of the entities used a magickal summoning beam to pull him towards them, whilst making him squeal in agony. Then, Charlie's arms flung upwards above his head, whilst his legs were forcefully being pulled downwards. Every bone stretched, cracked and elongated, like some cruel torture from a bygone age. Immediately, the wizard used a counter spell, pulling Charlie towards him. He then sent a silver energy to surround and protect Charlie whilst instantaneously repelling the dark creatures.

Without warning, the entities turned around and flew in the opposite direction, obliterating the door and disappeared into the night.

The wizard shook his head, looking disappointed, and then went over to Charlie. He leaned forward and touched his forehead with a finger. Charlie began to return to normal, if he could remain normal after that.

Charlie stretched to compose himself and he stood up.

'Thank you sir,' he said.

A kindly smile had now replaced the serious one and the man replied, 'No problem. Let us leave this place,' so they proceeded to walk outside.

'Charlieee!' shouted Imogen, Tom and Amanda. The magickal knights, Cosmolos, Hecate, Philbus and his inquisitorial lieutenants, surrounded them.

'He's mine,' said Philbus. Philbus sent some chains flying towards Charlie.

Sedrick went to protect Charlie when the wizard sent out a blast of gold energy, destroying the chains and sending Philbus flying. He was fuming and was about to attack back.

'Wait Philbus,' said Cosmolos, stroking his beard.

'This boy is under my protection,' said the wizard.

'The boy is a thief,' said one of the knights.

'He most certainly is not. He bravely returned one brother to its sister,' said the man. He held the prophecy, united once more. The tear that existed between the two scrolls had disappeared.

'Who are you?' said Imogen nervously.

229

'My name…is Lord Gideon Mortus. Just call me Gideon,' he said coolly as stunned faces just stared back at him.

Chapter 25

THE END OF YEAR

After the shock of the night, Charlie was fast asleep in his quarters, completely drained by his experience. Amanda, Tom and Imogen were all sitting in Imogen's room. It was decorated in Orberon posters and pink bedding, which amused Tom. They couldn't get over what had happened, though they were happy that Gideon intervened on their behalf. Gideon and Cosmolos went around the school placing additional protection in the form of ancient symbols that were magickally embedded into various rocks, trees and the earth. These were necessary, as the phantom-like creatures that had left were actually the Lordos, the closest of the Dark Keepers to Zordemon, and who might be tempted to return to the school. Their Phantom appearance was due to a time drain drawing on their life force. However, they would now be able to regenerate back into their human form.

Philbus, who was unhappy at Gideon's interference, left the school grounds and went back to the Great City uttering curses that he was denied the enjoyment of an inquisition. Hecate wasn't quite sure what to make of it, opening up a vintage brandy to steady her nerves, as did Randle who was also visibly shaken after being sent flying by the outbound Lordos. Unfortunately, reporter Graham Golden, who had sneaked onto the school grounds following Philbus, Cosmolos and everyone else who had descended onto the school, captured some of the events.

By the morning, everyone would know of the great wizard's return, and it would certainly send shockwaves throughout the Magicklands. Many questions would now be asked and Gideon, would soon have to go to the Political Quarter to explain what had happened. At least Gideon could now answer some of the greatest magickal riddles, for instance: what happened during that famous battle with Zordemon? What does the other half of the prophecy reveal? Why had he been cooped up through that perfectly preserved door? Why were the Lordos in there? What consequences would this have on the Magick World that had moved on uninterrupted, for nearly a millennia? What of Charlie…Why was he so important in all this? Why did he receive the guidance and clues that lead to all of this?

Gideon himself had much to adjust to also. He had missed centuries, but it only seemed like a few weeks to him.

The next day, Charlie woke up with a splitting headache. He groaned, holding his head. He turned to the side and dozens of scrolls had turned up spilling onto the carpet.

'Charlie,' said a voice quietly through the door.

'Enter,' said Charlie, and the door opened. Amanda, Tom and Imogen came in quickly.

'Are you Ok?' asked Amanda.

'Yeah, I guess,' said Charlie. 'A bit of a headache, though.'

'I bet,' said Tom. 'What happened?' Charlie explained all that happened in the Door of Mystery, the battle that happened and how Gideon saved him. Charlie also explained to Tom and Amanda about the sensations that he had experienced. Both Imogen and Tom were shocked by this, whilst Amanda looked saddened that Charlie went through this process again. Charlie did find a positive; he actually performed a spell more than competently, which cheered him up a bit.

'Are you going to tell him?' said Imogen.

'Tell me what?' said Charlie. Tom put on the Television and went to the news station. There before his eyes was his face splattered across the news, along with Gideon's. A clip of Philbus being sent flying was put on loop, showing every conceivable angle of his confrontation with the great wizard. It even projected out of the TV in 3D for extra emphasis.

'I bet he'll be happy,' said Tom laughing at Philbus being humiliated live on TV.

'Yeah, I'm sure he'll keep his own copy at home,' laughed Charlie. Charlie wasn't sure what to make of his face splattered across the news.

'Turn it up,' said Imogen. The report started.

'Well, as if the shock of the theft of the Half Prophecy by school children under the watchful eyes of the so called magicka knights wasn't enough, the return of Lord Gideon Mortus was certainly the icing on the cake for the day. Some are questioning whether it is him, after all, he supposedly died nearly a thousand years ago. There are some reports by some of the children who were awake at the time, of strange things flying over the school, though these can't be substantiated. The question remains, what is the meaning of all this? What is the story behind this Plainlander Magician in all this? I'm sure the truth will come out over time - back over to you Gloria.'

'Thank you, Graham…' Charlie turned off the TV.

'Well, you've made TV,' said Amanda, 'everyone certainly knows who you are now.'

Charlie completely ignored his mail and got ready. They all went outside to head up to the main canteen, when Winston came over and said, 'You four need to come to the headmistress' office to answer some questions.' All four of them looked worried as they accompanied Winston to Hecate's office. There seemed to be no let-up in all this Prophecy business, but questions were bound to happen.

'We're going to get expelled,' said Tom.

'Crikey, do you think?' said Amanda.

'He could be right. After all, we did some pretty dangerous things, not to mention stealing,' said Imogen.

'You're right,' said Charlie, and not for the first time Charlie looked dejected. *Surely, they aren't going to suspend me? What were they going to do, banish me to the Plainlands?* He really didn't like this line of thinking.

Minutes later, they arrived at the headmistress' office. Winston knocked at the door.

'Enter,' she said in her authoritative manner. The door opened automatically and they all went inside. Standing behind the desk was Hecate, with Cosmolos, Astrophos, Lord Balfour, Sedrick, Sir Anton Shine, Head of the Magickal Knights section, of the English Quarter, and Randle.

The presence of all these top officials staring at them seemed overwhelming, though Charlie was getting used to this.

'Cup of Tea,' she said, indicating to Randle to pour them some drinks; they dare not refuse. They sat very quietly; you could hardly hear their breaths.

Hecate walked around the front of the desk and spoke. 'Last night saw a momentous event happen - something that seems unbelievable even in the Magickal world. Through various bizarre happenings, we have seen the unity of the Prophecy and the return of an incredible wizard from our history. The world as we know it is about to change and unknown forces are let loose in the world. Many will embrace the change and others will fear and fight it. Whatever changes happen, it will take time to unravel these strange mysteries and why the fates have guided you. Ordinarily, all of you would be suspended without question for participating in highly irregular and illegal activities. On the one hand, you have shown cunning and ability way beyond your years. On the other hand, you have shown reckless behaviour endangering the lives of yourselves and, potentially, others. To be honest, I'm unsure whether to thank you or discipline you all. However, after an emergency meeting, we have agreed that you should stay. But as an example to others, you will all face detention, be banned from attending society work, and a curfew will be put in place for two weeks beginning at the next academic year. There is another condition,' she said, as Sir Anton Shine approached the front of the desk.

'Well, well. I never thought I'd see the day when my best knights would be hoodwinked in such a fashion – and by Children. Maybe, I should recruit you into security – but first, I'll cut straight to the chase – how did you do it? Bear in mind, a less than honest answer or a no answer will see you expelled from the school and other punishments will be handed out. 'Well then - tell me,' he said commandingly.

'Well Sir,' said Amanda. 'We figured out that the prophecy needed to be reunited and, the one in the museum was the key to stabilising the Door of Mystery. There was no option but to try and steal the other half. We knew that the prophecy was going to go to the museum so this was our chance.'

Imogen explained how she stole the key from her father and then managed to get into guard changing area.

'So what did you do then?' said Shine.

'Amanda sprinkled some Teleportation Powder on the armour.'

'Really, top grade armour is quite impenetrable to basic spell work, including powders,' said Shine.

'Yes, said Amanda, 'but at the opening of the Orberon, Imogen saw one of the knights use some Quickness Powder to speed towards his opponent. She pointed it out at the time, so I knew it could be used. The knight had a small opening in his armour, in which the powders could be thrown! This meant that any Powder could be used on the inside because all the protection work is done on the outside, to prevent pretty much anything piercing the armour,' explained Amanda.

'Quite brilliant,' exclaimed Shine.

'But why didn't the knights teleport as soon as they put the armour on?' quizzed Shine.

'Well, that was a problem. I came across a book on Advanced Powder Making, which said that the Powder could be activated using a spell command,' she said.

'Amazing,' said Shine. 'OK, but where did you teleport them to? My knights could swear that they were there in the museum. They knew something was up when the curator vanished and then reappeared unconscious on the ground,' he said with a confused look.

'This was a massive problem, but my favourite part of the spell-working. If they had teleported elsewhere, they could have easily made their way back raising the alarm, so we had to send them somewhere they couldn't. They teleported to the Wizopoly board,' she said. 'It has an identical replica of all the key places, roads properties etc. The new version lets you walk around the inside too. The powder had about a ten minute delay, so when it finished, they would teleport back, to exactly the same place.'

'That is incredible thinking, such cunning. So, it wasn't that the curator disappeared; it was the knights that had disappeared and never knew it. So when they reappeared, it was like the curator had suddenly appeared again.'

'Yes,' said Tom. 'We didn't think the curator or anyone else was going to be there, so I used a sending spell to throw an object to knock him out. Sorry about that,' he said quite

235

apologetically, but proudly. 'Once we had the Prophecy, we used some Quickness Powder once we got outside the museum to escape without anyone seeing us, but we were seen running on the inside.'

'Well, that is the most incredible plan I've ever heard. Of course, we will have to make various security adjustments, but I take my helmet off to you all.'

Cosmolos quizzed them about the door of mystery. Charlie explained what had happened, although heads turned when he said the room only went still when he used his magickal name and that he was also the only one that could enter. It was the reason why all his friends were on the outside. However, Charlie purposely left out the shadowy entity's help, as he didn't want to reveal quite everything to his teachers.

Cosmolos just twisted and stroked his beard reflectively, then walked away. Cosmolos knew there was more to come from Charlie, but didn't want to tell the others.

The meeting lasted over and hour and then they left.

The hours passed quickly, and whist he was out, Minnie and her helpers had cleaned the rest of the room and helped with the packing. Later, his friends came over to see him.

'Put the TV on,' said Tom. Tom grabbed the control and put another Channel on. 'Great, it's Sun Beach City, my favourite programme. Quick put your tanning lotion on.'

'Why on earth would I want to put tanning lotion on?' asked a confused looking Charlie.

'So you won't get sunburnt. With some channels you get the full experience of actually being there,' said Tom as Charlie just looked aghast as he smelled the sea air coming from the TV.

Later, Charlie had a shower, drank some warm milk and got into bed.

He was still no further in finding out what the shadowy entity was, the silver entity he saw that night at the Orberon, and why he was so important in all this; it was maddening to him. Charlie eventually fell asleep, dreaming about his exciting and frightening adventure.

Daybreak came and Charlie opened his eyes and screamed, nearly jumping out of his skin. There was a ghost-like figure of a child reaching out to him and then vanished.

'Oh no, not again!' said Charlie shaking his head.

That was it, the year had finished. It had been an incredible year of mystery and adventure for Charlie and he was now at the centre of the greatest stories to hit the Magicklands. Despite the fact that so many questions remained unanswered, it had seen the unification of the Half Prophecy with its sister and the return of a great legend. The world was about to change!

The adventure continues…

Dear Thomas Greenhalgh

Hope you enjoy
this magical
adventure.

All the best

J Shaw

11/10/14

Lightning Source UK Ltd.
Milton Keynes UK
UKOW050147110713

213543UK00001B/4/P

9 780956 250551